THE HONEY FARM

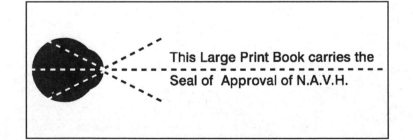

This Large Print Book carries the
Seal of Approval of N.A.V.H.

· THE HONEY FARM

HARRIET ALIDA LYE

THORNDIKE PRESS
A part of Gale, a Cengage Company

Farmington Hills, Mich • San Francisco • New York • Waterville, Maine
Meriden, Conn • Mason, Ohio • Chicago

LIBRARY OF CONGRESS CIP DATA ON FILE.
CATALOGUING IN PUBLICATION FOR THIS BOOK
IS AVAILABLE FROM THE LIBRARY OF CONGRESS

ISBN-13: 978-1-4328-5564-2 (hardcover)

Published in 2018 by arrangement with Liveright Publishing Corporation, a division of W. W. Norton & Company, Inc.

Printed in the United States of America
1 2 3 4 5 6 7 22 21 20 19 18

To Mary Nighy, for seeing it with me,
Rosy Lamb, for putting me in
perspective,
& Sylvia Whitman, for giving me a
room of my own.

Listen. It starts with the bees.

All day long the low, throttling hum of movement, the moment of liftoff — the bass note that never goes away. Then, swelling from the sidelines as day falls, comes the digital tick of tobacco-brown crickets — percussion — *chkchking* like an automated sprinkler, *chrpchrping* like needy birds. In come the fiddling grasshoppers — strings — from the balcony of trees, birch, poplar, and pine, followed by the lazy, peripatetic buzz of a fly. The high whine of mosquitos — the fugue — soars above the rest.

You will not be able to hear the bees whispering, and you would not understand their secrets even if you could. What you will hear is a hungry, unearthly cringe: the rub of wings as they fly. A science — no, a magic — that you will never know. The sticky slurp of suction, nectar, thirst, sex. It is nothing at all like love.

Look. The gluey honey is cracking from the cloud-grey hive bubbling from the branch; it's cracking too from the ceiling where the colony has swarmed.

Open mouth. Blood on the teeth.

It starts with the bees, and it'll end this way too.

■ ■ ■ ■
PART I
■ ■ ■ ■

Go up to this land that flows with milk and honey. But I will not travel among you, for you are a stubborn and rebellious people. If I did, I would surely destroy you along the way.

— EXODUS 33:3

I

The honey farm was in a valley in the northeastern part of the province, not far from the old river mouth. Islanded between Timmins on the Ontario side, La Sarre on the Quebec side, and the Abitibi Indian Reserve to the northwest, the farm was in the middle of a logistical no-man's land. The nearest town was Smooth Rock Falls (population: 1,316 at last count).

Though the region was not particularly known for its agriculture, the farm had always done well. However, that spring there had been a terrible drought, the worst in recorded history. Everyone suffered. The flowers were desiccated. The bees were restless.

Cynthia was the proprietor of the honey farm — she'd purchased the land about a dozen years ago. She had worked it, and worked hard, to make the cold, pebble-dashed plot yield more than anyone would have expected. She kept her dark hair cropped sensibly short, making her neck look even longer. Meeting her for the first time, you might be reminded of a tidy, highly polished operating theatre.

Cynthia had scatter-bombed specially made advertisements in an attempt to recruit extra hands to help during these tough times. The drought had made sand of her soil, wax of her honeycombs. She needed reinforcements; Hartford, her assistant, was not enough.

The idea was that people would work for free in exchange for room, board, and "life experience." Cynthia had asked Hartford to find relevant blogs and websites on which to post her ad. For the newspapers, she selected only those in cities and large towns, mostly the provincial capitals and their peripheries, and none in the surrounding area. Nobody from the villages in the region could be fooled into such a scheme. The ads promoted the farm as an artists' retreat, with a bonus: a chance to learn the apicultural trade.

Applications started trickling in immediately.

"We've had twelve so far." Hartford hovered in the doorframe of the honey house — wood-panelled, warmly lit — not want-

14

ing to disrupt Cynthia at work.

"Terrific," Cynthia said, without turning around. "Let's take them all." She put down the jar of honey she'd been labelling and turned to reach for the stack of forms Hartford was holding.

"They don't have any experience . . ."

"What did you expect?" She laughed. "At least artists don't expect to get paid." She took a large swig from an unlabelled beer bottle. "This drought is only going to get worse — we'll need all the help we can get." She started flicking through the papers, searching for something, she didn't yet know what.

After a moment Hartford said, as a last resort, "But where will they sleep?"

"You'll clean out the rooms up in the attic and we'll get futon mattresses from . . . from that place, you know, that place in Timmins filled with junk."

"No, I'm not sure I —"

"Oh come on, Hartford, the secondhand shops filled with evangelists where you can buy old tea towels and household —"

"I really don't —"

"The Salvation fucking Army, yes, that's it!" Cynthia's eyes were slightly farther apart than was proportional, and when she became angry, her eyeballs bulged and her likeness to an amphibian grew stronger.

They stood quietly, Cynthia a little drunk, Hartford a little afraid.

"Where's the twelfth?" Cynthia asked, flicking through the pages.

"Oh." Hartford reluctantly handed over the final form, including the optional photo the applicant had chosen to send in along with the paperwork. He'd held it aside for reasons he was sure Cynthia would understand. "A writer from Halifax, but she doesn't seem to have much . . ." He faltered, found his feet again. "I mean, she's not published or anything, and as it's so far away I didn't think she'd want to —"

"That's her choice, isn't it?" Cynthia spoke lightly, and then her eyes landed on the photo. "I see," she said, her voice changing. "Well, it will be good to have more people around." She stared at the photo; Hartford stared at her.

There used to be a river that ran into the valley. The remaining conduit still rippled with now-frozen fluidity, the memory of its function forever dictating its form. This was thousands of years ago. Now there was no water: there were wells. These days the river bypassed the region entirely, and instead of riffling around the north, it diverted directly

16

south, towards the centre of the province.

In the old hollow where the river once ran, ridges of sand drew topographical maps in the weedy ridges; fish had had to grow legs, becoming salamanders, newts, and toads. The word *amphibian* means, etymologically, "both sides of life."

The town had not yet accommodated this season's sudden drought. Patterns hadn't changed. No research had been conducted into ways either to find more water or to use less. This was partly because there was still hope, but primarily because the infrastructure did not exist. Wells, like habits, run deep. Cynthia was intent on changing this.

II

Silvia's bedroom is still decorated the way it was when she was eleven and obsessed with horses. She finished her final exams three days ago and her books, clothes, and empty teacups are all over the room. She's normally much more organized than this, but since finishing her finals — history, minor in English, at Dalhousie — she's found herself in a new kind of limbo. Everything is contingent, and everything is an option; there is no longer a predetermined path ahead of her. Before, she was a student. Now that she is out from under that umbrella, she could be *anything*.

She has no plans. This is partly what she tells herself she's doing: looking for a plan. After just three days she's got computer hands, cramped and stiff, from digging to the depths of the Internet. So far she's bookmarked teaching English as a second language in Korea, an unpaid internship at a literary magazine in outer Los Angeles, and an MA in cultural theory at the University of Edinburgh. She knows her parents wouldn't approve of any of these.

Her family home is a clapboarded three-bedroom home on Waegwoltic Avenue, just up from the Northwest Arm. The Arm is a wedge of Atlantic Ocean that cuts right into Halifax, though in this neighbourhood the city feels more like a suburb. Ever since she started walking herself to school (age nine) she'd walk down the hill to the end of Coburg Road on her way home, no matter the season, to crunch mussel shells under her feet or stare at the evolving families of geese or, if it was warm enough to have her fingers outside gloves or pockets, read. Though oceans don't often freeze, this sliver is shallow enough that during particularly polar winters, people can skate from her side of the shore all the way to the dinky Dingle Tower, presiding over the bay like a chesspiece.

This is where she's lived for her whole life.

Now she's skimming one of her favourite book blogs when she sees a simple advertisement — black text on a square white background — that intrigues her.

THE HONEY FARM.
Free retreat for artists, writers, thinkers!
Can't work in the city?
Come to the Artists' Colony for a month
or two (or longer!) and also learn how to
keep bees!
Start early May.
Contact Cynthia.

Like most, she doesn't consider herself the type of person who normally clicks on online ads, but this one feels different: it seems too simple to be manipulative. But mainly, she has a problem and this is a solution.

She clicks the link.

Silvia, sylphlike, is often limited by the annoying and reductive description of "cute." She is slender and springy and has short hair, an open face, and eyes that take in the world. They even change colour in different lights. Green, blue, grey. Her eyelashes are pale, indicating that as a child she'd been an angelic blonde, but now her hair has dulled to the colour of the underside of a button mushroom. "Fair Silvia." A girl led not by her longings but by some dated sense of duty.

This is false. She is hungry as anything.

Her parents named their daughter after Shakespeare's Silvia, the one from the sonnet. They used to read her the poem all the time, whenever she was sad or sick or restless.

Who is Silvia? What is she
   That all our swains commend her?
Holy, fair, and wise is she;
   The heaven such grace did lend her,
That she might admired be.

Is she kind as she is fair?
   For beauty lives with kindness.
Love doth to her eyes repair,
   To help him of his blindness;
And, being helped, inhabits there.

Then to Silvia let us sing,
   That Silvia is excelling;
She excels each mortal thing
   Upon the dull earth dwelling:
To her let us garlands bring.

Little Silvia had consequently grown up admiring an abstract version of herself, venerating this conjecture of what she might grow into. Though the outline was large and loose — even the poem lets the woman remain a mystery — Silvia, tidy even as a

21

child, knew to draw inside the lines. But the part that went "For beauty lives with kindness" stuck with her. *Where do they live?*

Just as she's about to Google the farm and see where it is and what exactly is involved, her mother opens the door. Silvia closes her laptop.

"Hi, honey, how are you, are you hungry? Can I get you anything? A snack?" She walks right into Silvia's room, looking at the messy floor and not at her daughter.

"I'm fine. Thanks."

Her mother has a plastic laundry basket tucked under her arm and starts roaming around the bedroom, crouching to pick up clothing and sniffing it to see whether it's dirty or clean. No matter what she discerns, she puts it in the basket.

"I can do that, Ma." Silvia prounounces it *Meehh,* an indifferent sheep bleating.

"It's no bother! I'm putting a load on anyway." Her mother is so busy with the task that she still hasn't looked at her daughter, who is sitting on her hands. Silvia waits as her mother retrieves all the clothes, knowing that there's more to it than this. Sure enough, as soon as the basket is full, her mom sits down on the bed: "When are you going to start applying for jobs?"

"I'm actually looking into that right now."

"Krista needs to know about camp soon, and she also said that Bruce said it could turn into a full-time admin job in the fall, so . . ."

"I'll think about it, Ma." She'd attended Daybreak Bible Camp for ten years as a camper — ages seven to seventeen — and had been an instructor there for four, despite starting to doubt the validity of the whole thing — of camp, but also of the world it represented — from the very beginning.

At vespers one evening that first summer, a ritual the camp extolled as "a nightly spiritual conversation" held in each cabin between the counsellors and their campers, seven-year-old Silvia asked what happened if you believed that God didn't necessarily make each flower open, or lift up the sun every morning by His own hands, or even heal her friend of his flu, but made it so that the world could operate on its own. Seasons. A spinning globe. Immune systems.

The counsellor thought about it for a second, snapped her cotton-candy-flavoured gum, and said, "Well, if you believed that, you'd go to hell."

The conversation swiftly moved on, and minutes later they were all expected to go to sleep.

But Silvia lay in bed staring at the cabin ceiling. She couldn't understand. This wasn't rational. An eighteen-year-old could tell her that she was going to hell because she believed in deism?

And so after that, Silvia started seeing holes everywhere. The heavy doomsday feeling of doubt was so terrifying that she never mentioned it to anyone. It cracked the foundation upon which her entire world had been built.

"Of course," her mother says now, trying to act as though she is cool with the possibility of Silvia's *thinking about it.* "It's just . . . well, life has to start sometime, you know."

Hasn't it already started? Silvia wants to say. *Isn't this it?*

Her mother looks around the room at the preserved image of her eleven-year-old daughter. Dolls, Black Beauty, a clock that has long since run out of batteries inscribed *Blameless Before Him in Love (Ephesians 1:4).*

"Dinner will be ready at six."

"Great." Dinner was always ready at six.

Standing in the door now, clearly wanting to say something more, Silvia's mother — tall, self-contained, so nearly very beautiful — looks at her daughter with a love that is forever laced with concern.

When her mother is finally gone, Silvia is left with a familiar vague yearning and so, spontaneously, without further reflection or investigation, decides to give it a try with the honey farm. Her half-hatched idea is forced fully out of its shell as she fills in the online application:

1. What is your artistic practice?
2. What do you want to work on for the duration of your stay?

Because she has no other artistic inclination, she puts

1. Writing.
2. A series of poems.

She's written exactly one poem in her life, but maybe this is all she needs. Everybody has to believe in something.

The idea is still too effervescent to talk about, and she doesn't want to have to see her parents right now, so she sneaks quietly out of the house, down the eggshell hallway and through the living room where the only decorations are framed professional photographs of her — the same pose throughout her childhood — to go to the Trident, her favourite bookshop, which faces the other side of the ocean.

The air is crisp as paper. She feels happy, self-sufficient in some small way.

When she gets to the bookshop — right around the corner from the terminus of the national VIA Rail line, a path of wood and metal that reaches all the way to Vancouver — she says hi to Dan, the owner she's known since before she even knew how to read. She gets a mocha, then spends two hours just flicking through things, following the wandering. She wonders if she has the right to participate in this, in the making of *this*. It all feels perfect, overwhelming — apart from her.

A hundred and twenty-nine of her parents' dollars later, she carries a paper bag full of new words and the remains of her coffee so chocolatey it barely tastes of coffee down to the harbour, where she sits and cracks the spine of *The Making of a Poem*. There's a salty fog materializing on the horizon, but the Dartmouth side and McNabs Island are still perfectly clear. She likes it here because of how the view is of everything — water the same colour as the squat glass skyscrapers, sailless masts spiking the sky like crucifixes — but also of nothing at the same time. It's open, a blank canvas. From here it's a straight shot to Spain, Portugal, even France if the current took her slightly north. All those places are the same to her in that she's never been, cannot pin one apart from the other. It's mind-blowing, if she really thinks about it, that it's the exact same ocean here and there. She could swing her feet into the water here and, connected in the way that everything is, she'd be touching Europe (she thinks of it that way, as one big exotic thing: *Europe!*).

She puts the book facedown in her lap and looks out into the growing fog. Spring on a honey farm, she thinks. That could be nice.

III

At any given moment there are literally *tons* of free cardboard in the city. Twined into bundles on the streets, stuffed into garbage bins, stacked behind restaurants and shops. Tons. And all of it freely available. Ibrahim would never take anything that belonged to anyone else, but this belongs to nobody, and so, by consequence, it also belongs to him.

Ibrahim and his family live near the train station, a stone's throw from where his father alighted thirty-two years ago — the plane tickets from Marrakech were cheaper if they flew into Buffalo, so he and his wife took the train from there to Toronto — and where they've all stayed ever since. Although Ibrahim moved into his own place a few years back, it's just around the block from his father, also called Ibrahim, and his brothers and sister.

The streets behind the station — on a map, the lines are so fine they crosshatch,

28

like shading — form a neighbourhood the locals call the Marmite. *Mar-MEET.* The French were among the first people to arrive, and for them, *une marmite* is a pot in which you cook any old thing. A village stew made up of all the leftovers. A kind of stone soup.

The Marmite now houses the Arabs, the Poles, the Chinese, the South Koreans, the Somalis, the French, the Irish, the Cubans, the Bengalis, the Tamils and other Sri Lankans, the Balinese. The whole world.

If they'd come off a boat from the Atlantic they would have hopped on the train out east, heading west, and stopped here: Toronto! Tdot! The Six! And if they came from down south they'd have stopped in what was effectively the first city across the border. No need to reach beyond the necessary. Besides, everyone knows it's too cold farther north.

For all the development happening, condos and complexes and tramways and all that, they don't touch the little shantytown casting its low shadows behind Union Station. And everyone stays, no matter how much disrepair the houses fall under or how much cleaner and cheaper it might be to live elsewhere, the suburbs maybe. They stay where they landed, out of convenience and fear. They'd already come so far, Ibrahim the Elder said, there was no reason to risk it all. Risk what? Ibrahim the Younger never asked.

Nights, Ibrahim goes round the city — all over it, from the theatre district to the old textile factories, from Chinatown to Little Italy — to collect all that cardboard, but the best stuff is right by the train station. All the shipping crates for furniture, pianos, farm supplies, car parts, wheelchairs, bicycles, textbooks, hospital equipment, grain. He stops here last, on his way home, arriving moments before dawn, before the first trains come in from out West.

He uses it for canvases.

His paintings are big, abstract, bright. If you know where to look you'll see all the weighted Moroccan symbolism he disguises in them. The lion, the pentagram, the hand of Fatima. It doesn't matter if you can't see any of it outright. Most people can't.

He has yet to sell any, but he also has yet to try.

Ibrahim first sees mention of the honey farm on the public announcement board in the departures hall of the train station. It is morning and he is on his way home to sleep. (He works nights and early mornings, sleeping all afternoon.) He has sheets of cardboard strapped to his back with a carefully devised system of bungee cords, and he's carrying a box of hardly broken bottles in both hands. He has nothing particular in mind for the bottles but will find a use for them. To store his brushes, maybe.

A pigeon — no, a whole family of them — has strayed into the station, and they are now busy creating a nest for themselves above the coffee shop that hasn't yet opened its wrinkled silver lids. Ibrahim watches the one that seems to be the mother fold slender bits of food into the mouths of her young.

The postings on the board are all pretty standard — yoga classes, guitar lessons, lost dogs, and basement sublets — and then he sees this one, ripped from the classified section of a newspaper and tacked onto the cork:

THE HONEY FARM.
A free retreat for artists, writers, thinkers!
Can't work in the city?
Come to the Artists' Colony for a month
or two (or longer!) and also learn how to
keep bees!
Start early May.
Contact Cynthia.

He scribbles the email address onto one of the sheets of cardboard on his back and then begins the walk home, across the sleeping steel tracks already starting to vibrate with the national repercussions of movement. The sky is veiled with thin clouds — cirrocumulus, combed so high as to be in practically another stratosphere, a whole different universe — starting to pink with the first inkling of morning.

His pack is heavy and he feels full of this contented feeling. A feeling of largesse. He is excited to start work, proper work, with paint on his hands and jeans, in his hair and pores. His mind is already preparing for his next piece, and the world begins to parcel off into colour swatches, alternating and contrasting blocks of neon and matte metal that make up his palette. The world becomes as he would paint it: simplified, brightened, stratified into a kind of unity.

Get him going and Ibrahim will talk your ear off about how things get spoken into creation — his faith system is a personalized mashup of ancient Egyptian and Islam — and how he believes this is also true for his paintings. Nothing exists for him until he paints it.

Near the lakeshore, on the leafy boulevards that encircle the water, the houses are made of brick and spread apart, each with its own fenced-in garden. He and his brothers worked as landscapers around here for pocket money when they were younger. As he gets farther away from the water, the yards shrink until the houses are attached — townhouses connected two by two — and the trees turn to stout bushes, always only almost in flower. In the Marmite, bricks are used on only some of the houses, and only ever as a façade. The sides of the buildings are all clamped with aluminum clapboard, and residents take turns scrubbing off the graffiti that springs up like mould.

Walking up his street, he passes his father's house and brings the newspaper to the front door. It's been getting farther and farther from the mailbox, and now Mikey, the paperboy, stupid little lazy-ass kid, thinks the bottom step of the porch suffices.

Now Ibrahim turns the block, and as he rounds the corner, the sun breaches the horizon. He feels, with the tiniest bit of sadness, that he is no longer the only person in the world.

Once home, he disregards the first floor and goes straight up to his attic studio. This is where he works, usually until about noon (his midnight). Though his paints and brushes and thinners and sponges are nearly impossible to find in all the mess, it is here that he stretches the boards flat and tapes them into one patchworked canvas.

Once he's located them, Ibrahim lines up the paints he's drawn to that morning and splotches red and blue and yellow, gold and pink and neon-orange, and black and white and silver onto a palette of waxed card, and then, finally, he starts to paint.

As he paints, shapes emerge from colours: the line of a horizon volleys, peaks, and turns, the stroke unfolds and meanders as a river does and then continues, bending into the first letters of the Arabic alphabet: alif, beh. One slight stroke for a dot beneath the cupped line of beh.

Alif, beh; aleph, bet; alpha, beta. The first letters — the first words.

Ibrahim is getting into the rhythm of it now; he starts to feel alive in the painting, as if its motion and his motion are one, as if he is the colours and they are coming out of his fingers. This is why he paints. To see things differently, but to *be* different too.

After a while he pulls back from the canvas to see the bigger picture. He is happy with it; he feels it in his chest. He puts the brush down, pulls out the spare one from behind his ear, pushes back his straggly hair

— his longish curls tend to puff out with the morning humidity — and motions to crack his knuckles. His knuckles don't crack but his father's do, and Ibrahim inherited the gesture. Both Ibrahims make to crack their knuckles either when there is a situation that needs to be controlled or when they are satisfied with a job well done. This is the latter. It's time for coffee.

He boils the kettle, presses the grounds, then sits in the window cupping his mug, milkless, looking out over the tree- and rooftops.

Spring on a honey farm, he thinks. That could be nice.

IV

Silvia is astonished when she gets the email saying her application has been accepted, especially since it has been only two days since she sent it off. The acceptance includes an attachment with instructions on how to get to the farm, and that's it. No notes on scheduling or what to pack. She doesn't bother Googling what the farm looks like, or even to check the weather — it is *happening,* she is *doing* it. The rest doesn't matter. With uncharacteristic recklessness, she signs off the future, at least this part of it, to "inevitable."

She makes the announcement that night at dinner — baked salmon and new potatoes — after her father has said grace. She decided not to present it as a question.

"It's called the Honey Farm," she says, taking a sip of her iced tea. "It's an artists' residency in Ontario. I'll help with making the honey and stuff too."

"Ontario?" Her father looks at her mother.

"I'm going to leave in seven days," says Silvia. "I booked my train."

"But what about camp?" her mother asks. She, who doesn't have paid employment. Silvia's father's dentistry business has always been enough to support the family, but her mother keeps herself occupied with volunteer work at the church, the Women's Club, the Children's Hospital, the board of Silvia's old elementary school, the Refugee Welcome Committee, the church lunch club, and, of course, occasional recruitment services for Daybreak Bible Camp.

"I never said I was free," Silvia says.

"But honey" — her mother turns to Silvia and puts her fork down — "even if we did let you go, what would you . . . I mean — you said it's for artists, so I —"

"I want to write." Then, more assertively: "I was accepted as a writer."

"Oh," her mother says. Her parents are stunned into a moment of silence before her mother says, "Is it free?" at the same time her father says, "Don't think that we're going to pay for it."

Later Silvia overhears her parents talking in the living room as she's looking for her rain gear in the cupboard under the stairs.

They're drinking chamomile tea and trying to whisper, but her father, being half deaf, finds this difficult.

"I didn't know Silvia was a writer," he says, holding his favourite mug — a stripey one that Silvia painted for him at Glaze Craze — in both hands. His hands are enormous but graceful: elegant, with long and slender fingers that Silvia inherited.

"I don't know *what* she is anymore," her mother replies.

There's silence for a breath, then her father asks, "Will we let her go?"

"Well, I don't see how we can very well stop her."

The next few days are taken up with packing her school things into boxes to put in the basement, packing her summer clothes — and some sweaters and jackets in case it gets cold — into the most enormous suitcase she can find, and transferring her toiletries into miniature plastic bottles from the drugstore. She stacks the books she definitely wants to take in a pile next to the books she maybe wants to take, but the piles gradually become a single pile of definites as she decides that she absolutely can't live without Austen, or Updike, or Pullman.

She tries on outfits to see if she can find

the right self to present on the first day and all the days after that. Jean shorts, striped T-shirt? Hair tucked behind her ears or clipped back with a barrette? Does she want to be the kind of girl who wears an emerald-green cotton Lacoste tennis dress?

Though she's been finished with classes for what feels like an age, it's only late April, and public schools are in the full swing of their final term. In the afternoons, as Silvia lies in bed in a paralysis of *what to become,* time extending before her like an eternal diving board, she hears the cries of children playing during recess in the schoolyard on her block; they seem to have no problem at all with the fluidity of *being* and *becoming.*

On Saturday — nine days after Silvia found the ad — Silvia's mother calls up the stairs as she's drafting her autoreply email, which she plans to leave on for the duration of the summer.

Silvia shouts back down.

When there's no answer, she knows she simply has to go downstairs; her mother will not engage in call-and-response.

It's dusky early evening, and Silvia sighs her way to the family room. When she's at the threshold she sees Bruce, their minister, who baptized her, sitting on the pink sofa with his hands in his lap. He stands as she enters.

"Hello, Silvia." He smiles and extends both of his hands to enclose her own.

"Oh — hi. I'm sorry, I didn't —" She shoots a glance at her mother, who shrugs, smiling. "It's so lovely to see you." She takes a seat next to her mother on the opposite pink sofa.

In Silvia's mind, her minister has always been more of an awkward but benevolent uncle than the image of a sombre, robed priest she sees in movies. He has the right shape and colouring to be a shopping mall Santa. He is kind. He is good. She knows he loves her exactly the same way he loves everyone. But being around him now makes her feel squirmy, melancholy, exposed.

"Your mother tells me you're going on a bit of an adventure," Bruce says, his tone, as ever, as though he's speaking to a toddler.

"Yes," Silvia says, holding her voice close. "I'm sorry about camp."

Bruce looks between her and her mother. "That's not a problem, Silvia. We'll miss you, but I'm sure we'll manage."

Silvia can see from the corner of her eye that her mother is nodding at Bruce and gesturing towards her daughter as she stands up. "I'm just going to pop out and put the kettle on. Tea? Coffee?"

"Decaf would be lovely, thank you," Bruce says, coming over to take Silvia's mother's place on the couch as she disappears, as had clearly been the plan all along.

"I wanted to check in with you, Silvia," Bruce says, suddenly serious, "see how you're doing."

"How I'm doing?"

"You're in a major transition period right now. A time of uncertainty, a time when you might perhaps feel overwhelmed at the number of choices you have to make."

Silvia, still listening, looks slightly behind Bruce's head, finding the gilt mirror in the bookcase. She meets her own eyes.

"I want you to know that God is with you for all of this. And so is your family. And so am I, of course. God is with you wherever you go."

She feels as though she's at the bottom of a swimming pool, the weight of water compressing her.

"Do you have anything you'd like to talk about, Silvia?"

She blinks, and realises she's been staring at her reflection this whole time, unrecognizing. "No, I'm good. But thank you."

"You feel prepared for this journey before you?"

She does not even know what preparation would look like, but she nods. "I'm excited," she says, as hopeful and dismissive as possible.

Bruce looks at his watch. "I've enjoyed watching you grow into a wonderful, composed young woman, Silvia, and blossom in the love of our Lord. I'm going to give you my direct phone line should you need anything while you're away. I've also looked up some churches in the region your parents said you'll be staying in. My colleagues there will look forward to meeting you."

"Thank you," Silvia says, that guilty feeling pulsing underneath her heart. "That's very thoughtful of you."

"That was nice of Bruce to drop by, wasn't it?" Her mother catches Silvia on her way up the stairs. She'd never even put on the kettle.

"Very nice."

She falls asleep early that night and has incredibly cinematic, terrifying dreams she forgets as soon as her eyes are open. She tries to brush away the foggy feeling, but it lingers all day.

■ ■ ■ ■

Later that morning her father drives her down to the train station at 6:15 a.m., too early for Trident coffees.

"Do you have everything?" he asks, handing Silvia her second suitcase. The morning is mist-thick; at his insistence, she is forty minutes early.

"I think so."

"When do you get back?"

"I told you, I haven't booked my return yet."

"Well —"

"I'll let you know, Dad."

"Right."

She can practically see something growing in his throat.

"I've been away before, Dad." But this will be the farthest she's ever been from home, and she hadn't considered what that might be like for them. "So you have the address, right?"

Her father pats his breast pocket and looks at his feet.

"I'll let you know when I get there," she says. "And I'll write to you. Once a week at least, I promise."

He finally looks up at her. "Be back by

the end of summer," he says, his shaky voice betraying his stern command.

"It only lasts for the summer anyway." She's soft, but unwilling to concede. She hugs him, takes the bags, and walks towards the train platform. "Love you."

Freedom is being without an anchor, and she feels like she's floating. Doubt has a way of ripping a hole through which, eventually, the whole sky can fall.

Silvia settles into her single front-facing seat for the twenty-five-hour train journey and leans her head against the cool, wide window. She wonders what the other people will be there for. If they'll be *real* artists.

As the train hugs the side of a body of water, then cuts through another, everywhere a different body that she can't identify, she starts to lose her sense of place. She doesn't know if they're in New Brunswick or northern Quebec, or maybe still in Nova Scotia. She doesn't even know what time it is. There's a strange feeling of being in the land but outside it. Moving through it, over it, in every place and no place at the same time. She's getting farther and farther away from what she recognizes, all she's ever known, and the names for things are starting to dissolve. She didn't bring a map, she can't follow along to acknowledge the borders or name the rivers and lakes; ties are stretching to the point of breaking and the train is in motion, there's no stopping it or going back now.

V

It's only April, but by nine o'clock in Toronto the day is as hot as summer. Ibrahim's throat is scratchy — his allergies always start at the beginning of spring.

His dad probably won't be awake yet, but Ibrahim needs to talk it over with him first. This is how they always do it. Hash out ideas over coffee and clove cigarettes, with their dusty taste of the Old World.

The lights are out in his father's house. Ibrahim wipes his feet on the tatty *Bienvenue* mat his father bought thirty-two years ago (it was cheaper than the *Welcome* version) and brings in the newspaper. Walking through the unlocked front door, he encounters a yeasty smell of warmth and mildew. It's possible that it smelled like this when he lived here, but he only notices it now that he's left.

A half-eaten sandwich sits on the staircase next to a scummy glass and a ball of tinfoil.

The ball almost has the shape of something else, as though someone started to make a sculpture and then abandoned the idea. Ibrahim picks all this up and takes it into the kitchen. The absence of his mother is evident in small ways: in the forgetfulness, in the lack of care and of consequence.

"Morning."

Ibrahim jumps, startled, to find his little brother folded up like a cat on the armchair in the kitchen. "Hey, morning, buddy," Ibrahim says. "You scared me." He goes over and kisses Aziz on the top of his peach-fuzz head. Aziz keeps his head shaven like their other brother Mo's. Ibrahim is the only one to let the curls grow. "You sleeping down here now?"

"Mmm."

"How come?"

"Mo started snoring."

The two boys, fourteen and seventeen, share a room. Their choice. Besides the master bedroom suite, where their father sleeps, and the attic room belonging to their sullen and dreamy nineteen-year-old sister, Isadora, there are three rooms. One has been turned into their father's study, never used, and the other two are ready to serve as guest bedrooms, should any guests ever drop by.

"Is Abouya still sleeping?"

"Mmm," murmurs Aziz. "But he won't mind if *you* wake him up."

"Okay. Go back to sleep, Zizi. I'll come see you on my way out."

Aziz whacks Ibrahim on the back of the knees for using his little-boy nickname, then curls back into the position in which his brother found him and promptly returns to his dreams.

Climbing the stairs, Ibrahim notices that the carpet is sagging at the lip of each step. The house is not in total disrepair — it's old, it was cheap, a certain crumbling is normal — but none of the family either notices or cares about details like carpet or shingles or paint. It doesn't bother them and there's nobody else for it to bother. Still, Ibrahim can't help but feel something — pity, or maybe shame at not being there — swell between his ribs.

"Abouya?" he calls before reaching the top of the staircase. A warning; no answer expected.

Ibrahim knocks — a gentle pushing tap — on his father's door. The latch is up, so the door slides open with this small force. As Ibrahim's eyes adjust to the velvety light in the bedroom, he sees his father's silhouette on the bed, wide and opulent as a maharajah's. While the rest of the house may be in a relative state of poverty and/or decay, the master bedroom remains palatial, swathed in past excesses. This is because most of Ibrahim's mother's purchases are still there, and Ibrahim's father feels that it is not only his duty but his calling to preserve these relics. Nothing in the room has changed since her death, nine years ago last month. Indigo brocade curtains she selected still hang from the four-poster bed, which has little sleeping space between all the pillows (Ibrahim the Elder likes to sleep propped up by at least four of them: one under each shoulder and a couple wedged between his knees). Her antique paintings in gold frames, her hand-painted tiles in turquoise and coral and egg-yolk yellow. Her book-cases and her tasselled armchairs and her tea trays decorated with tin teapots and narrow glass cups (a collection she bought in her youth from the Marrakech souk) assembled at the ready, just in case.

As Ibrahim enters, the shape of his father twitches, still sleeping, into a sudden tussle with the blankets.

Ibrahim walks over to the bed. "Abouya, good morning," he says, confidently but softly, knowing not to touch his father yet.

The shape jerks about again and snaps

into a seated position. "Ibrahim?" His father's eyes are still closed.

"Yes, Abouya, it's me."

"Come here."

Ibrahim slides into his father's bed, a wall of pillows between them, as his *abouya* comes slowly into consciousness.

Ibrahim the Elder tenderly strokes his son's hair. After a few minutes of silent, slow movement, he says, "This is getting too long."

"I like it like this, Abouya."

"You like looking like a girl?"

"I don't look like a girl."

"You look like your sister."

"She should be so lucky." Ibrahim looks up with a cheeky grin.

"Or a terrorist. Terrorists grow their hair long."

"Dad."

"What?"

"You can't say that!" Ibrahim sits up and looks at his father. Ibrahim the Elder has a chubby face under his sandpaper beard, an affectionate imitation of the Italian Mafia neighbours. His eyes glow in the unlit room. Ibrahim's do too, but he can't see them for himself. All the Abdullahs have the same tigers' eyes, orange-brown and radiated like quartz. A tinge of chatoyancy, especially in the dark. "How did you sleep, Abouya?"

"Terrible. Ever since your mother died I can't sleep, you know. No sense of rhythm anymore."

"I know, Abouya." To dislodge this familiar conversation, Ibrahim gets up and opens the curtains.

"Ibrahim! Slow! It's bright!"

"It's day." Ibrahim turns to look at his father, hooded like a turtle under the sheets. "Can I make you some coffee?" His father keeps a kettle and a French press next to his bed so he can make coffee and tea and boiled eggs and Cup-a-Soup without leaving the room.

"Yes."

When the kettle boils, Ibrahim pours water over the coffee grounds until the pale swell calms and the coffee sinks.

"So what brings you here today, Ibrahim Abdullah Junior? Anything good from your collection walk last night?"

"Some bottles. Hardly broken. And all the cardboard stays dry in this weather — it's perfect."

"Well, Ibrahim, there are always two sides —"

"But I also saw an announcement for something I want to talk to —"

"Is the coffee ready? Pour me a cup."

It is ready; Ibrahim pours it.

"You're not having any?"

"I already had some, Dad, but thanks."

"I don't like it when you call me Dad — sounds so trashy in your mouth."

"Sorry, Abouya."

"So. What is this announcement?"

"Oh, yeah, so at the train station, on my way back home, I saw an announcement for an arts residency on a honey farm, starting basically now. Next week. The beginning of May."

A pause as his father swallows his first sip. "Too weak," he says. And then: "What is this *arts res-i-den-cy*?" He says it slowly, as though the familiar words in unfamiliar conjunction have completely fuddled him.

"A place where artists can work on their, you know, work. But at this one, 'cause it's a honey farm, you can also learn how to, like, farm bees."

"Bees!"

"And you can stay as long as you like, and I could spend some time painting, really *painting.*"

"Where is it?"

"Where? Oh. I'm not sure, actually. It didn't say."

"Well."

"But I wrote down the email address from

the paper and I can write. I mean, I *will* write. To find out all that stuff." He's so excited he's practically pleading, though he knows his father will enourage him as he always has. "What if you don't like the other people? Will there be other people?"

"I'm sure I'll get along fine, Abouya."

"Of course you will. But *what if,* is all I'm saying. Like I was saying about your card-board staying dry because of this drought. There are always two sides to a situation and you have to consider both justly." He looks at his son; his eyes narrow. "How much?"

"Nothing. It's free. Work in exchange for room and board."

"Well, not exactly free then."

"Yeah." Ibrahim searches. "But it's no money."

"Bring me a clovie."

Ibrahim gets the clove cigarettes from the basket where they are kept and Ibrahim the Elder puts one in his mouth. His tongue navigates the base, just for a taste; he doesn't light it. "You don't want one?"

"No. Thanks."

"So do you want to go?"

"Yes, Abouya."

His father pauses. "What's the weather like today?"

"Hot and dry. As usual."

Shifting the position of the pillows beneath him, Ibrahim the Elder grunts.

This would be the first time Ibrahim has been away for any period longer than a weekend. He stayed close to home longer than he might have otherwise after the death of their mother, but it's not like he can stay around forever.

After what feels like an eternity, Abouya says, "Fine. You go. Go."

"Really?"

"Ibrahim. You do as you wish, always."

"But do you think it's a good idea?"

"I think it's a very good idea if you want to do it. You are good with paints, you are good with your hands. A change of scene will be good."

"Okay." Ibrahim slides back into bed and pulls the covers over his head like a child. His eyes won't close and he wants darkness. The navy covers become like eyelids, and he sees images playing out on the silk. "You won't need me here," he states, not asking, getting to the point he is most concerned about.

"Of course we don't need you, don't be ridiculous. Go, *inshallah.*" He pats his son's head through the covers. "We'll pray for rain."

■ ■ ■ ■

Though he's lived in this country his whole life, Ibrahim has never been north of Aurora. His nose piggied up against the window-pane, he stares out at the view, dizzied by the beauty of it. So stark, so wild. So unlike the city.

Ibrahim tries to follow the map he printed off the Internet as the train noses forward into the forest, past the millions of lakes. On the map they look like peeling paint, or a rash — haphazard and unhealthy. From the window, though, the lakes are glowing with the afternoon sun, pockets of liquid gold just floating there. There are so many of them. There must not be a drought up here, he thinks. What he doesn't know is how many there used to be: the water dissipates; the rash heals.

Things are starting to feel indistinguishably different. He has crossed no borders, but something's changed. Not the air. Not the sky. But something. And he's not even there yet.

Ibrahim's stop is Onakawana. He gets off there and takes a bus east and back south in the direction of Val Gagné, still this side of the Quebec border despite the Francophonic name. (This far north, all the borders overlap: French, English, First Nations in a nationwide Venn diagram.) He gets off the bus before Val G though, at a bus stop where County Road 634 meets Highway 11.

Off the air-conditioned bus, the heat is like hot breath.

WELCOME TO SMOOTH ROCK FALLS! THE BIGGEST LITTLE TOWN IN THE NORTH.

From Smooth Rock he has to walk about two hours. The farm is in a place that has no name, but it falls under the same municipality: Smooth Rock houses the nearest post office.

Looking at the map, he traces the line that leads to the farm. It must be the smallest road on the whole map. Like a vein or a root it bifurcates, then stops. It's not the kind of road that needs to be claimed, maintained. It's like a part of your body that's so tiny and familiar it doesn't even need a designation.

The landscape is starting to thicken. No path cuts a straight line. Though the forest is sparse, shrubby in parts, it seems untamed. All pines and needles. He looks up. The denim-blue sky is so wide up here.

When the path forks he stays left. He's

not really thinking about what it will be like
when he gets there.

VI

Posters for a carnival in Smooth Rock Falls are peeling, their tails tattering in the wind. Silvia is waiting on a bench with a large red suitcase, her high school backpack, a tote bag, a purse that slings over her shoulder, and a Panama hat on her left knee. She feels caught in that awkward space between posing for a photograph and posing for real life. She doesn't know what to do with her hands, and the hat looks like a dumb prop there on her knee. Looking closer at the nearest poster, she notices that the carnival is at the end of June, weeks away, but seven years ago.

With a sudden surge of panic, she scans and counts all her bags and possessions as though somehow, in the moments when her mind and eyes were elsewhere, something could have disappeared. But no. Everything is there.

She takes her phone out of her leather

purse and sends her parents a text: *Here, in Smooth Rock Falls. Train journey was long but nice. It's sunny, waiting for taxi to the farm. Excited.*

The taxi she booked finally arrives, twenty-eight minutes late. The farm is thirteen kilometres from the town, but with all these bags weighing her down, Silvia never thought about the option of walking it.

"You go to Honey Farm, *c'est ça*?" The driver's accent is thick Québécois.

"Yes."

"For Cynthia?"

"Yes."

"You know Hilary?"

"Nope."

"You look just like 'er. She used to live 'ere, with Cynthia."

Silvia shrugs. "I don't know Cynthia yet either."

The driver is still staring at her in the rearview mirror. "You could be sister of Hilary, it's *bizarre*," he says, pronouncing "bizarre" the French way.

Silvia looks out the window, trying to ignore him, watching the low rolling hills become higher mounds and deeper valleys. They are getting into the land of stark contrasts.

"A lesson for you: bees smell fear. When

you afraid, ferry-monies get aroused and come out your skin like *parfum,* so you must be calm."

"Thanks," Silvia says, still staring out the window.

The road forks, and when they arrive at the end of the long dirt road on the left, lined with evergreens, the taxi stops before the lane gets choppy. "I don't go up," he says, nodding up the road. "Bad ferry-monies." He drops all her luggage on a patch of grass, takes her money, and reverses. *"Bon courage,"* he says out the window with a laugh straddling pity and gentle mockery.

"Merci."

Confused and increasingly sweaty, Silvia walks up the "road" — waxy shrubs growing between two dirt-worn paths of tire treads — until it turns to a cleared, dusty track. She's pressing her hat onto her head so the wind won't take it. The track bends up a small hill, and right at the crook the farm comes into view.

It's more impressive than Silvia had imagined. The farm looks like it's from a book or a movie, or even from her imagination. Anything but real life — at least the life she's known up until now. The main, labyrinthine building is the perfect old English or old French country house: thick grey stones all veined with vines; white-framed windows, the panes of glass warped like bad dreams; overgrown lavender bushes on either side of the front door, their heavy purple heads falling all over the front path.

She notices the buildings — sheds and shanties connected by gravel paths scarring the lawn — scattered around the property in what seems like an arbitrary manner. Everything looks done by hand but done well, and the add-ons and outbuildings make the whole place seem . . . more approachable. Less rigid. Like a fun aunt instead of a stern grandmother.

She can see, behind the house, fields fading into the distance. Some fruit trees in the back lot, a corner of a vegetable patch. It's Edenic.

VII

Hartford has been bustling about all morning, assembling and personalising Cynthia's
welcome packages including a map of the
region; a legend of the property describing
what's what; directions to the local shops
but a reminder that no purchases are necessary, everything will be provided; a quick,
clever narrative illustrating the anatomy of
bees and the production of honey, with
Cynthia's own doodles of combs and drones
and clover; and finally a netted hat, for
protection. After tending to all sorts of last-
minute tasks, he is now sitting on a striped
green lawn chair at the top of the driveway,
drinking from a tall glass of lemonade, ready
to welcome the guests. Everyone is set to
arrive that day.

Hartford's hair is the colour of dusty
straw, and he's wearing one of those floppy
beige sun hats that are not fit for safaris. He
looks brighter than he feels: though he's

gotten over much of his initial resentment, he still feels territorial about this place.

"Silvia?" he repeats, though he remembers exactly who she is. "Silvia . . ." He taps his pencil, looking through the list he wrote. Then he looks up, remembering something. "Welcome to the Honey Farm. I'm Hartford, and Cynthia and I are pleased to have you here." He looks back down to his clipboard. "Ah yes, here we are. You're in the loft" — Cynthia had decided to call it the loft rather than the attic. "Follow me."

The way his nostrils flare when he smiles reminds Silvia of webbed feet: they tug downward with the furrows that lead to his chin. It wasn't clear exactly how Hartford had wound up living here, but it was known that he had started out as Cynthia's singing instructor and ended up living here full-time to help out.

Following Hartford up the gravel pathway to the house, Silvia sees a shadow flick across the window. She looks up, thinking it was maybe the reflection of a bird, but there is no bird.

"And Cynthia, where is she?"

"Cynthia is not available right now, I'm afraid. If you have any questions, I can help you." His voice is like a friendly automated voice-messaging system.

She's confused — it was Cynthia's name that had been on the application form, no mention of this Hartford man — and she's flustered too, the intense heat starting to get to her. Her bags seem to have grown heavier and bulkier in the past ten minutes, and sweat is darkening her mouse-coloured hair, sticking her bangs to her forehead.

Pushing the front door open, she scans the scene: lots more doors, three long hallways, a dark staircase on her right, and what looks like a dining room down the corridor before her. She readjusts her bags, then Hartford points her up the enclosed staircase.

There is a woman standing by the window on the landing; Silvia thinks this perhaps was the shadow.

"Oh, hi." Silvia smiles and, embarrassed, tries to blow her bangs away from her sweaty forehead as she approaches from below.

"Cynthia." The woman extends her hand.

"I was just wondering where you were."

The expression on Cynthia's face is bewildered, almost irritated. Silvia feels a flash of guilt, as if she shouldn't have been wondering about this, as if she has no right to wonder where Cynthia will be at any given moment. "Well, here I am! And you are?"

"Sorry, right, I'm Silvia." She finger-combs her bangs, trying to make them smooth.

"Ah yes, the writer. I remember. Lovely." Her expression opens up and becomes instantly warmer, familiar, and yet her eyes focus, the way a camera's lens focuses, on Silvia's face. "You look a bit different from your photo."

"Do I?" Silvia tries to remember which photo she sent and how she could possibly look all that different. She's looked exactly the same her whole life.

"Well, welcome," Cynthia says. "Hartford, help our guest with her bags. I'm so sorry" — she smiles — "you'll have to forgive him, it's all new for us. Oh, and put her next to Ibrahim."

Silvia's waiting for more, like a description of who Ibrahim is or why she'll be placed next to him, but that's all there is to it. Cynthia goes down the stairs, and Silvia watches her, aware of Cynthia's undeniable magnetism even beyond her physical beauty. Hartford grunts as he picks up her heavy bags.

"Here you are," he says, delivering her to an open door. "There'll be a bell for dinner." And he's gone.

The walls of Silvia's bedroom are unfinished wood. Pine, probably, though she isn't the kind of person who can distinguish one wood from another. The room is larger than she expected. Two thin twin mattresses are placed, monk-like, straight on the floor. The view is over the garden, and in the distance she can see endless fields, yellow and scorched. There are four doors: one to the hallway, which she had come through; one to an empty cupboard; one which she presumes is to Ibrahim's room; and one closed with a very small padlock.

She dismisses the encounter with Cynthia and tries to forgive herself for her awkwardness. *Everything will be fine,* she thinks, a secular prayer. It's gorgeous here, the house is massive, everyone will have plenty of space. And maybe she'll be able to write, maybe writing will be fun; maybe she will find inspiration.

She opens her big bag to get her eye mask, thinking to take a nap, and the first thing she sees is the family copy of the Bible with a note from her mother sticking out. *Love you, xoxo.*

She stuffs the Bible back in and checks her phone, wanting to see if her parents responded to her text, wanting to dispel the thrum of weirdness she feels. No reception.

Too exhausted to act on her curiosity, she

pulls the cotton bedcover over the mattress and lets herself flop onto her back, practically flush with the hardwood floor, where she sleeps until there is a knock at one of the doors.

VIII

Ibrahim puts his paints in one corner, drops his materials in another, then evaluates the place. Not bad. The man who let him in — what was his name, Henry? Something that reminded him of Robert Redford, but he can't remember why — said he'd be next to a girl, a writer, called Silvia. He decides to introduce himself and knocks.

"Hello? Is anyone there?" he calls, knocking harder this time. "Anybody home?"

After nearly a minute the door finally opens, revealing the girl he feels it's safe to assume is Silvia.

"Oh. Hi." Ibrahim smiles a smile that he's practiced.

"Hi." She seems caught up in sleep: her eyes are dream-soft and she's got pillow creases on her cheeks. The stamp of sleep suits her, he thinks.

They look at each other, knowing they'll be sharing a significant amount of time.

They look with scepticism and hope, in equal parts.

"Ibrahim." He puts out his hand and sneezes.

"Bless you."

"Thanks. Allergies."

She takes his hand. "Where are you from?"

"Toronto."

"I mean, where are you from *originally*?"

"Uh, Toronto."

Silvia looks down to her knees. "Oh, right."

"And you are?" He leans in through the door, gripping either side of the frame, and then walks into the room.

"Me? Sorry, yeah, Silvia. I'm Silvia." She looks around at the twin mattresses behind her and remembers what Cynthia said about being put next to Ibrahim. Next to — on that same bed? Are they meant to be . . . ? "Are we sharing —" she starts.

"A room?" he continues, moving towards the two mattresses and turning his head to look back at her. "Didn't they tell you?"

She moves her head in a way that's both a nod and a shake.

"Which side do you want, window or wall?" He sits and stretches out on the mattress nearest the window, watching her discomfort grow, a red stain up her neck.

"What, don't you think it'll be big enough for the both of us?"

Silvia does something with her bottom lip, sucking it through between her teeth. Her skin looks *dewy*. Ibrahim has heard people use that word to describe nice skin, and he thinks this must be what they meant. Her skin looks as though it's resting above a thin layer of water, her eyes the open pools.

He stands up. "Sorry," he says, laughing. "I couldn't resist. My room's through there." He gestures to the door from which he came. "You've got the bed all to yourself."

"Right. Of course." Silvia feels very aware of her feet and their position on the uncovered wood floor. "So, what are you here for?"

"You make it sound like a prison sentence."

"I mean, are you an artist?"

"Sort of, yeah." His face twists halfway to a frown. He walks over to her window. A little too tall for the frame, which is placed right underneath the sloping roof, he has to bend to put his eyes to the smudgy glass. Dust and cobwebs make intricate, animate patterns.

"So not a beekeeper?"

"Can I be a bit of both, please, miss?" He

70

turns around and gives her a full beam, showing the spaces between his teeth. He has the feeling that he wants to win.

His teeth are surprisingly small, she thinks, like milk teeth. His hair is longer than hers, and his face, when she examines it, is actually pretty handsome. His skin is the golden brown of wet sand.

The energy between them is chaotic; she doesn't understand this sort of magnetized tension. She thinks about the word *subject:* a painter's subject, subject of discussion; subjected to; the opposite of *object.*

Since she doesn't answer, he continues, trying to fill space. "What are your plans for while you're here?"

"Plans?"

"Like, what are you working on? I heard you're a writer."

"You heard — ? Uh . . ." How to explain, what to say, should she *lie,* could whatever she says now be a promise to herself to write that thing? It's not writer's block if it's blocking nothing. "I'm still figuring that out, I guess."

When she turns her head, he can see that her hair has been cropped to reveal the mole at the top of her neck, placed there painterly. His first impression is that her hair is too short, boyish. It looks like a toadstool, but then he thinks, *It will grow.*

"Do you know how many people will be coming?" she asks, but what she's actually wondering is why Cynthia has paired her with this man, whether she can request a room change to be next to a girl; something about Ibrahim gives her a twist in her stomach.

There is a bell, and a voice that follows: "Suppertime, everyone!" Ibrahim looks out the window and sees Hartford's floppy hat floating in the middle of the patch of grass that forms a sort-of courtyard between the outbuildings.

Everyone. That means everyone must have arrived.

"No idea, but I guess we'll find out now. Let's go," he says, but she's already two steps ahead of him.

Neither of them bothers to lock their doors.

IX

Everyone arrives at the same time, and supper is already on the table when they get there. Ibrahim notices the colour of the cold boiled ham, lipstick-pink, the rim of fat gone white. There's a jug of milk too, and all the glasses are already full.

A starched white tablecloth has been laid over all the mismatched tables that make up the communal eating area. There are additional pitchers of milk, and candles that reflect their warm light off the wooden wall paneling.

Everyone takes a place wherever he or she was standing. And then they wait, full of first-day nerves. The evening light sits yellow on the table, a corner falling onto Ibrahim's face.

"Well, everyone," Hartford says, presiding at the head of the table. Ibrahim sees that the other end of the table is empty; Cynthia hasn't arrived. Hartford opens his mouth, swallows whatever he was going to say, then tries again. "Bone appa-teet!"

The people at the table serve themselves from the porcelain bowls that line the surface: potato and lentil salads, both smothered with store-bought mayonnaise, fresh bread with fresh butter, and spinach from the garden with zucchini, shelled peas, baby radishes, the first wisps of carrot. Though it's still spring, Hartford explains that the unseasonable heat has advanced some of the produce to summertime size.

The milk tastes of cow. The peas taste of green. The ham tastes as ham should — Ibrahim has never had pork that tastes so good. (He and his siblings have eaten pork ever since their mother died; any semblance of practicing their faith dissolved after that, though none of them drink very much alcohol. His father still prays fairly regularly, but mostly conversationally, finding comfort in talking rather than the whole *salah*.) Everything is *delicious;* they all say so. A buzz of chatter rises.

On Ibrahim's side of the table are two similar-looking men and one blond woman. The men must be brothers, maybe cousins. They look like they might have sat around playing video games as children, and their skin, now pulled taut over bulging muscles, still holds the memory of their former chubbiness. Even though they've now got broad shoulders and tapered waists, grapefruits buried in their shoulder sockets, you can always tell from the face. The way chin meets neck.

The blond woman is drinking quickly and eating copiously. She's pale and plump as a Vermeer lady. Abnormally pale. Her eyes, eyebrows, and eyelashes are almost albino. Her name is Alicia.

Silvia is sitting opposite Ibrahim. On one side of her is a married couple, Marie-Juliette and Jean-Baptiste, who explain that they go by MJ and JB respectively. On the other is a pair of young girls who look like art-school hipsters. Ibrahim doesn't say anything, but he frankly does not see the point of neon-green nail polish on a farm. Both girls are silent; Ibrahim wonders if they are afraid.

In fact, the only person who seems to talk comfortably is a girl who's narrow, pretty, and pointed as a bird, a heron maybe. She has platinum hair with dark roots and a wide mouth revealing big teeth.

"How many days has it been since it's rained, then?" the bird girl — Monique, they've learned — asks Hartford.

"About forty-five days now, I'd say. Yes,

forty-five days." Hartford wipes off his milk moustache with the back of his wrist.

"What will we do about it?" Monique asks.

"There's nothing much to do," says Hartford. "We adjust."

"Does it affect the honey?" Ibrahim asks from across the table.

"Bees aren't personally affected by water, no, but if the flowers are dehydrated, then the honey, the little that can be made from the meagre nectar samples, will be lacking in flavour. Not to mention quantity."

"So yes?" Ibrahim glances across at Silvia with a tricksy half-smile. "It does affect the honey, then?"

Hartford coughs. "Well, I suppose you could say that, consequentially, yes, in one way or another."

"And when can we expect Cynthia?" Ibrahim persists. "Or does she not travel among us?"

As an answer to his question, the screen door to the garden swings open and a tall column of a woman is there. "Good evening, everyone. Hello, hello." Cynthia nods to each side of the table, sighing like a gracious but slightly put-upon monarch. "Welcome." Her shirt is crisp, tucked into her trousers, and she is carrying nothing. Or at least her hands are empty, though her pockets look full. "Thank you all for coming. I hope your journeys were fine. I know we're not exactly conveniently located, but I am very happy to have you here and look forward to getting to know each and every one of you."

Another general mumble. Cynthia looks around at each person's face. "Ten, have we?" she asks Hartford.

"Yes," Hartford replies. "Two haven't arrived, and I don't believe they will." He passes her two bits of paper. She stuffs them into her pockets without looking at them.

"Right. So, we make our living from our honey, as you know — last year we sold two thousand pounds — and with your help this year, and a few new hives, we're hoping to double that. There's also the livestock and the garden, and some general maintenance to do. The day starts with breakfast at a quarter past seven, and you'll alternate chores in the afternoon. I'm sure you'll do very well. That's why we picked you!" Cynthia fetches a jug of water. "For when you finish your milk," she says, and places it in the centre of the table before walking deliberately to take her place at the opposite end of the table from Hartford.

Everyone settles into the dynamic of their collective relationship. They help each other to seconds, make tentative gestures at passing condiments and water; they bounce around pleasantries and generic background questions, unintentionally cross-checking each other. Where are you from, what do you do, how long do you plan to stay. Nobody gets into the whys yet. Whys are for later.

"Hey, can you pass the . . . ?" Silvia reaches for the water.

"You haven't finished your milk," Cynthia says.

Silvia retracts her hand. "I don't like milk," she replies.

Cynthia raises her eyebrows. "Nobody else is complaining, Silvia."

For a moment there is silence at the table. Then Cynthia continues: "Does anyone else have any questions?"

One of the brothers next to Ibrahim pipes up. "I do, actually, a quick one. Where can we get cell reception? I noticed there isn't any in the —"

Hartford jumps in. "You'll find there isn't any at all on the property," he says. "Maybe in Smooth Rock."

There's an unhappy mumble around the table.

"In any case," Hartford continues, "cellphone use is not encouraged. The radio waves can interfere with bees' communication."

"Wait — are you serious?" the other brother asks. He's holding up his phone, and the one next to him is jabbing at the screen of his own.

Monique laughs; Hartford looks at her sternly. Ibrahim notices that Monique's irises don't have a solid edge but are ruffled, the colour bleeding, as if water had gotten into her eyeballs before they'd finished forming. They're the colour of rust, and veined with blue and black. In fact, her eyes look exactly like the quartz of the rocky shield beneath them, but rock made somehow soft, diluted, what with the undefined borders. Monique is definitely an artist, he thinks.

"There's a pay phone at the end of the road," Cynthia continues, "before it forks off to the highway. You can make and receive calls there." She grins. "I'm sure you'll get used to it. Now, I suggest you all go up to your rooms and get a good rest. Early start tomorrow. Hartford will clear up tonight." Cynthia smiles at Hartford, then takes her leave.

The group around the dirty dining table is left sitting there like an unassembled jigsaw, and piece by piece they go back to their rooms.

X

Silvia rummages through her still-not-unpacked suitcase to get her toothbrush. She didn't bring toothpaste, figuring there would be some here.

The common bathroom is at the bottom of the stairs. The corridors are conspicuously bare. Most people have art or photographs or some kind of identity hanging on the walls of a home. Family pictures. Framed maps. Horseshoes or antique washboards. Here there's nothing.

As she opens the bathroom door she's listening for sounds upstairs, so she doesn't expect the sound inside: "Hey!" A blur behind the door.

"Sorry," Silvia says, letting go of the handle.

A second later Monique opens the door just enough to peek through. "Oh, it's you." She is wearing only her underwear and an off-white wife beater, baggy around the armholes. "Come in." She opens the door wide so Silvia can pass through. "I'm just brushing my teeth."

"Me too," Silvia says, holding up her toothbrush like it's a white flag. "Sorry," she says again, trying not to look at Monique's unshaven armpits or the rounded peach of her butt. "Do you have any —"

"Toothpaste? Yes." Monique squeezes some onto Silvia's brush, jawing down on her own between her molars. "So what do you think?"

Silvia looks at Monique in the mirror. "Of what?"

Monique spits into the sink. "Cynthia! Hartford! This whole thing!"

"Oh . . . fine?"

"I can't place Cynthia. I'm usually really good with people, but I don't know, there's something about her that's just unreadable." Monique examines her face close up in the mirror. Silvia notices how she goes over her skin with her fingerpads as if she's painting it.

"Oh." Silvia doesn't find herself caring very much — it doesn't seem relevant. "She seems professional, I guess. Like she's doing her job."

"Her job? How many farmers do you know who dress like that?" Silvia doesn't

82

respond, so Monique goes on. "Anyway, what're you working on here?"

"Can I get to the sink, please?" Silvia speaks through the toothpaste in her cheeks.

Monique steps away. "All yours." And then: "Pretty fucked that there's no reception, too."

"Maybe we'll be able to concentrate on our work better."

Monique stops what she's doing and eyes Silvia's reflection, her combed hair and cotton pyjama set buttoned right up to the collar. Monique takes her toothbrush in her fist. "Sleep tight."

Silvia goes back to her room and falls asleep straightaway. No dreams.

XI

Everyone is on time for breakfast the next morning, sleepy but alert. Silvia notices how their clothes smell of their detergents from home. The table is laid, and an impressive selection of cereal, fruit, bread, milk, jams and honey, tea, and coffee is lined up on the kitchen counter. A note says "Serve Yourself."

Silvia sees Ibrahim, and her first thought is that he looks nice in the morning. He's talking to everyone and seems comfortable, relaxed. He's standing by the serve-yourself station and just taking handfuls of random things as he chats. Shoving Shreddies into his mouth, he points to some suitcases by the door. "Whose are those?" he asks, mouth full.

Kate and Lauren, who had introduced themselves as the art-school students from Nova Scotia the night before, are standing at the end of the table drinking water.

"Ours," Kate says.

"Need help carrying them up?" he asks.

"No," says Lauren. "We're leaving."

"Oh," Ibrahim says. "Forever?"

The girls look at each other, then at their bags, then back at him.

"How come?"

"This is just not what we expected," Kate replies, frankly. She applies lip gloss, slowly, without a mirror.

Ibrahim looks at the others. They don't look at him; they look at the girls or at their food. "What are you going to do?"

"I've got family in Calgary," Kate says. "We'll take the train west and spend the summer there. You know, like *actually* working."

"We've got school assignments and stuff," Lauren elaborates. "I mean, we can't just become beekeepers all of a sudden."

"We're going to go now," Kate says. "Before they get here."

"Will you tell them for us, please?" Lauren asks Ibrahim.

"Tell them what?"

"Tell them we . . . I don't know. Just tell them we had to go," Kate says, pushing air away with her hands.

"Okay," says Ibrahim. "Safe travels."

Then the girls are gone. They didn't take

any breakfast for the road.

Silvia looks into her cereal bowl. She's sitting in the same place as yesterday; everyone else has taken the same spots too, leaving two empty seats to Ibrahim's left. Everything is the same except for the table-cloth, which is gone, revealing the assortment of mismatched, water-stained tables.

Partly because it is early, partly because they haven't yet formed an opinion about the whole thing, nobody talks except to exchange banal formalities.

Please pass the milk.

Please pass the honey.

It's Cynthia who is late: she doesn't show up until after 8:00. (Though she might not have been late, they realise afterwards. She never said she would be eating with them.)

"All done here?" Cynthia appears from behind them, from nowhere. "Where are the others?"

"Kate and Lauren?" Ibrahim asks.

Cynthia pauses. "Weren't there ten?"

"Yeah. The two girls . . . aren't here."

"Right — are they coming?"

"Well, actually, they had to . . . leave." Ibrahim swallows his last huge spoonful of Shreddies.

"Why?"

He empties his mouth, which takes a moment, then replies. "They . . . they couldn't stay, they said. They left ten minutes ago. To Calgary," he says, as though Calgary is the missing link.

"I see," Cynthia says. "Let's go into the garden then."

Silvia doesn't finish her breakfast, but she didn't feel that hungry really.

XII

Hartford is waiting in the ineffectual shade of a very small tree. When everyone arrives he smirks into the sun, eyes closed, lips stretched across his teeth. His beige hat doesn't do a very good job protecting him from the sun either; judging by his already glowing face, he'll have a burn across his nose by midday.

"Good morning, everyone." He speaks with the forced, formal cheer of a camp counsellor.

"Good morning," they chorus.

"I trust you all slept well." He pauses and looks around. No response. "So," he continues, "I have here a rota for daily chores." He taps his clipboard with a pencil Silvia can tell has been freshly sharpened. "We've done our very best to divide them fairly, and you'll be paired with a partner." While speaking, he makes the necessary modifications for Kate and Lauren. "Tasks are

varied, and you'll be supervised for some —
for example, I'm sure you all know how to
water plants and weed a garden, but I doubt
very much that any of you have previous
experience in requeening a hive or moving
a swarm of wild bees."

Silvia notices Cynthia lock eyes with him.

"Right," Hartford says, following direction and shifting gears. "Silvia, you're first
up with Cynthia."

Silvia is slightly taken aback: she'd expected her partner would be another resident. She looks over at Cynthia, standing
placidly under a birch tree in her crisp white
shirt. Ibrahim is on her other side, slightly
apart from the rest of the group, his head
bowed as if the weight of the sun has
become a physical burden. Maybe it's just
because of the proximity of their rooms, but
Silvia had somehow thought that she'd be
working with him. She wonders if this is
what he's thinking too.

"Silvia?" Cynthia starts walking away, and
Silvia is pulled, as if magnetically, to follow
her.

Cynthia leads her round the back of the
house to the greenhouse, where she retrieves
pieces of white cotton from a trunk. "Here."
Cynthia hands her several separate items
that make up a full beekeeper suit. There

are zippers and pockets, veils and gloves, a hat and a carabiner. "No, put the suit on first," she says as Silvia squashes the broad-rimmed white hat over her mushroom hair, adjusting the black netting that zips onto it.

"Sorry." Silvia takes off the hat.

The material is thick but airy, the suit so large it doesn't cling. She puts her legs into the leg holes — keeping her shoes on — and bends her knees. She zips up the middle and slides her arms into the long tubes, elastic at the wrists. Her hands look so tiny and pink down at the bottom of the white pipes. There are pockets at the hips, and a small gold-and-black bee embroidered on the left breast. "Pretty," Silvia says, touching it gently.

"You like it?" Cynthia, bent over some metal tools, looks up. "I did that myself."

Silvia looks at the bee again, closer this time.

"Don't forget the gloves," Cynthia says, closing the box of tools.

The gloves are on the countertop: rubberized like gardening gloves but long enough to cover her elbows; yellow leather palms and a ventilated panel above the wrist. "Do I put them over or under?" Silvia has the left one on.

"Here." Cynthia comes over and pulls the

elasticated top of the glove over the baggy cotton arm, snapping it tight at the elbow. "You have beautiful hands," she says. "So delicate."

Cynthia lets go of Silvia's hand and turns away, and Silvia feels as though she's been set adrift. "Don't you need a suit too?" she asks.

Cynthia is walking towards the forest, away from the hives Silvia had noticed behind the vegetable patch. "Nope, no need. Bring the hat and veil — you can put them on once we get there."

It's hot in the suit, but as they walk into the forest, the shade of the scrubby trees protects Silvia from the beating sun. She doesn't know where they're going but doesn't want to ask, even though following in uncertainty makes her feel nervous. The bark of the trees is reddish and ragged, as though cheaply made; the trunks are spindly; and pine needles, dead as hay, carpet the ground.

"Nearly there." Cynthia looks back at Silvia as she sidesteps a fallen, rotten log.

Silvia steps over the log a few paces later and notices that the wood has been tunnelled into a complicated home for ants, or termites; she has absolutely no idea what kind of bugs would live here.

Cynthia is wearing hiking boots, and Silvia is wishing she'd known to bring more suitable footwear: she's wearing white Keds with no socks.

"Here." Cynthia stops abruptly beneath a tall deciduous tree, and Silvia, having been looking at the ground to track her footfall, nearly walks right into her back. "Put your hat and veil on now," Cynthia says, looking up at the sky.

Silvia cranes her neck to see what Cynthia is looking at and notices a droopy lung suspended on a branch at shoulder height. As soon as she sees it, she hears it — the way lightning always precedes thunder — and the dull buzz turns into a vacuuming roar. The shape moves with such smooth subtlety it seems like a single, complete organism. Then an individual bee separates itself from the rest and darts upwards, sideways, and disappears.

"My trap worked," Cynthia whispers, more to herself than to Silvia.

"What trap?" Silvia's voice too has become subdued.

"Your hat." Cynthia turns around and watches until Silvia puts on the hat, and then the veil on top of it. "I'll help you with that," she says when she sees Silvia fumbling with the zip that attaches the veil to the neck of the suit.

"Thanks." Silvia turns her head to feel the new pull of material connected to her, like a tendon.

Cynthia guides Silvia's glance. "See the wooden plank?"

Silvia looks, and though her depth of vision is compromised by the black pixels of the netting — like the compound, mosaic eyes of a fly — she can see the plank Cynthia is pointing to.

"It's part of a box, which is a swarm trap I set up for wild bees. Half my bees died this winter — it was an especially rough one all across Ontario — so I was hoping to catch a swarm that was looking for a new home. And here we are."

"Why the trap, though?"

"So I could find them more easily," she says. "Bees are expensive."

"You have to buy them?"

"Unless you trap them." Cynthia speaks with a logic that frustrates Silvia: she doesn't understand, something about it bothers her, and Cynthia intuits this. "They don't belong to me, no, but they also don't belong to anyone else."

Silvia squints, looking for the connecting thread.

"But the bees have a lot of nectar this time of year, and they want a new home to make their honey in. And I can give them that."

Silvia can hear her breath amplified in the chamber created underneath her cotton hood. She doesn't feel afraid.

"Right." Cynthia steps forward and puts her bare hands into the buzzing mass of bees. "Here we go."

"Won't they sting you?"

Cynthia's head swings around. "I'll need you to be quiet for this, Silvia." She turns away and moves her hands slowly, reminding Silvia of tai chi. "Can you bring me the box?"

Silvia notices the wooden box on the ground beneath the tree.

"Put it by my feet." Cynthia pulls her hands out of the swarm. Her hands, cupped, are full of bees. "They're so warm." She speaks softly, maternally. "Now," she says to them, "down you go."

And with that, the bees flow off Cynthia's hands and into the box. As the bees separate, the buzzing amplifies.

Cynthia's focus on the job is so intense that Silvia feels as though she's become invisible. Cynthia once again puts her naked hands into the bulging swarm, thinner now. Silvia holds her breath within her echo chamber. This time the bees seem to flow down from the wild hive and into Cynthia's hands instinctively. Some clamber up her arms, making mechanical freckles all the way up to her elbow.

"There we go," Cynthia says.

On command, the bees flow down into the box.

Still not looking at anything but the bees, her bees, Cynthia says, "The lid."

Silvia passes Cynthia a flat piece of wood that Cynthia quickly slides over the box, closing the bees inside. She steps back, and Silvia lets out her breath. "That was amazing."

Cynthia nods. She looks tired from the effort, the excitement.

"Did you get stung?" Silvia asks.

"They don't want to fight."

Silvia feels a tickle of sweat as it drips from her neck to the hollow of her lower back. "Do you ever wear a suit?"

"It's just about confidence. Bees know when you're frightened, so you have to keep calm. And this is a young swarm — they're pretty easy to control."

XIII

Finished with her chores for the day, Silvia goes back to her room and lies on her mattress, staring at a single point on the sloping ceiling. Was that theft, or was it simply cunning? If the bees belonged to nobody, could they belong to anybody? Could things exist without being owned? Who does *she* belong to, now that she's left home? Is it possible that she belongs to herself?

The way that Cynthia knew exactly what she was doing — and did so with a strength that seemed divinely appointed — created in Silvia a feeling of reverence. This was a woman who belonged to herself.

She opens up her empty notebook, hoping she'll be able to translate her feelings into words. The way the bees moved under Cynthia's direction. The way their buzzing came from all around, from within. The way she felt like a magnet, drawn to everything. Her pencil hovers over the blank page.

■ ■ ■ ■

That night Dan and Ben are on the rota for preparing dinner. They had the day off and spent it "exploring." The kitchen is old-fashioned but open plan. The cupboards are wooden and the room has a worn, scrubbed-clean look. The others are sitting round, not attempting to help. Silvia brought down her notebook, mostly as a prop.

Filling a copper pot with water, Ben speaks loudly, his back filled with all the emotion his face is hiding. "So Dan says to this woman we're filming, 'Yes, of *course,* ma'am, I swear I'll never tell a *soul* about all the freaky things your secret Internet persona does, hand on my heart!' but he didn't mention that we were making a documentary on catfishing and we'd already signed a contract with a station!" He shakes his right hand until his fingers snap. "The rushes were going to the boss in real time."

Monique, grubby from sodding the back fields, perks up, pushing a blond tuft behind her ear. "The documentary you made was on TV?"

Dan takes the pot from his brother and puts it on the stove to boil. "Yeah. Our stuff's been on TV a bunch of times."

"That's awesome." Monique, energy crackling off her body, crosses her legs the other way around.

MJ and JB arrive in the kitchen after having finished weeding for the afternoon, pulling their rubber boots off and kicking them onto the mat inside the screen door. They sit next to one another at the table. MJ's hair is dyed bright red, and JB is bald. An attractive, stylish bald. Silvia is intrigued by them.

"And are you working on something here?" Monique continues, looking from one brother to the next, not sure which to address, or even which is which.

Ben and Dan look at each other. The awkward moment passes, and Ben winks at Monique. "Kind of," he says.

"We've got some ideas," says Dan, elusive.

Cynthia enters, and the atmosphere shifts — everyone stands to varying degrees of attention. "Hello," she says.

There's a murmur of greeting from the group.

"Ben, Dan, are you finding everything you need?" she asks, and they nod. "It's past seven o'clock — is dinner nearly ready?"

"Ready in ten, Cyn. Sorry." Ben starts pulling plates from the cupboard and, with one arm full of crockery, fishes in the drawers looking for the cutlery.

"Right. I'll be in my office, then." She starts walking, then turns back around. "And it's Cynthia."

Silvia catches Ibrahim looking at her and quickly opens her empty notebook and flicks through it with false intention. She wants to tell him about the bees but doesn't know where to begin. And how to get to beyond the bees to whatever it is that the swarm represented. Her words haven't come yet.

XIV

The next morning, Hartford leads the way to the animal pens. The group walks towards the hedge-stitched fields about a hundred yards behind the farm. Wisps of morning cloud have already been burned away by the sun, and as Hartford walks, encumbered by the large bags of feed he carries, sweat pearls on his lip.

While his hair isn't actually receding, if Silvia were to think back on Hartford years after having met him, she would remember him as being afflicted with a mild baldness. This is not the case, however — in fact, his hair is quite lush. The impression of being a little threadbare probably comes instead from his pallor. It's difficult to distinguish Hartford's hair from his skin except for where he's sunburnt. His colourless eyebrows disappear into his forehead, and he seems to favour pinky-cream clothing just a few shades off his skin tone.

When they crest a hill, the animals appear: five pigs and about twice as many sheep. As it's spring there are lambs, some with their bendy legs knitted up beneath them, others jumping in the ridiculous way that baby sheep jump.

"Cute!" Monique squeals. "Are there any little piglets?"

Hartford explains, "All the pigs are gilts."

Monique looks blank.

"Lady pigs. Unmated. For food."

"Oh." A tinge of horror appears on her face.

"Here's the bag of food," Hartford says, handing a huge plastic sack to JB. "Just fill up the troughs."

And here the group splits off as had been previously coordinated: Monique, Silvia, Ibrahim, and JB go to feed the pigs, while MJ, Alicia, Ben, and Dan stay with Hartford to shear the sheep.

Ibrahim and Silvia walk next to one another, just behind the other two.

"How are you finding farm life so far?" Ibrahim asks.

"I like it here. I mean, I think? It's different."

"Good. Me too. Different is good, right?" he says, as though picking up a baton she'd passed him. "I'm just exhausted," he says.

"Back home I paint at night and sleep in the day. I think it'll be hard to get used to the rhythm here."

"Oh." She's not sure whether she's meant to feel sorry for him or admire him for his passion, his persistence.

"I'll be right back," Monique says as JB spills feed into the buckets and the enormous pigs come barreling over. "I forgot . . . a thing." She gestures vaguely towards the house and walks back as quickly as possible.

"You think she's vegetarian?" Ibrahim asks Silvia once Monique has disappeared.

"Maybe just a city girl," Silvia responds, swinging one leg over the wooden slatted fence, then the other.

Hartford, in the sheep pen, sees Monique walk deerishly back up the hill and then resumes demonstrating how to shear the sheep he's got gripped between his knees. Ben, Dan, MJ, and Alicia stand in a semicircle around him.

"You have to keep the sheep calm," he says, "so that it doesn't move around." Hartford's movements are gentle and efficient, and the fleece comes away easily. "The idea is to do it as quickly and closely as possible." He brings the electric clipper's blade to the sheep's neck without ever cutting the delicate skin. He stands up and holds out the device to Alicia, simply because she's nearest. "Give it a go."

Alicia gets confidently down on her knees and waits as Hartford manoeuvres the next sheep into position. She turns on the clipper, brings it to the sheep's belly, and wicks away the fleece with ease.

"Excellent," says Hartford, clearly surprised.

"What are you gonna do with all the fur?" Ben asks, watching it peel off as Alicia mows the sheep's body in neat stripes.

"The fleece," Hartford corrects. "We sell it."

"Right. I bet we don't get a cut of that profit either," Dan mutters to his brother.

Alicia finishes quickly and Hartford points to Dan. "You're next."

After half an hour blistering in the sun, Silvia walks back to the house to fill up her plastic water bottle from the garden tap by the back door. She turns the tap on, then lets her eyes wander. She hears laughter and turns to find Monique standing with Cynthia by the tousled carrot tops. Monique is chatting animatedly, and Silvia can't hear the words, but she notices Cynthia smile.

"Stop it."

Silvia turns and sees Hartford right behind her, holding a bundle of fleece.

"The drought." His voice is stern.

Silvia looks down and sees that her full water bottle is overflowing. Hartford turns off the tap.

"We have limited reserves," he says.

"Sorry, I —" she starts, but Hartford is walking back to the pens, having left the greyish pile inside the back door. She returns to the pigpen where the others, though finished with the feeding, are lingering, not sure what's next.

There's still light in the sky after dinner that evening — the orange stripe along the horizon sets the clouds aflame. The farm is farther north than Silvia's ever been, and she's amazed at how the light lingers: it's nearly ten o'clock, and still night has not yet killed the day.

The group gathers round in the library. After dinner there is no rota, no chores to do, and they are not tired — of work, of each other — yet.

The library looks just the way a library should: bookshelves from floor to ceiling; lamps that cast a warm, uniform light. There is nondescript but pleasant wallpaper. Greenish, floralish. A brown corduroy couch big enough for three — four if you squish, and Silvia squishes in with three of them now; two comfy chairs to match; and two red stools that pull out from under the coffee table. Ibrahim and JB sit on the ground.

"Anyone bring a guitar?" Ben — or is it Dan? No, Ben, he's got slightly lighter hair — asks. He's clearly afraid of silence, Silvia thinks. Or maybe of conversation.

Nobody did, but Monique spots a guitar case in the corner, propped next to a bookshelf. She goes to it.

"You think we . . . ?" she says, asking nobody in particular, reaching out and touching its neck with her fingertips.

"Yeah, I'd say so," Dan says. "Until they tell us not to." He smiles around the room.

Silvia notes that both Ben and Dan have an unobtrusive familiarity that must make them excellent at their jobs. It's as if they smile just to open a window onto how other people are feeling.

Ben opens the guitar case and holds the instrument as if he's hugging it. "Sweet," he says, and zigzags a few chords as he tunes it. "Any requests?"

Nobody says anything, so Monique says, "Play what you feel like." She stretches the "feel."

His chords turn into a medley of Bob

Dylan songs. The music creates a background, not a focal point. An excellent tactic for documentary filmmaking.

Ibrahim gets out a pad of paper and some charcoal pencils of varying thicknesses and, without saying anything, starts sketching objects in the room. Silvia, sitting behind him on the sofa, watches as images appear on his page. A cup, a foot, the neck of the guitar. It's incredible, she thinks, how things can appear where there once was nothing.

"Give it to me," Monique says to Ben, holding her hands out for the guitar. The Dylan was deviating into a dull but dizzying melody as he listened more to the conversation than to his own rhythm. Monique sits on the arm of the sofa and retunes the instrument. "I write songs," she says, clearing her throat. "*La la LA la la* . . . ahem . . . okay, so then —"

Her song is about love and suffering and the moon. It hits all the clichés in the right key, but the tune is nice and she's got a pretty voice. It soars above her; her face screws up and her eyes squint as the notes get higher. She turns a string of misery chords into a punchy, ecstatic riff, and when she's finished, everyone claps.

"Thank you, thank you," she says, making an awkward curtsy. "What are you drawing?" she asks Ibrahim.

"Nothing," Ibrahim says, putting his sketchbook facedown. "Just stuff in the room. But hey, you guys wanna be my subjects?" He's holding his pencil in one hand, and with the other he rakes his hair with his fingers. "It could be . . . fun. For you!" He looks around the room. He got ahead of himself, and now he's realising that he has to follow through on the offer. "And good practice for me."

"Ooh, yes!" Monique says, rushing forward. "Do me, do me!"

"Okay," he says. "Sit down, then."

"Just my face, or — ?"

"Yeah, the face," he replies, oblivious. "I could do, like, five-minute sketches of each of you. You can keep them, or we can leave them here when we go. As, like, a, a memento or something." He stumbles over his words; he's unusually nervous.

"Great idea," Ben says.

"Totally," echoes Dan.

"Hey, me first!" Monique rushes to sit on a pillow at the foot of the couch. "This can be the model's cushion," she says.

"Fine," says Ibrahim. He picks up the pad. He holds the charcoal above the page. He looks at Monique's face, making mental measurements.

"That's such a good idea," MJ says. "But easier for a painter," she continues, no jealousy in her tone. "I'm a potter and didn't bring my materials — it's too much with clay and spin tables and all that." She gestures as though she's doggy-paddling or DJing. "I am here just to collect my thoughts a little bit. Get ideas for my work from textures and colours in landscape." Her turntables get wider as she gestures beyond an LP's circumference. Though she speaks clearly, her French accent sneaks in slightly, sticking to the vowels.

"And bees," JB says, his voice falsely sarcastic. "In landscape and in bees. Is what she writes in 'er application."

Before Ibrahim can begin — the page is still clean as fresh snow — a knock at the door presents Cynthia. "Hello," she says, holding two small brown-paper rectangles. "I brought chocolate."

Silvia feels suddenly uncomfortable, and she can sense the others do too. It's as though a mom has crashed a high school party. The chocolate works well to create a bridge, though: the eight of them immediately scramble for it as though each piece could have Willy Wonka's Golden Ticket within the wrapper, as though each of them could win — what, the ticket to leave? The ticket to stay?

"Oh *god.*" Monique moans. "I forgot about chocolate. It's like fucking *ambrosia* or something." Her face is in pained raptures.

"What are you up to in here?" Cynthia asks.

Silvia can't tell if her tone is accusatory.

"Ibrahim is drawing me," Monique says, going back to her position on the pillow, turning her head on her long neck. She swallows.

"I'm gonna draw everyone," Ibrahim says, democratically.

"Oh," Cynthia says, "lovely." She sits down in the armchair opposite Alicia and watches as the group settles back into their places.

The two bars of chocolate disappear before Ibrahim is finished with Monique's portrait.

"Are you done?" Monique asks, fidgety.

"I think so," Ibrahim says, each word hitting a different note. He holds the paper at the length of his arm, squinting. "Yeah."

"Show me, show me!" She jumps up and goes around to see. Her face scrunches like one of his discarded, balled-up drafts. "That's *me*?"

"Uh —"

She pulls the paper from his fingers. "Does this look like me?" She holds it in both hands and displays it for everyone.

Everyone is silent. Ibrahim is mortified.

Silvia thinks it's incredible — though she can see why Monique might not like it as a figurative representation of herself. There are sharp lines dividing the regions of her face — top, middle, bottom, but also left cheek from left eyebrow, and dimple from jaw — and the features are rendered as if etched from stone. Even if it doesn't look like Monique all that much, it somehow feels like her.

"I think you look hot," Ben says.

"Is that related to the portrait, though?" Monique asks, her sarcasm verging on smugness. "This doesn't even look like a woman. Or even a *human,* really."

"I wasn't going for a specific likeness." Ibrahim is going the colour of a sunburn. "It's just a little game. Maybe I'll do more representative stuff for the next ones."

"I think it's wonderful," Cynthia says, standing. She walks towards Ibrahim. "Incredible, really. The confidence in your lines, the boldness of your vision. Congratulations, Ibrahim. Monique, what an honour."

"Well, yeah, that's what I was trying to

say before . . ." Monique trails off and looks at the drawing again, tilting her head.

"I think it's nice too," Silvia says.

"You do?" Ibrahim asks.

Silvia nods. "It's amazing that you can make something from nothing."

Ibrahim looks at his sketch afresh, smiling. "Thanks."

A mellow quiet settles over the group. It lasts a second before Monique gets up and asks Ben if he wants to go get some water.

"I'm not thirsty."

She puts her hands on her hips. "Well, *I'm* thirsty," she says. "Come with me."

"Oh, right. Okay." He gets up so quickly he falls over his feet.

Silvia looks around to see what time it is, but there is no clock on any of the walls. She has no idea whether she's been sitting in this room for ten minutes or four hours. She has no idea whether she's been on the farm for a day or a lifetime. Time feels oceanic — too big, impossible to measure — and at the same time it's metonymic: one second of her life, just as one drop in the ocean is representative of the whole. She looks around at the people, at the books, at the way the light paints the same gold over everything, and feels a smile from inside.

"Shall I do you next?" Ibrahim asks, looking at Silvia.

"Me?" Silvia looks behind her, where Cynthia is leaning against the sofa. Silvia can feel Cynthia bristle at his question, though she doesn't understand why.

"Yeah, you."

"Okay." She sits on the cushion Monique left and softens into place.

"What should I do?" she asks. "Where should I look?"

"Wherever you want."

Silvia's face is pale and open. Like a child with a life of opportunity lying ahead. She sits facing forward, eyes on Ibrahim. Still. There's something pure about the connection of artist and subject that she doesn't want to break, but also she doesn't want to look away from Ibrahim because she can't bear catching anyone else's glance. The feeling of eyes on her is tangible as cloth. She's never liked being made aware of the unknowability of others, or the impossibility of others truly knowing her. If they're looking at her, they're forming opinions of her that she can't control. She has the feeling that in being drawn like this, she is understood, somehow, in a way she's never experienced before. She tries to focus on the strength of Ibrahim's gaze and forget about the others.

As she sits there on the pillow, her senses

become attuned to the sharp sound of charcoal on paper, shaping contours and scratching shadows as it itches through the chatter in the room. She watches Ibrahim's face scrunch as he concentrates, his long hair falling in his eyes. She is also aware when the sounds of talking dull down and the only sound — and seemingly the only thing — in the whole room is Ibrahim's charcoal on the thickly woven paper.

She has no curiosity about what the drawing looks like. That doesn't feel like the matter at hand. The only thing she's thinking about is this moment of sitting, and watching, and being watched.

XV

Breakfast. Ibrahim comes down, wolfish. He hasn't slept all night. The others are halfway through toast and cereal when he lopes into the kitchen, his eyes red-veined like another planet. His face looks hollow, cavernous.

Back home he didn't usually go to bed until well after dawn, and now, what with the rigorous schedule imposed on them — rising with the sun and working all through the day — he isn't performing to capacity in any aspect. Plus, here there is no garbage to rifle through at night, no new material to move him onto some unplanned path. Though he arrived with enough supplies to last him through to autumn, he's realised that it's the routine of the hunt that inspires him. It's the air; the dirty streets; the people who, like him, lurk in the night; all the evidence of life he sees and collects as he roams.

Standing like a zombie in the kitchen now, Ibrahim takes it all in — orange juice, oranges, the radio tuned to something Québécois — before he takes a seat.

"You all right?" Silvia asks.

"Fine. Coffee?"

"Here," says Monique. "There's a little left in the jug. Milk? Sugar?"

"Black."

He'd been working all night, making good on his five-minute sketches from the evening before — five minutes is nothing, five minutes isn't even coffee and a clovie — softening the edges with his fingers, erasing lines into highlights, crosshatching shadows. He likes the one of Silvia the best; this is the one he cares most about. Of all eight sketches, hers looks most like her, but also most like him, his style. Part of it, for him, comes in the moment, but another important part comes in making it his own, after. The final product is equal parts him and his subject. It's just like bees, he's coming to realise: the honey isn't sitting there inside the flowers, ready to be sucked; the bees have to work to turn it into that sweet syrup. The solitary work, the magic that happens in the cells.

"Aig?" Ben asks.

"What?" Ibrahim's confusion sounds angry.

"You want some aig?" Ben repeats, pointing to his breakfast. Runny yolk and ketchup make an abstract painting of his plate.

"Oh, *egg*. No. Thanks." The thought of food makes him feel like vomiting.

Now everyone is looking at Ibrahim, concerned. He catches Silvia's eye but looks away, too tired to think.

"I have to go back to bed for a few minutes," he grumbles, making his voice gruff to try to mask the panic of the sleepless. He walks out of the kitchen, holding his coffee in both hands.

Back in his room, the eight charcoal-grey faces lie face up on the floor, a protective line in front of his bed. Ibrahim falls asleep, thinking of Silvia's grey eyes.

XVI

Silvia's morning job is to tend to the garden. It's a simple job and doesn't take two, so she's happy to cover for Ibrahim, her partner for the day. Transitions have always been easy for her; she doesn't think too much about things. Like water, she takes a little while to fill her surroundings, but inevitably she fills them wholly.

The sky is bare. It's only nine o'clock, but beyond the shade of the greenhouse, the sun feels naked, as if it were noontime. Despite the water shortage, irrigating the plants twice weekly is essential. More than that is unnecessary — overwatering leads to plant rot, Hartford explained, and overfertilizing leads to root burn — but less than that and the plants will be endangered.

Today is a watering day; tomorrow will be for weeding. She gets the plastic watering can from where it lives by the hosepipe and pours small green beads of fertilizer into

117

the bottom, eyeballing a one-to-six ratio, and then fills it up with water from the hose. There is a well at the bottom of the yard, but its pulley is no longer functional and the bucket's purely decorative; the water system now works through a series of pipes and cisterns and taps and hoses that connect this well to the others in the area, extending all the way to the nearest village. None of the wells have been private for years, Cynthia has explained. In this case, codependence means strength.

Drop a stone in the well and it will sink, an echoless sigh, for two and a half seconds before the tiny *plink* when it finally hits water.

One alligator
Two alligators
Thr—

Straining slightly to hold the heavy watering can, Silvia walks back to the garden. The whole thing is planted in perfectly straight lines — probably Hartford's doing, she thinks. Peas curl up bamboo posts, their new shoots clinging tight; star-shaped yellow flowers preface as yet miniature cucumbers, also vining their way up pale bamboo. The clusters of tomatoes are still young and let off such a familiar smell: they smell so perfectly of green.

The water absorbs quickly into the earth, and as soon as it's gone the dirt looks dry again. Silvia touches the ground but finds it damp, spongy, as it should be. Seconds later the furled leaves stretch flat to face the sun and the stalks straighten as they fill with the water. It looks as if the tomato plants are breathing, the way they move and sway on their own. Watching this, she feels a little bit heroic. Her back is sweating, so she ties the bottom of her striped T-shirt in a knot above her navel. Wind catches the wet skin and turns it cold.

A bumblebee blunders about the lavender stalks, pulling the flower heads down with it as it lands on one, then another. It's actually the closest she's ever been to a bee in nature. Or maybe it's just the first time she's looked closely. The bee is encased in fuzzy armour, much more black than yellow. Its antennae are as long as its legs, but the back legs are squat like a quarterback's. The wings, muddy-pellucid, remind Silvia of reused cling film.

As she's checking to see if the carrots are orange beneath the earth, a large grey thing runs straight for her ankles and weaves between her legs, purring like a revved-up machine. It's a cat. It's a cat without a tail.

"Hey, little guy," she murmurs, petting his

back. "Where did you come from?" His fur feels greasy; it comes out in clumps. Though he has only a small stub where the tail should be, like a rabbit's scut, his back arches and the stunted tail flicks from its base the way an ordinary cat's would. After she's stroked him tip to tail he runs off to the zucchini plants and stares into space, completely still, as though he can see something that she can't. She'd read somewhere that cats have eight times more light-sensing rods in their eyes than humans, and that this greater vision is more remarkable than can ever be fully comprehended. Some people think it means that cats can see ghosts.

Returning the fertilizer to its place in the greenhouse, Silvia sees Cynthia there through the window, sorting some papers. She drops the fertilizer to undo the knot in her top, re-covering her abdomen, then goes in.

"Hi," Silvia says, hovering awkwardly by the door.

Cynthia jumps — the moment before fear finds its object, when the heart is caught in the air — then sees Silvia. "Goodness, you startled me."

"Sorry," Silvia says, "sorry — I should have knocked, I was just, the fertilizer —"

"Not at all." Cynthia rights herself, her hands shifting off a stack of papers, and smiles uncomfortably.

"Who's that?" Silvia sees the thing that Cynthia's hands had been covering up: a photograph of a woman, slightly older than herself.

"Who's who? Oh." She sees what Silvia is pointing to. "That's Hilary."

Hilary. The woman the taxi driver said she looked like?

"Sorry," Silvia apologizes again. "I thought it was — for a second it looked like me, and I didn't — that didn't make sense, obviously." She laughs.

Cynthia nods.

There's silence for a moment.

Silvia mentions the cat.

"Oh," Cynthia says, turning to open a blue file folder. "That's Toby."

"He's yours?"

"Sort of."

"He doesn't have a tail."

"I know."

"What happened?"

"We had to do it for his sake."

Silvia starts walking backwards, making her way out of the greenhouse, too stunned and filled with dread to probe any further, but Cynthia continues, reeling her back in:

"Silvia, I was wondering — how is your writing going?"

"My writing? Oh! Fine, thanks."

"Really? You're finding it inspiring here?"

Silvia, standing still, looks around at the tools on the walls, the empty Mason jars, the bags of dirt tipping onto the ground. She nods meekly.

"What exactly is it that you write?" Cynthia pauses, waiting. When Silvia says nothing, she continues: "Short stories? Poems? A novel? Or — ?"

"Poems," Silvia says. "I'm not very . . . experienced or anything, though. I haven't really written anything yet. I'm still settling in, I guess."

"Right." Cynthia nods knowingly, but unlike with most people, Silvia can tell she really does understand. "Well, thank you, Silvia."

It's clear that Silvia is being dismissed now, so she leaves, walking out backwards, feeling like she's seen something she shouldn't have and cannot unsee.

Back in the house, on her way to her room, Silvia pauses at the window in the upstairs hallway to see if she can see the part of the forest where Cynthia took her to remove the swarm. She wants to see how it all fits together, to see if from this bird's-eye perspective (albeit that of a low-flying bird) she can get a sense of the land. She stares and stares but can't make any more sense of it from here. She looks down instead, where she can see Dan, Ben, and Monique in the garden. Then a sound brings her perspective even closer: there's a buzz-banging right before her, and she suddenly sees a bee, which must have been dormant, come to life on the window ledge. It's trying to fly out the closed window, and every time it bangs into the glass it drops down in the air by an inch or so before catching itself, buzzing back, and thrashing against the glass once more. She quickly tries to get a grip on the wooden window frame and lift it up, but it's jammed, she can't even budge it. The bee keeps banging, the buzz of its wings getting louder. She puts her finger near the back of its body, and the bee stills. She moves her finger, and the bee moves.

"Wow." She lets out a breath.

She lifts her finger up and the bee follows, lifting off the ledge and hovering by the still jammed window. She drops her hand, and the bee drops too.

"Ibrahim!" She calls into his room. "Can you help me open this?"

"What's up?" He ambles to the doorway,

then sees her clutching the window frame. "Fresh air?"

"No, this bee, it's stuck, I'm trying to free it."

"I wouldn't worry," he says. "There're a few thousand more in the garden."

"Please?"

"Okay, sure," he says, sensing her concern. He comes over, bends his knees, grips the handle, and as he stands he lifts the window with the posture of a heavyweight champion.

The bee hovers, its wings beating so fast they're invisible, until Silvia gestures out the window. "You're free." As if understanding, the bee flies out, and Silvia feels immense relief. "Thank you," she says to Ibrahim.

"No worries."

She smiles. They're both hovering in space, drawn between their separate rooms and the common hallway.

Ibrahim rakes his fingers through his long hair. "Well, I was just coming up for a nap before dinner," he says, though that's not what he'd planned on saying.

Silvia looks at him, at his eyes. They hold each other there. "See you at dinner then, I guess?"

He nods, backing into his room. "Later."

She goes to look out the window, making

sure that the bee has in fact flown away. There's no sign of it. She puts her hands on the ledge, about to close the window again, but decides to leave it open.

XVII

Dinner is homemade meatloaf, though Hartford clarifies that it wasn't made in this home. There's a quiet inertia to the group, and Silvia can't tell whether it's due to exhaustion or intimacy. Everyone eats in silence, serving themselves salad and seconds.

At the end of the meal, Cynthia breaks the peace. "I hear you're having trouble sleeping, Ibrahim."

He swallows his mouthful, nodding. "I've been painting, yeah. Night's the only time I can work."

Cynthia pauses as if to mull this over, though it's clear that in raising the subject she's already made up her mind. "I'd like to give you the mornings off, then. You're so talented and devoted, I think you need time to work on your personal projects."

A different kind of silence follows.

"Uh — thank you," he says, stumbling

over his words. "That's really . . . kind."

"Not at all." She smiles modestly.

A mumble circulates around the group and Ibrahim catches Silvia's eye questioningly, but Silvia shrugs, as if to say, *It wasn't me.*

XVIII

The next day they are assigned a group task: to repair broken hive frames and clean out all the combs. The sound of grumbling can be heard above the dull buzz of bees all the way to Smooth Rock.

"We have to degunk all these?" Ben groans when he sees the teetering pile of framed honeycomb.

"And Cynthia expects this will only take a day?" Monique says, looking not at the pile but at the rest of the group, imploring.

Cynthia isn't sure whether the problem is mould or wax moths, tiny papery things that feed on the honeycomb and are a sure sign of a stressed hive, but whatever the problem is, it needs to be aborted before it develops any further. The bees have been getting agitated.

"Well, many hands make light work, right?" Silvia says.

"Save it, Silvia," Monique snaps. "Cynthia's not around to hear you."

At the beginning, none of them knew very much about bees, or honey. They are learning from doing — and a few of them from reading the information Cynthia has provided. The foremost fact is this: each bee has its role.

First, of course, there is the queen, the largest of them all. In any colony there is only one queen, and her sole purpose is to lay eggs. Once a new queen has been introduced and accepted, she takes a mating flight, during which she'll lose her virginity. She flies straight up, about thirty feet in the air, followed by a whole pack of drones. Ten, twenty, forty — as many as a hundred. This typically occurs over a couple of days, but unlike most organisms that mate over and over again for the production of each offspring, this singular incident provides the queen with a lifetime of viable eggs. She'll store the sperm collected over these few days in an internal sac and use it to produce fertilized eggs for workers or unfertilized eggs for drones. By mating with a large number of drones, the queen assures the hive of genetic diversity, and this, according to both Darwin and Cynthia, helps promote flexibility and longevity. The biological desires of bees, as with any animal, are 1) to survive, and 2) to procreate.

Drones have only one purpose too, and this is to mate with the virgin queen. Until then they loaf around the hive, and once their task has been completed, they die. Their purpose has been fulfilled. Drones are all males, and they neither work nor sting.

Then there are the worker bees. Worker bees are all females, and as their name suggests, they do all the work. They have three main jobs, depending on their age. Immediately after hatching they become nurse bees, looking after and feeding the new eggs and larvae. Inside the hive it's completely dark, so in the combs they work in blindness. Bees are deaf too, so in their early days in the hive, touch is their only sense, and they rely on this for all communication.

The nurses work for about ten days before becoming house bees, keeping the hive clean and clear of debris and storing the nectar that has been brought into the hive by the foraging workers. House bees fill the comb cells with the nectar, then seal them off with a wax lid. Inside the cells the nectar is transformed, as if by alchemy, into golden honey.

Another rank of house bees produces the

wax and shapes it into the thin, miraculously hexagonal cells. Another still will guard the entrance to the colony and keep it cool by fanning their wings. They take their turn as house bees for another ten days and then become foragers themselves, going out to collect pollen and nectar for the colony. This is their first experience of the outdoors. Imagine, all that light and colour must be . . . startling. A zillion flowers in every hue, and the three foremost colours: green grass, blue sky, yellow sun.

The bees work so hard at this last task that after three weeks of foraging they have literally worked themselves to death.

After an hour or so repairing the frames, the assembly-line aspect of group work has established itself organically: each person has a task, and the work goes quickly.

Alicia picks up a frame, gives it a wipe with a wet cloth, then hands it to Ben, who checks the wood, then hands it to Dan, who sprays it with Clorox, then hands it to MJ, who looks for live moths. If she finds any, she throws them in a pile behind her, but if she doesn't, she hands it to Monique and JB, who sit down with the frames in their laps and pick away the wax, handing the frames to Silvia, who sprays them with mint and fresh lemons (wax moths hate the stuff and avoid it like the plague) before adding the frame to the pile neatly to be stored in a freezer, to kill whatever might remain.

Nobody talks except to utter the occasional question or express exasperation. "Pass it to me"; "Did you see anything on that one?"; "It's so hot, eh?"; and then, eventually, as the grumbling mounts, "This is impossible" and "Such fucking bullshit."

"It is *so* not fair that Ibrahim doesn't have to do this." Monique stops working to pick out wax from under her fingernails.

Nobody replies. Everyone continues working until the work is done, but it's enough.

The seed has been planted.

XIX

The group files in, all sweaty and dirty from working, as Hartford is straining the spaghetti for dinner, steam obscuring his face as if he were in a film noir. Someone's tuned the radio to a smooth, dinnertime jazz station.

Monique is the first to sit down, and she takes her chair backwards, her legs around the seatback. "So," she says to Ibrahim, "what did *you* do all morning?"

"Worked," he says, filling up a glass of milk from the jug.

"Oh yeah? On what?"

"A painting." He makes it clear that he doesn't want to talk about it.

"Right." Ben sits down next to Monique and twists the top off a beer bottle with his bare hands. The bottle gasps. Something about this is menacing. "About that" — he necks it and looks at Cynthia — "when will we get a chance to do *our* art?"

Cynthia looks back at him. Ibrahim looks at her — everyone looks at her — but nobody can tell what she is thinking. She says nothing.

"I thought this was supposed to be an *artists'* colony." Ben stands up halfway, his thick thighs supporting the weight of all the hesitation in his muscles, then sits back down. "And only *Ibrahim* is getting to work on his art."

Ibrahim: "Hey!"

Dan: "It's really not fair that *he* gets mornings off while the rest of us work."

Ibrahim: "But —"

Ben: "We wanted to make a documentary about it here, artists and bees and stuff, those kinds of artistic connections, you know, but nobody would want to watch a bunch of inexperienced youth hoeing away in the dirt."

"You have free time every day." Hartford is quick to the defense, but he isn't quite sure what he should be defending. "But do any of you work on your art?"

"Obviously," Monique interrupts, eager to get involved. "This isn't just about *art,* it's about the *freedom to make art,* and none of us have any freedom."

"If you show the same level of productivity and talent," Cynthia says, speaking calmly, practiced, "then we can discuss adapting your work schedules too." She looks from Monique to Ibrahim, then catches something in her periphery: Ben is standing just outside the candlelit ring around the table, holding his phone. Looking steadily at him, she says, "Will you shut that off, please?"

He doesn't stop filming but flips the phone around to capture the reaction of the group.

Dan looks at his brother, gestures, and Ben starts circling around the table, keeping the lens trained on Dan, who's now standing, as if at a podium. "We've been here for over a week. We're doing all your chores and heavy labour, but if we don't have time to ourselves, what exactly is in it for us?"

The silence that follows is clear as glass.

Cynthia's voice is smooth as marble. "Look, I don't really know what to tell you. What did you expect when you came here? Some kind of summer camp?"

No one responds. The question hangs in the air.

"The creative work you do in your own time is your responsibility — how much you get done, what you want to make. You can leave any time you want."

XX

Silvia wakes early, before the bell. The light comes through her window like a veil, gauzy and fleeting. She has eleven minutes until she has to go down for breakfast and chores and interactions, which will all pull her out of herself, so for now she lies in bed, thinking. About who she was just a few weeks ago and who she is now. Is she the same person? Do people ever really change? Does it matter?

There's a sense of inevitability that comes from living in the moment: things flow smoothly into one another without forethought or preparation. Organic, authentic. This seems to make sense with her understanding of religion, if one is living in Christ, but her personal feelings are at odds with the greater implications of this. She's not sure whether the complicated Christian system of cause and effect really applies. What if one thing doesn't lead to another?

What if you make each thing happen for yourself, all the time? What if each thing is separate? For now it feels slightly treacherous even to articulate this thought in her mind, so she blanks it out.

She stretches out under the thin white sun-warmed sheet and looks out the window. Cynthia is out there already, working near the hives on the back lot, wearing a straw sun hat and a sleeveless button-down shirt. Her arms are surprisingly strong. Silvia can see her biceps beneath the skin as she lifts large hive boxes into a stack.

Soon Silvia will join her, but for now she luxuriates in her two remaining minutes of stillness, closing her eyes in the pleasure of it, thinking of Ibrahim only in the most abstract of senses.

All the others have remained with the partners they'd been assigned initially, but since Ibrahim's schedule has been adjusted, Silvia continues her partnership with Cynthia. Nobody envies or questions this position.

Requeening, Cynthia has explained, is often necessary at the beginning of a new season. If a queen bee conks out, she must be replaced with a new one. Like light bulbs. Sometimes the queen dies; sometimes she disappears, often taking her hive with her in a swarm; sometimes she just gets old and unruly. Signs of a queenless (or just anarchic) hive include especially noisy bees, a steadily decreasing population, and wild and distracted drones.

Without a mother, the colony becomes aggressive; without a properly functioning queen, a hive is doomed.

Silvia has put on the same protective suit she wore for the swarm, and Cynthia is wearing her normal clothes, not even a sun hat anymore.

"So." Cynthia hands Silvia a small cardboard box the size of a thick book. "Here's our new queen. All the way from California."

"FedEx? Crazy." Silvia takes the box in her gloved hands.

"It only takes two days, and the bees don't mind. The California ones are hardier than the Europeans. Must be all the kale." Cynthia smiles, but Silvia doesn't understand the joke. She nods seriously.

Cynthia continues: "Before you open the box and insert her in the hive, you must find and destroy the old queen."

"The old queen?" Silvia asks. "I thought you said it was queenless."

"That's just the term for when a queen

has stopped being useful. This one's still there."

"Why do we have to kill her?"

"Because you can't have two queens at once." Cynthia speaks calmly. "They'd fight each other to the death."

Later Silvia will learn that it's often the virgin queen who defeats the incumbent monarch, but not always.

"How do I even find her?" Silvia is understandably baffled.

"Put this" — Cynthia holds out a pipette — "in front of the entrance. It's sugar water, and queens go mad for it. She'll come right out."

Silvia stares at the pipette. It looks fragile and impractical.

Cynthia opens the latch on the front of the hive, and a door the size of her palm flaps down on its hinge. Silvia squeezes three droplets onto the wood.

Almost immediately the old queen dodders out onto the drawbridge of the door. She's enormous and unbalanced-looking. Her torso is so long. All yellow-gold, no black. Her wings don't even go halfway down her body. (Most mature queens can't fly. They're used to having everything done for them.)

"Is that her?" Silvia asks.

"Yes!"

Silvia puts out her hand and the bee climbs onto her index finger. "She came right to me!" She brings her hand to her face and peers at the bee through her black veil. The queen does not flap around or struggle. She perches on the thick cotton of Silvia's glove, calmly awaiting her fate.

"Great. Now kill her," Cynthia says.

"Can't we just put her somewhere else?"

"Just squish her. You're wearing gloves, she can't sting you."

Silvia flashes back to ten days earlier, in her childhood bedroom surrounded by horse posters, and thinks about how she never would have imagined standing in a field in the middle of nowhere murdering a queen bee. She closes her fist and feels the plasticated crunch of wings.

"Done?" Cynthia plucks the broken queen from Silvia's glove, examines her briefly, and tosses her off to the side.

"Shouldn't we bury her or something?"

"If you want to, go ahead and make the hole."

Silvia quickly, maniacally, digs a small fist-sized hole with her gloved hand. She retrieves the discarded queen's carcass, her carapace holding whatever regal soul still lingers, and places it into the hole, keeping her hands there for a moment as if feeling for a heartbeat. She scoops back some of the dirt from the pile and smoothes it flat. Nobody would know this was the burial ground of a queen.

"Okay, quick now," Cynthia says. "We only have a few minutes until the drones get cranky."

Before opening the cardboard package in which this mail-order bride awaits, Cynthia explains that they have to spray it — box, queen, everything — with a vanilla-scented spray.

"Seriously?" Silvia asks.

"It makes them calm." Cynthia pulls out a bottle of perfume. "Once we put her inside we have to spray it again, over the whole hive." By the time the scent has disappeared, Cynthia explains, the new queen will be accepted.

Everything happens as it should. At least, as far as Silvia can tell. The virgin queen gets out of her box and shuffles into the hive. Gone. She looked just like the old queen. Just as long, just as yellow, wings just as stubby. They can't yet tell if the others have accepted her, though. That will take another few hours.

"Good work," Cynthia says as they walk

back to the greenhouse to return Silvia's suit.

"Thanks," Silvia says, taking off her veil and hat. "It was sort of weird to kill the queen like that, but I get it." She repeats what she's learned: "For the good of the hive."

Cynthia tilts her head and looks at Silvia as though she's looking at a painting. "Can I show you something?"

Silvia replies lightly, "Sure."

Cynthia smiles with her lips closed, then pivots, guiding Silvia in the opposite direction.

Silvia feels sweat liquefying her lower back and ringing the armholes of her tank top underneath the heavy cotton suit.

When they get to the top of a lowly rolling hill, Cynthia stops. The boundary of the lot is marked with a dried-up hedge where yellow dandelions sprout carelessly. Lion-yellow, bee-yellow.

"This is my favourite place on the farm," Cynthia says. "On a clear day like today you can see all the way to the Quebec border there" — she points — "and the Abitibi reserve that way." She looks at Silvia.

"It's . . . it's beautiful." Silvia doesn't know which way to look, or how she would tell the difference between here and there.

It is stunning, though — there's something perfect, complete, about it. "I see why you love it."

"Here," Cynthia says, pulling a slim book out of her pocket. "For you."

Silvia takes the book and looks at the cover. It has Cynthia's name on it, and an illustration of what looks like either a tree or a woman. "You wrote this?"

"Practically a lifetime ago. I thought it might interest you, as a fellow writer."

"Thank you." Silvia looks at the book, turning it around with reverence.

Clouds come from a corner of sky, tracing shadows as they pass over the fields. White, decorative, they hold no illusion of rain. Silvia blinks, and keeps her eyes closed a second longer than necessary.

"I want you to find your voice, Silvia." Cynthia speaks with authority and kindness, like an elementary school principal. "I know you have a lot to say."

Silvia is about to respond, but a humming sound starts rising from all the way down at the bottom of the hill, where the hives are; the buzz clouds her thoughts.

XXI

On Sundays they all sleep in, or not, and can come down for breakfast at their leisure. Supplies are laid out on the table; there's no set time for anything. There are no chores. No weeding, no requeening, no cleaning, no mowing, no honey categorizing, paper filing, muck room demucking, honeycomb dewaxing. On the seventh day, everyone rests.

That second Sunday morning, dried and dressed, Silvia has gone down to fetch coffee and toast to bring back to her room, and now she wants to try to write. A poem. She wants to write a poem about . . . about everything. Splayed stomach-down on her mattress, she thinks.

She reaches for Shakespeare's "Silvia," in the middle of the bedside pile, and looks at it. First at each word individually, then scanning it as a whole. She tries to think about what happens in poems, what they are about. She'd covered some medieval and Renaissance poetry in her English lit coursework, but it all felt pretty cursory. Lots were about love, lots were about God. Lots were about the love of God. She wrote a poem when she was little, but it was basically just copying the Silvia sonnet, so she'd decided it didn't count. She'd written another poem when she was a teenager, but it was about nothing.

Instead of a poem, then, she starts a list about what a poem should be.

POEMS:
-

Distracted already, she starts looking at herself in the small mirror in her room. She turns her head one way, then the other, looking from the line of her jaw to the smooth curve of her hairline.

She shifts around on the bed, front to back. She looks around for answers as if they will be in the room with her.

She props her legs vertically against the wall and stares at the ceiling, then out the window, trying to get something moving in her bloodstream.

Then she remembers the book that Cynthia gave her. She opens it for the first time,

taking a moment to appreciate the bookish-
ness of it, noticing the details: publisher
(Black Moss), date of publication (1990),
and dedication (to Hilary and Leila).

Silvia flicks through the book. There are
poems called things like "The Root of
Things" and "Inner Heart," lots more with
words related to bees. "Comb," "gold,"
"hive," "home." Many have titles that are
clearly about love. Cynthia knows so much
about so much. The book feels like it's a
part of this place; the phrases and images
Silvia picks out as she flicks through seem
to perfectly capture the atmosphere and
feeling of being here.

What does Silvia know about? What could
she write about? The stories that come to
mind are all related to God.

*Active rebellion against anything incorpo-
rates that which one rebels against.* That was
her parents' argument to invalidate atheism.
Is that what being here is about? And if she
is rebelling, will there be punishment?

Silvia wonders if this is the sort of thing
she could talk to Cynthia about. Not the
religious stuff, but maybe Cynthia could
help her write poems, give her answers to
more general questions. Her mind scans, a
flashlight beaming through fog.

Then that feeling comes, and now she is

able to give it a name: magnetism. She feels physically drawn to the next room, where Ibrahim is working. *Maybe Ibrahim could help me find answers.* But she knows this is not truly what draws her to him. It's the effect, not the cause. Minutes pass and she wavers in indecision, trying to think of that beam of light in her mind, until she finally becomes so restless and annoyed with herself that she gets up and knocks on Ibrahim's door.

XXII

Because so much of life on the farm is shared, their rooms have become private, sacred places. Everyone has been extremely careful not to cross any territorial lines. This is the first time Silvia has actually been inside Ibrahim's room, and she's floored: it looks more like a full-blown atelier than a bedroom. Cardboard canvases stretch all the way to the top of the ceiling and are propped on every surface. Colours, chaos. No pine — or nondescript faded wood panelling, whatever it is — is visible. There must be *dozens* of paintings, in varying states of completion. Or maybe they're all done; she has no idea.

"So," she says, her eyes moving quickly across all surfaces, "you're definitely an artist, then." She speaks with only the slightest undertone of envy. It's more a tone of surprise, of admiration.

He nods at her, then at the room. It's true

that he works quickly: all these in the weeks since they've arrived. Since Cynthia let him have his mornings, Ibrahim's been able to work through the night like he used to. Silvia can sometimes hear him — not the sounds of him working, specifically, but the sounds of him living. He's a very loud person; he occupies a lot of space. He grunts, sighs; his joints creak. He doesn't seem to snore, but as Silvia is such a deep sleeper, she can't be sure of this. He talks when he eats, and at the dinner table, while she is efficiently mopping up her plate with bread, Ibrahim hardly takes two bites because he's chatting to whomever he's sitting near. His laugh is loud and liberal, whereas hers is perfunctory, succinct. The two of them must have very different backgrounds, she thinks.

Now his forearms are splattered with paint — cyan, magenta, cadmium yellow — and he's got two spare paintbrushes, narrow ones, sticking out behind his ear, masked partly by his thick hair.

"None of these are finished yet," he says, going up close to the painting he's working on and, to her surprise, touching it with his fingers. "It's all just the background work."

But of course artists are allowed to touch their own paintings. That's how they make them. She feels foolish. She's self-conscious in front of him. She feels suddenly that she really doesn't know anything about this, or him, or anything.

The canvases, which he calls "figurative but expressionist," represent figures she can nearly recognize. "Who are all these people?"

"You're not here, if that's what you're asking," he says quickly, perhaps willfully misunderstanding her. "Most of them aren't real people. But I'd be happy if you wanted to pose for me again one day."

She blushes and goes to the window. It has the same view as the one in her bedroom. Almost.

"Get much writing done?"

"It's more of a thinking morning."

"Thinking is good, right?" He steps closer to her; she feels his breath on her right ear. "You must be getting good material just by being here too. Even if you're not actually writing yet. It's all valuable."

He's really being so kind, she thinks.

"What is your stuff about?"

"Nothing," she says. "Just, no, nothing."

There is silence for a moment. He smiles, playful. She wants to disappear — into the woodwork, into him. Then the sounds return: the hum of bees, the homely creak

150

of wood, the muted muddle of speech in a distant part of the house.

"Hey, wanna go for a walk?" he asks.

"Aren't you working?"

"I'd like to hang out with you, and I don't think I'll get much painting done now anyway."

"Okay, sure. I'd like that too."

They don't lock their doors; they don't tell anyone they're going. It's a difficult thing here, to balance public and private, spoken and unspoken. They were never told they weren't allowed to leave, but do they have to ask?

They go straight down the gravel path until it forks and then walk out into the short grasses. Ibrahim has brought the Google map he printed out for the train journey. The lakes they are looking for are less than a kilometre away.

"How old are you?" He looks sideways at Silvia, guessing, unable to.

"Twenty-two. You?"

"Twenty-nine."

No wonder he's more in possession of his own body, she thinks — he's had more time to grow, to fill his skin.

As they get farther from the property there are fewer paths tamped down amongst the grasses. Here, they make their own.

"These lakes aren't named, far as I can tell." He points to their destination on the printout. "Google doesn't have names for them, at least."

"We can name them ourselves, then," she says, looking at the map.

"They look a bit like splatters of bird shit, don't they?"

Silvia smiles. "Well, I don't think we should call them that."

A trough cuts through the valley; the path water once carved has left a muddy scar. They follow this path.

"There must have been a river running through here, feeding the lakes," Ibrahim says, following the worn conduit. They listen to the wind in the trees.

The sludge slouches thickly through the reeds, through an obstacle course of fallen logs and thatched grass. Lost branches and upturned roots are tangled up like Medusa's hair. There's not enough water to call it anything — not stream, not brook, not even rivulet. The damp dirt is the colour of rust.

"Doesn't it look sort of like blood?" Silvia points with her whole hand. "Blood that's gone all dry and scabby?"

"Yeah, it does, actually."

I will show you that I am the Lord. Look! I will strike the water of the Nile with this staff in my hand, and the river will turn to blood."

"What?" Ibrahim looks baffled.

"Exodus. The story where God turns the river to blood — you know it?"

"No, but I'm impressed you do."

"My family is Christian."

"Full-on Christian or, like, regular Christian?"

"Full-on Christian."

"Oh. And are you?"

"Um, I don't know. That's why I came here, really. I needed some space, I guess. They even sent me to a Christian camp every summer. I was a counsellor there." She tries to laugh, but it comes out false.

"So were you allowed to have, like, boyfriends and stuff?"

"Not really, no."

Ibrahim nods.

"But I'm not against the idea."

He smiles sideways at her. "Good to know."

She's worried he'll see her heart beating through her shirt, hear it beating in her ears, but if he does, he doesn't comment.

On the trail she can see skeletons of fish that look like pencil drawings of themselves. Everything is halfway fossilized already. Silvia bends down to look more closely at the reddish muck, but something pulls her back.

She looks up at Ibrahim.

"I'm sure it's nothing," he says, "but maybe it's best not to touch it."

Quiet as they walk, they listen to the different lives playing out in the forest. They don't see any animals other than flashes of flitting birds, but they know they're there. Bears, foxes, wolves. Moose and caribou. There like your shadow on a cloudy day.

The first lake is bigger than they'd expected. Although the river, if there had even been a river, has all but dried up, the lake seems healthy, deep. The glaciers — limbless monsters — made footprints and left them full of water, still cold even now.

"Freezing!" Silvia dips her hand down and shudders, then shakes her hand dry.

"It'll warm up by the end of summer — we can come back and swim then."

Cloud reflections skirt across the surface of the lake, and reeds, thick as straws, punctuate the water-clouds. The life underneath the water is invisible too, though they know it's there.

They wander on to the next lake. They couldn't see it from where they were — the land is flat and the grass is high — but find it's only about twenty paces away. This lake is smaller, so less cold.

"I think we should call this one Hartford,"

Ibrahim pronounces.

"Do you think he'd like that?" Silvia stands on her tiptoes to get the lay of the land. "He'd probably call them Big Cynthia and Little Cynthia."

Ibrahim smiles. Silvia sits down, then he follows suit. Neither laughs at the other's joke. The grass is papery and cold. Silvia watches an ant climb up a great flat blade that bends with the weight of even such a small body. A second ant crawls onto her hand, its feet the faintest tickle up the inside of her wrist. He's close enough to touch her, and she finds herself wishing he'd brush the ant off her arm, even though the ant isn't bothering her.

The air suddenly gets cold and quiet; it's as if silence had a feeling. She looks up to the sky, which was blue five minutes ago and is now filling in with billowy, charcoal-coloured clouds.

"We should probably get back," Silvia says. "It looks like . . . like rain?"

And it's true: there's a wind in the trees and that vacuum sound of air suddenly descending. Black edges encroach on the crinkled tinfoil sky. Then a filament of light flashes, as if tracing all the wrinkles in the foil, and lights up the whole land.

"A storm," Ibrahim says.

They sit next to each other, facing it. The hungry rumble follows, fifteen or twenty seconds after the light. The air is staticky. Electric.

"Do you think it will rain?" Silvia asks.

"I don't know." A pause. "But let's go back."

Neither moves for another few moments. Something else electric.

The trees seem smaller on the way back, in the way that the journey home always seems shorter. The pine needles make canopies and carpets: green above, brown below. They hear a giant crack in the sky. It sounds like something broke, something immense and irreparable.

By the time they return to the farm, the storm has passed and there was no rain. The world breaks and heals itself again, eternally.

XXIII

Back at the farm — nobody yet calls it "back home" — Silvia feels suddenly parched. Her throat is sandpapery. It's probably the heat, but she feels a little light-headed too. "One second," she says, and then remembers that Ibrahim doesn't have to wait for her. "Or actually, don't worry, I'll just see you later."

"It's no problem," he says. "I'll wait."

She puts her mouth under the garden faucet and turns the blue plastic handle, letting the water run right onto her face. It tastes a bit funny and feels a little thick — dusty, almost — but it does quench her extreme thirst. She gulps it, like a landed fish finding water again.

Ibrahim is facing the backyard, shading his eyes from the sun and watching the others puttering around in the garden. It's nearly dinnertime. Dan and JB are in the herb garden, and Monique is following Ben as he films plants in close-up.

"Ready," Silvia says, standing up.

Ibrahim turns around, ready to go inside with her, but then he sees her face. "Oh my god!" he cries. "Are you okay?"

Silvia's face is covered in blood, trickling straight lines to her chin from either side of her mouth as if she were a nutcracker. There are red splatters around her right temple and across her cheek, and red patches are staining her T-shirt too.

"What?" Her hands fly to her face, feeling the dampness around her mouth. She wipes the water with the back of her hand and brings it down to look at it. "Holy."

"Sit down," Ibrahim says, rushing over.

The others from the garden look up to see what the commotion is all about. "Silvia," JB says, rushing over, "what 'appened?"

Ibrahim replies for her. "We just went for a walk and then, I don't know . . ."

Silvia is looking at all the faces of the people appearing in a circle around her, looking at her as though she's a medical experiment.

"Are you okay?" Monique asks, touching her shoulder. "Does it hurt?"

"I'm fine," Silvia says. "I don't know what . . ." She looks at her red hands and remembers the rusty earth by the lake. *By this you will know I am the Lord.* She turns towards the house and spots her reflection in a window. "Is that . . ." She looks down at her shirt and then up at the others again.

Ibrahim, still right by her side, says, "It's okay, just stay still for a second." He puts his hands to her head gently and says, "I'm just going to check for an injury," as he delicately moves her hair around, examining her scalp.

"It doesn't hurt, though. I don't feel — I don't feel anything."

Ben, who dropped his phone when he ran over, picks it up again and starts filming as JB goes and turns on the tap. He lets the water run, but nobody is watching him, focused as they are on Silvia.

"Hey," JB calls, "look." As the others respond he points to the red water running out of the faucet, dark and silty, looking almost exactly like blood. He dips his hands in and out of the stream, and they come away just as red as Silvia's face. "It is the water." He holds up his hands, palms facing outwards as if in apology.

Ibrahim pulls his hands out of Silvia's hair and looks at her, both of them baffled. "I'll go inside and get you a towel and some clean water, okay?"

Silvia nods. "Thank you."

When Ibrahim has gone inside, Monique walks between JB and Silvia. Her hair, white-blond and tufty, looks like a baby chick. "This is not right. Blood in the water?"

"It's probably not blood," Dan says. "I mean, it's more likely iron deposits in the pipes or something."

"Whatever," Monique says, "it's fucked up."

Alicia interjects, "Iron deposits can cause stains in laundry. For high levels of iron, a filter needs to be installed."

"We'll have to use bottled water for cooking tonight," Ben says.

"Is that allowed?" Silvia asks. "I thought bottled water was just for emergencies."

"This *is* an emergency," Alicia says.

"Let's go find Cynthia." Monique takes Silvia's arm and pulls her, not very gently, to the garden. Silvia allows herself to be led, wiping red liquid off her face with her other hand.

The girls walk to the end of the garden and find Cynthia digging troughs in the vegetable patch to help the water get down to the roots: any water that makes it that far needs to have its potential maximized.

Hearing them approach, Cynthia bends

up from the waist and wipes her hair off her face with the back of her bare hand. "Is it dinner already?"

"Look at Silvia!" Monique cries out.

"It's just the water," Silvia says, holding her arms over her stomach. "Does it often run red?"

Cynthia's lips move as she slides them over her teeth. She thinks for a second. "Well. No, not that I am aware of."

Monique looks over to the well. "Could there be some kind of problem with the pipes? Iron deposits or something?"

Silvia adds, "Alicia said something about a filter —"

"If we've got iron deposits it'll need something way more serious, in my opinion, than a *filter,*" Monique says, looking back at the house.

Cynthia drops the spade she was holding and puts on the beige cardigan she had tied around her waist. "I'll come in and take a look," she says, not giving any emotion away.

As they're walking back together, Silvia sees what looks like slime on the earth by the well. She stops, bends closer to it. "Hey," she calls out. The other two, already a few paces beyond her, stop and turn. "What's this?"

"What's what?" Cynthia asks.

"This, this sludge." Silvia is crouching. She touches the earth and raises her finger. It's red. "It looks like blood too."

Monique takes a step closer to Silvia so she's standing between the two women. "Ugh, it *totally* looks like blood."

"Well, that *is* blood," Cynthia says. "I had to kill one of the pigs."

"What?" Monique jumps back.

"Why?" Silvia asks.

Cynthia looks baffled. "For food, of course. And because she was getting old." She looks at the two girls. Both of them stare back at her with sad eyes. "Welcome to life on a farm," Cynthia says, laughing genuinely for the first time.

"So it's pig's blood in the water?" Monique is incredulous but willing to believe. "Maybe it sank into the well water?"

"That wouldn't be possible — not so fast, at least. It's probably just mud from the bottom of the well seeping into what's left of the water supply. We're so low on water that half of what we're getting is silt."

"But the dirt by the lake is red too," Silvia says. "I went down there earlier. Could that be linked to the water colour?"

Cynthia smiles at her. "No. The high quartz content colours the earth this high in the Canadian Shield, that's why it's red.

I think it's rather pretty, don't you?"

"I . . . I . . . It is pretty, I guess, yeah." She wants to trust Cynthia's explanations for this. She wants to take all her faith and put it into this woman, who seems to have such an innate understanding of and control over the natural world.

"Anyway," Cynthia says, wanting to move this along, "let's get you cleaned up." She walks between the girls with her arms open as though pushing them forward, on to the house.

XXIV

Later that night, Silvia — her stained clothes soaking in Tide and her hair still wet from its washing — is sitting at the table with the others for dinner. Cynthia brings out a massive portion of roast pig on a platter and puts it on the table to applause. Ben and Dan start filming the scene with their phones.

Silvia has the strange sensation that she's underneath a bell jar — as though she is on display, and set apart. She stares at the roasted head before her — its rubbery snout, its cheeks gone caramelized, the hairs on its face shaved away. She looks away quickly, feeling squeamish, and notices that Hartford, who is sitting next to her, has turned away as well.

"Anyone thirsty?" Cynthia asks, holding up a pitcher of water.

"Can I have a glass of juice?" Alicia says.

"There isn't any juice," Cynthia says.

"I'm not drinking that water," Alicia says.

Cynthia holds the pitcher to the fading light coming in from the garden-facing window. The water is clear. "The water is fine, Alicia."

"Iron can sometimes be invisible," Alicia says, "but the internal corrosion it causes remains the same." She looks around the table for validation, but everyone is silent, having given up the fight already.

"There's bottled water if you'd rather," Cynthia says, her voice heavy, nodding to the pantry.

Alicia doesn't move.

Nobody else moves either.

The shadows of the candles shift slightly as the sun makes its final descent. When they have stopped eating, whether or not they've finished, they leave the table, one by one.

XXV

The next morning Alicia arrives at breakfast with her things. One small cabin-sized suitcase, four wheels, an ergonomic design. She's wearing mascara and has drawn in her eyebrows; she looks completely different.

"It's just not for me," she says, beady eyes to the ceiling. Alicia is the only one of them who seems to have gotten fatter since arriving; the rest have rarefied.

Silvia is confused. More than that: she's let down. But, she wonders, what makes it more than this? Why does this feel like more than just a business arrangement?

Toby the cat runs after Alicia as she walks down the path, but he stops where the driveway ends and the road begins. He knows his limits.

Cynthia has always been proficient at separating the wheat from the chaff. A hive isn't about how many bees but about how well they work together. Some say that honey production is less dependent on the acreage of blossom available than on how effectively the bees can drink up all that nectar.

The water returned to normal the next day. Whatever the problem, pig's blood or iron deposits or some other mystery, it passed, and everyone except Silvia seemed to forget about it immediately.

XXVI

The first honey harvest happens in late spring. At this point the nectar in the flowers is fresh, unripe; the resulting honey is pale and silvery, with a fragile spume — called, rather ironically, the *flower of the honey* — which has the most exquisite flavour. This early honey is of a different, rarer consistency from the mellifluous golden substance generally sold in shops. Flowers that start blossoming in this period include apple, strawberry, and, a little later, purple loosestrife, the beautiful invader.

For chores that afternoon, Ibrahim and Silvia are paired with JB and MJ, and their task is to harvest this first late-spring spume. The four of them stand idly in the shade of one of the silver birch trees, waiting for Cynthia to come with instructions.

"But why did she leave?" Ibrahim asks again.

"That's all she said," Silvia repeats. "That

it just wasn't for her."

He seems personally offended. His forehead crumples, puglike; he pulls his fingers through his hair. He grunts but doesn't say anything. He hadn't painted that morning, couldn't get into work, was too sleepy and distracted. It felt like he had an antenna elsewhere, wasn't fully present in his own body. It's not that he misses home — he doesn't think that is it — and though he wouldn't want things any other way at the moment, change has always been hard for him.

They expected Cynthia nearly half an hour ago. Drones are at once children and pupils, dormant without the commands of their queen.

When she finally arrives, she neither apologizes for nor excuses her lateness. "Everyone all right?"

"Alicia left," Ibrahim blurts, sounding wounded.

"I see."

"What, did you know?" he asks.

"Know what, Ibrahim?"

"That she was leaving."

"No," Cynthia says, walking over to the shade of the tree. "I did not." She sounds upset, more upset than Ibrahim would have expected. "Everyone is free to leave whenever they wish, as I've said, but I do prefer to be notified, at the very least," she says, not looking at anyone in particular. "This is my home, remember. As well as my livelihood."

Everyone shifts positions slightly, chastened. Ibrahim sneezes, breaking the silence.

"Anyway." Cynthia looks like she's doing math in her head. "Let's get started." She pulls a small sample of honeycomb from her pocket. "To test whether or not the honey is ready to harvest, you slide a knife along the wax caps of the cells, then gently crush the comb with the back of a large spoon and tip it into a bowl. Like this." She goes through the motions: slide, crush, tip. Her eyes are like wet stones.

"That's the honeycomb?" Ibrahim asks, going closer.

"This? Yes."

"And the bees made *that*?"

"Bees make honeycomb, yes."

"But it's perfect. All those tiny little perfect shapes!" He doesn't touch the honeycomb, he just marvels at it.

She fights a smile as it flits across her face. "As I was saying. When you press the wax, the cells of the comb will split, and if the honey is ready, it will be released and flow smoothly into the bowl beneath."

They have none of the modern equipment: uncapping forks, heated knives, extractor machines. They have no need for such technology, Cynthia says, when the old tools work just as well.

"And if it's not ready?" Silvia asks.

"It will be," Cynthia says, leaving no room for doubt.

Before Ibrahim, Silvia, MJ, and JB can get near the hives and the honeycomb, they have to suit up in their astronaut gear. There are only four uniforms, which is why only four can harvest at a time. The suits are all one size, so it doesn't matter who wears which. There are around fifty hives in each of the three designated apiary areas, and the goal is to complete this first harvest in three rounds.

In matching baggy white coveralls, with their clasped ankles, elbow-length gloves, and veiled hats, it is impossible to tell the four apart. The only distinction is JB. He's exceptionally tall and has to hike up his socks to cover the bare space left where the trousers end, two inches above his ankles.

First thing they have to do is drive the bees into the lower part of the hive so as to extract the top frames. To do this, they use the smoker Cynthia left.

"It looks like an old-fashioned fire extinguisher," Silvia says.

"Or the Tin Man's oilcan," says MJ, swinging the smoker between two fingers. It's a small silver can with a funnel top and ribbed sides. There are bellows at the back. MJ is right: it's exactly like the Tin Man's.

"If I only had a . . . what is it?" Ibrahim tries to sing the tune. "Brain? Or heart?" He's never even seen the movie, but he knows the songs nearly by heart from his brother Mo singing them all day every day for an entire summer.

"The smoke is meant to calm them." Silvia pushes the bellows but nothing happens; it hasn't been filled yet. "Or maybe it confuses them? I can't remember."

Ibrahim takes the brown bag of pine needles that came taped to the can. He and the others are meant to stuff the bottom of the smoker, the burner part, with the needles and then set them on fire. The needles will burn slowly, and a blast from the bellows will set them aflame again to sustain the smoke.

MJ handles the smoker, puffing the bellows as needed. The smoke comes out thickly, like a theatrical effect, and the clouds keep their shape for longer than normal smoke. Silvia's eyes have gone small from concentrating. She moves closer to the hive and everyone watches, waiting for the smoke to filter to the bottom.

After a minute, hoping the bees have all descended, drugged, Ibrahim opens the lid.

There are no bees there.

"It worked!"

He goes to pull the first frame out but finds it's sealed to the hive with something cement-sticky. Propolis. Cynthia said this might happen. JB, standing behind Ibrahim's elbows, is at the ready with a hive tool that looks like a miniature crowbar and pries away the upper honeycomb. Once JB has removed the frame, Ibrahim lets the lid slam shut. MJ extinguishes the fire in the smoker; Silvia takes the honeycomb and brings it to the crooked table under the birch tree, where a spoon and a bowl have been placed. Every motion is calculated. They work together like cogs in a clock.

Silvia lifts the veil from her face so she can clearly see what she's doing. Her eyes are narrowed with focus, her skin rubbery with sweat, her pupils constricted to pin-pricks against the brightness of the sun, even under the trees. Carefully she peels the waxy hexagons away from the wooden frame and smacks the comb with the spoon. It makes a suctioning sound: *suck, pop.*

"It's flowing!" she cries, laughing. She props the honeycomb on top of the bowl to let it drain, then cracks off a corner of comb and brings it to her mouth. The golden taste of it coats her teeth and tongue, and the resin of each capsule cracks softly, pleasantly, every one of her nerves receiving more stimuli than it's used to.

"The bees don't seem to be affected by the drought, so?" JB asks, coming over. He lifts his veil and takes a corner of comb too. "Oh, is go-*oo*-od!" he says, mouth full, surprised.

The honey, as Cynthia had said, is pale, more white than yellow. The colour of a sponge. And it tastes of garden, of greenery, of life and death. It is the best thing Silvia has ever tasted.

Ibrahim watches Silvia, enjoying her pleasure vicariously, then takes a fingerful for himself. If he believed in heaven, this is what it would taste like: sweet and gold, sunshine and love. He wants to kiss her mouth.

After the first frame has drained — it flows slowly, effortlessly, from the comb into the bowl: they don't even need to whack it — they will extract the other nine from the top box of the hive, down to where the bees have descended. (They'll leave the lower box full for the bees.) Then they will lower their veils again.

In the morning there will be a pot of the fresh honey for breakfast, and the four of them, the harvesters, will eat it with the particular pleasure of knowing that they had been there, involved, like worker bees proudly assisting their queen.

XXVII

Cynthia has prepared a special dinner to celebrate the success of their first harvest. There's honey-glazed pheasant, and roast vegetables from the greenhouse, and vanilla ice cream with honey for dessert. Her face is shiny and red with both pride and the heat of the oven.

"This is fucking fantastic," Monique says, mouth full of bird.

JB, already finished, serves himself seconds. "Anyone else?"

MJ holds out her plate for more, even though she hasn't finished her first serving yet. "Don't want you eating it all," she says, swallowing.

"I'm glad you like it," Cynthia says delicately; she said she'd already eaten.

Scattered along the length of the table are bottles of Ontario wine, both red and white, and something homemade, unlabelled. Silvia fills up her glass with this one, not for the first time. She spills some over the lip of the glass and brings her mouth to the edge to catch the rest of the overflow, giggling. "What is this? It's so weird. Delicious weird."

"Mead," Hartford says.

"What's that mean?"

"It's honey wine," Cynthia explains. " 'Mead' is an ancient Slavic word for honey. It's the oldest alcoholic drink in the world."

"I love it," Silvia says. "I love old things!" She laughs at herself.

"Hey there." Ibrahim takes the bottle from Silvia — it's splashing all over the floor as she's waving it around.

"I'm fine! I feel nice. Really, really nice!"

Ibrahim smiles.

"What?"

Ibrahim notices Monique and Ben sharing a look at Silvia's expense. He stares at them, partly curious, partly challenging.

"People live their whole lives doing the same stuff every day," Silvia continues, "following these rules they say are absolute, being sorry for stuff they don't need to be sorry for, stuff which for all they know is just stories in a book, when they could be living like *this.* Free."

Monique laughs; Ben and Dan smile.

Ibrahim glares at them.

"What?" Silvia looks around as if she's only just become aware of the other people at the table.

Monique stage-whispers to Ben at her side, "See? I told you she escaped from a cult."

Silvia's face starts burning.

The air in the room shifts when Cynthia draws a breath. "Monique," she says, her voice hard, "that's enough." Then she speaks perfectly normally to Silvia: "Are you from a religious family, Silvia?"

Silvia nods.

"And are you a believer?"

Silvia murmurs something.

"Sorry?"

"I said I'm working that out."

Cynthia nods. "Well, I'm very glad you like it here."

"It's beautiful," Silvia says, finishing the glass. "This whole area, so . . . beautiful, yes, that's the word."

Ibrahim downs a thimbleful of the honey wine and makes a face: it's incredibly strong. "Did you set up the farm on your own?" he asks Cynthia, moving the bottle of mead farther away from Silvia.

"No, I was with my partner."

"What did he do?"

178

"She. She was a gardener."

Maybe it's the alcohol clearing her brain, or maybe it has just allowed her to lose certain inhibitions, but Silvia twigs something. "Hilary?"

Cynthia looks at Silvia and nods. "She set up the vegetable patch and got that side of the farm started, but the bees were mine. And still are. Thankfully." Cynthia gets up before anyone can say or ask anything else. "Well, good night. I'll leave you kids to it."

Ibrahim calls after her, "Good night."

Once Cynthia has left, Monique opens her eyes wide and looks round the rest of the group.

"Cynthia's a lesbian!"

"So?" Ibrahim asks.

"Oh, come on!"

Silvia says, "Does it matter?"

"No!" Monique becomes defensive. "I'm not saying it does, I'm just saying . . . well, I hope she doesn't fall in love with me or something."

MJ looks at her through her glass of wine. "I wouldn't flatter yourself, Monique."

There's a second of silence as everyone processes this, then Monique stands up and puts her arm around Ben. "I'm gonna head to bed," she says.

MJ and JB stand up, holding hands.

"Good night," they say as one.

"Me too," Dan says, knowing he'll be the only one of the five sleeping alone that night.

Silvia looks across the table at Ibrahim, her eyes unfocused. It's just the two of them remaining.

"You feeling okay?" Ibrahim asks.

She nods, smiling like a Buddha.

"You're not used to liquor, are you? That stuff is at least twenty percent."

"It's nice."

"Let me take you up to bed." He goes to help her out of her seat and takes her hand, but it slips from his grip. He tries to lift her instead, but her body is too wriggly. "Come on, just go limp."

"What does that mean?"

"Stop trying."

"I don't know how to do that!" She hiccups, then laughs.

"Here, get onto my back." He crouches like a linebacker awaiting the snap. She jumps up once, slips down, then jumps again, and this time he catches her. "Now, don't let go."

He feels her muscles squirm against his back, each one separate and alive, seemingly unconnected to limbs and ligaments. Behind him, invisible, she is an abstract work of art. He goes up the stairs slowly, as each step up causes a bump-slip-laugh, and shushes her as they shuffle down the corridor shared with JB and MJ and Monique.

"Here you go," he says, slipping her down and dropping her off at her door. "You gonna be okay?"

"I already am okay, Ibrahim," she says.

"Okay, well . . . good night," he says, still standing close enough to feel the heat coming from her mouth.

"You don't sleep at night though, do you?" she asks, leaning against the wall. "So what are you gonna do?"

"Well, I might paint a little bit, I guess."

She looks up at him. Her face is so close to his face she can smell his skin, feel his breathing. "Do you still want to paint me?"

"Now?" he asks.

She nods, eyes half closed and hungry, and they tumble, each pushing and pulling, into his room.

XXVIII

Ibrahim puts down his paintbrush and takes a sip from his sweat-salty bottle of water. "You want some?" he asks Silvia. "You should probably hydrate."

She reaches out her hand to take the bottle, but instead of sipping from its neck, as he did, she pours a little into her cupped palm and flicks it onto her face, neck, and shoulders. She draws a line along her forehead from temple to temple, making a halo of water. It dries in an instant. "That feels good," she says, smiling to herself.

With a slick of pink paint on the bristles, he pulls his brush across the canvas in one broad stroke, adding large leaflike wings to her body. They connect to her shoulders and he outlines them in red.

He's not used to painting from life. He doesn't like the idea that he has to follow what's before him instead of what's in his mind. The face he's painted on the canvas is only a shape so far. At least he's got the fresh peach-pink of her skin. Her body, her body . . .

Let this be clear: lying there before Ibrahim, stretched out on a tartan blanket, Silvia is naked as they come.

"How's it going?" she asks.

"Fine." Ibrahim's mouth puckers around an imaginary cigarette.

She closes her eyes. She feels so unshy. It doesn't even feel like she's not wearing clothes. She's not aware of his eyes on her, not in a way that feels invasive — she can feel him looking at her, creating her for himself, admiring the creation that she already is. It feels as though she is being seen for her true self. She is loving lying there, calm and purposeful, doing nothing and yet doing so much. Her nothingness is being elevated into art. She trusts him completely. This is so much easier, so much better, than making art herself. "I'm fine too," she says. "I feel so good, so . . . myself."

Ibrahim smiles. "Good." But after a few minutes he puts down his brush again. "I can't concentrate," he complains.

"Want me to switch positions?" She's wriggling, not unlike a cat, on the blanket.

He stands up and goes over to where she is lying. He crouches next to her. The light is making her skin look purple, sweet, edible. From up close he can see the goosebumps dotting her shoulders, down her chest, between her —

"Maybe if you could move . . . Can I?" he asks before touching. She nods, and so he places his hand gently around her elbow and pushes it back. She had been propped up on her right elbow, her legs curled underneath her. Like a mermaid, or a cat. The same way Ibrahim's little brother was tucked up when he woke him before leaving. But Silvia looks — she doesn't look like his brother. Her hair is growing out, nearly at her shoulders now. No longer propped, she's lying on her back, fingers spinning circles round her navel. She lifts her legs and pulls her knees towards her so the soles of her feet press into the floor. This creates a barrier between him and her.

"I can't concentrate because —" He opens his mouth, his little teeth spread apart in his big mouth. He leans his head on her shinbones, feels their warmth. "Because you're just so beautiful, lying there looking at me, and it's so stupid —" He stops there because it's not his style to eulogize a moment, but he so wants to be tender.

The alcohol is wearing off and she has in an instant become very aware of her nakedness. She is naked. In a bedroom. With a man. It's an interesting in-between feeling she has now, with this belated, obvious realisation. She still wants to be here, just . . . Licking her top lip, she finds it salty. She turns her face away, pressing her cheek to the blanket and covering her (small, she thinks; perfect, he thinks) breasts with her other arm, bent in a V to hug her shoulder. He turns his face away too, red, shamed.

"Sorry," he says, reading the change in her body language. "I didn't mean —"

"No, not like — no." She reaches to him. "I don't mean — you have an unfair advantage, is all." She fingers the ragged collar of his shirt, then lifts it over his head.

They still haven't kissed.

Silvia dresses herself as she undresses him. Shirt, pants, socks. The same order, backwards and forwards.

When he's naked and she's fully dressed, they stand facing each other. His body is so unfamiliar without the cover of clothes, a new composition of muscles, flesh, hair, bone.

"Now we can start again," she says, chin up, jaw hard.

He holds her face as one would hold a breakable vase and goes for her neck, licking, thirsty; like a horse, he finds not water but salt. He stitches kisses up her neck, and when he finds her face again her mouth is open and damp and finally their lips touch.

"You can start taking my clothes off now," she says after a moment. Her voice is changed by the kiss: deeper, more steady in itself. Like he put something inside her.

So then Ibrahim unwraps her. One layer at a time.

Shirt. Buttoned, collared, blue. First he flips the collar back down, smoothes it over her shoulders. He unbuttons from the bottom up, ending again with the goosebumps on her neck. Each bump an uncharted topography; each dot a star. Her ribs, just visible, are the same size and width as piano keys. He can see her heart beating behind them, her skin, so thin, pulsing like the skin of a drum. Her nipples. Her nipples he takes into his mouth whole, feeling them turn on, like light switches, against his tongue.

Pants. Levi's, tight in an unconsidered way (she's had them since she was sixteen). A little tear here at the pocket, another there at the knee. With his teeth he tugs the tufts of heavy cotton unthreading from the holes and, moving up, unzipping the fly, he kisses the thin cotton underneath.

Underpants. Before he pulls them down her legs — pipes, branches, he is running out of metaphors — he touches his hand to the dip, damp, between her legs. He makes mental notes of her sounds and motions as if he's a scientist, aiming to understand wholly so as to better the experiment in the future.

Socks. Her feet are hardly bigger than his hands. The intricate boning on the tops is opposed to the smooth, marbled arches on the bottoms. It is only when looking at her feet that he realises how small she is, how compact and complete.

Now she is naked. Newly unveiled.

"Are you sure you want to do this? We don't have to, we can wait."

"No," she says. "I'm sure."

He starts kissing her all over, trying to find the heart of her.

Starfished on the bed, she keeps her eyes open and looks at the ceiling, out the window, at the top of his soft, dark head. His skin tastes of salt, and his body — his body is taut, hard in the right places. His muscles still hold the memory of school sports; his legs are slim from long walks.

He touches her with hands that feel gentle and strong. His body glows with heat. His kisses feel intentional, each one planted specifically in its place, each one specially for her. He lifts her body and kisses the side of her upper thigh, the back of her knee. "You're perfect." She smiles, but he can't see. "Shall I . . . ?" He pulls a square foil packet from somewhere she can't see. She nods; he opens it. She is not afraid, not self-conscious, just hypersensitive, with tuning forks for bones, as he makes his way up and kisses her belly button, her chin, her cheek, then looks her in the eyes. Then a feeling she's never felt before. She's not thinking about anything, not a single thing, except what is happening moment to moment. It's different from the freedom she proclaimed, drunk at dinner: it's similar, but different. That feeling was like a dependent clause, but this is self-contained. Later she will have the expected waves of confusion and guilt, but for now it is pure, embodied pleasure, the delight of being seen.

XXIX

The next morning, bruised with her first hangover, Silvia wakes up with a panicky start to the sun blazing through the window. Which window? Not her window. She sits up quickly and looks around, piecing the night together. Ibrahim is still next to her, his body starting to groan with movement too.

His window.

"Hey." He pokes his face out of the sheet and squints into the sunlight.

"Hey," Silvia says, pulling the sheet up to cover herself.

"How's it going?" He puts his arms behind his head.

Silvia rolls her head and lets out a low sound. "Everything hurts."

Ibrahim smiles. "Everything in moderation."

She's not sure what he means, whether he's trying to tell her that she did too much, that she indulged and should have been more moderate. She must have done it all wrong. She looks at him, ready to offer an ambiguous apology, but his face is full of warmth — there's no judgment there.

"We'll have to lay off the mead next time," he adds, and brings his head close to her thigh to find a crook in which he can nest.

Her chest puffs with the words "we" and "next time." Then the panic returns. She looks around the room for a clock, then out the window, trying to see where the sun is. "What time is it?"

"Don't worry," Ibrahim says, nuzzling deeper into the sheet by her hip, "there's still half an hour till breakfast. We're good."

She flops back onto the pillows, lying down next to him. Yesterday she was a virgin. *Virgin.* Is that still a word that means something to most people? Now that she's not a virgin, has anything changed?

"How are you feeling? Other than the hangover, I mean."

She opens her eyes. "Good." Different but the same. The same, but different.

"Good," he says, delaying, trying to find the right words. "I enjoyed last night," he finally says, bringing his face closer to her face, putting his cheek next to her cheek.

She nods quickly. "Me too." Then, looking at him sincerely this time, she adds, "Thank you." She wants to ask him all sorts of questions — what does this mean, how many girls have you slept with, do you love me, will we be together forever — but knows enough not to. And besides, she is learning that want is different from need.

Ibrahim leans forward and kisses her on the mouth. "Hey, why don't you read me something you've written, from before?" he asks.

She groans, a smile making plums of her cheeks. "I told you, I'm not a real writer."

"Please. It could be anything." His fingers stretch across the ivories of her ribcage.

"Okay, fine. I'll go get something." She hops up, and he admires her agility. She's stronger than she looks. Wrapping his shirt around her body without buttoning it up, she goes through the adjoining door to her bedroom.

She comes back after a minute or longer. "I've got one poem I didn't write, and another I did. The one I didn't write is called 'Silvia,' and it's by Shakespeare. It's why I'm called Silvia."

"Heard of him. Read the one you wrote."

She looks at him. "I wrote this one years ago. In, like, my first year of university. Just don't — don't even say anything when it's done. I don't even want to know what you think."

He closes his eyes and nods like a philosopher. Then she starts. He watches her read. Her mouth making shapes around the words. The whole thing seems fated, as though it couldn't be any other way. It doesn't even matter what the words are; he thinks she's brilliant.

"What do you mean, not a real writer?" he says once it's done. "You're amazing."

"Shut up," she says, pleased.

"No, but really. Real — I mean what is *real*? If you're not a real writer, then I'm not a real painter."

"Yes you are!"

"Then what makes someone a 'real' artist?"

She looks up, around the room, at all his canvases propped against the walls, and his painting supplies scattered all over the place. "When you *do* it. Like you're doing it, like this."

"Well, look at you — you're doing it too."

"It's not the same at all. This is one thought. It took ten seconds to write, I wrote it years ago, and I haven't done anything else. I've never had one published."

"Well, I've never sold any of my paintings."

"Really?" She pauses and looks around again, trying to find the one he started of her last night, but she can't. "Well, you could. You should. People would want to buy them. You can feel the . . . urgency of every single one."

"Would your parents buy the one of you, you think?"

"I don't want to think about my parents right now." She is suddenly serious, and it startles him.

"Oh, sorry," he says, and wonders if he should tell her about his parents, his mother, how much he loved her, and his father, how much he misses him.

"First," she says, softening, "you'd have to put some clothes on me."

"But I like you like this." He puts his hands around her, all over her.

They begin again.

Silvia is twenty minutes late for breakfast.

XXX

Monique and Silvia are paired together that morning to clean the kitchen. This is an easy job, comparatively, and Silvia's happy to be inside today, as there's a sharp wind ripping through the leaves, as if summer got cold feet. No matter the weather outside, though, the golden place inside Silvia is undimmed. She thinks about Ibrahim, about last night, and it glows.

The girls are gossiping about all the people there, and in talking about other people, they're able to feel close to each other for the first time. When Monique laughs, it sounds like a pipe clanking; she doesn't try to be quiet about it. Silvia notices the purple circles sagging under Monique's eyes. They look pretty, though — gaunt suits her. She's wearing very short white shorts and her legs are as thin as bamboo but stubbly.

"So," Monique says. "What's the story?"

"What?"

"Don't *what* me, you know what I'm talking about. Ibrahim! I'm just two doors down."

Silvia's face peels open.

"Oh, don't be a prude, I hardly heard anything."

"Do you think Cynthia knows?" Silvia asks quickly.

"Knows what? Are you together?"

"I don't know."

Silvia is cleaning the sink when she sees Cynthia come out of the honey house. She's wearing the same brown trousers she always wears, and a large straw hat that hides her face. She stops, her body facing the house — facing the reflective kitchen window that Silvia is standing behind, though she can't tell where exactly Cynthia is looking. They could be looking at each other and neither would know. Both women are still for a long moment.

Then Cynthia looks up to evaluate the sky, holding on to her hat. Coming to some conclusion, she walks on.

The girls continue to work. Instead of rinsing the cloths, they fold them over and respray a new corner with Javex. The work goes quickly, pleasantly, until something in Monique shifts.

"This is bullshit," she says suddenly, dropping her J Cloth. Her voice has gone up an octave.

"What?" Silvia stands up — she had been on her knees, scrubbing a patch of floor by the oven.

"Cleaning up after other people's shit. I'm sick of it."

"Yeah, but —"

"But what?" Monique snaps.

Silvia waits. "I guess, well, we have to earn our keep. Right?" Monique looks back at her blankly. Silvia wonders if Monique has ever cleaned her own kitchen. She could be either very spoiled or very dirty. Monique didn't do her hair that morning, and Silvia thinks she looks like a leaking feather pillow, her hair mostly flat but with white tufts sticking out in the wrong places.

"Listen," Monique says, coming close in a confidential way, "have you even used the pay phone yet?"

"No, actually." She's been avoiding calling her parents.

"You haven't used a phone in how long — like, three weeks?"

"It's been that long?" Silvia thinks, letting it settle in. "No, I guess not. Why, have you?"

"No! Why is that?" She sounds like she is trying to prove a point, as though she knows the answer and is just seeing if Silvia does too.

"I guess I haven't thought about it."

"Well, I hear it doesn't even *work.*"

"Oh? Says who?" Silvia feels like it's her job to placate Monique, to dispel this doubt and bring her back to where she was two minutes ago.

"Ben. He and Dan went to call their parents the other day and the phone just had that dead dial tone." She pauses for effect. "And we don't have Internet or cell phones or anything. We're completely isolated in this backwoods, bloody-water, you know . . . It's like . . ." Monique looks up, scanning the corners of the ceiling as if there might be security cameras there. "It's almost like we're trapped here."

Silvia sees Monique's eyes flash silver, like fish in water. "Trapped? Really? Do you feel trapped? I don't feel trapped."

"Maybe that's 'cause you don't even know what freedom is."

With this sting, the girls turn their backs to each other and get on with their tasks. The static fuzz of passive aggression builds up; each scrubs harder.

But after a few minutes it seems as though the storm within Monique has calmed. It leaves as quickly as it came. Her eyes look normal again, no longer turbulent. From the way the trees are gently swaying, it looks as though the wind has calmed down too.

"Sorry about that," Monique says suddenly, turning to Silvia.

"It's fine," Silvia says. She doesn't want to push for reasons for Monique's behaviour, but she's a little unsure of how to act.

"I don't deal well with isolation, apparently," Monique explains, smirking. *"All work and no play makes Jack a dull boy."*

At that moment Cynthia enters the room and scans the stacks of unclean dishes and the piles of rags that Monique pulled out of the drawer, thinking to fold them later. "Is everything all right?" she asks, looking specifically at Silvia.

Silvia, strangely bashful, looks at Monique for an answer.

"Yeah, we're fine," Monique says.

Cynthia inhales. "Silvia, you're looking a little tired. Are you feeling okay?"

Silvia blushes. "Yes, I'm fine." She feels she should apologize, but refrains.

Cynthia maintains eye contact. "Why don't you two take a break? It looks like you've done enough here for the morning." She looks back and forth between the girls, then leaves.

XXXI

Later that day Silvia walks down to the lake by herself. Though she still feels hungover, she is surprisingly alert. She wants to have a moment alone, truly alone, but more pressingly, she wants to see what the water looks like.

She passes the well on her way and stops to look down. Leaning on the stone structure, she sees nothing but tunnelled darkness. She whistles, then waits for the echo. Looking around, she finds a rock the size of her palm. She drops it, and counts:

One alligator
Two alligators
Three alligators
Four alligators
Five al-
Crazy.

The forest is calm. Nature feels almost sympathetic to her tenderness — the birds coo rather than chirp; the small creatures move slowly, and twigs do not snap under-foot. She looks up rather than down, and doesn't see the creek she'd stumbled upon with Ibrahim.

There's a huge tree that she hadn't noticed the first time she came down here. She stares at it, moving slowly up from trunk to top, so high she can't even make it out. She is still for a moment, thinking about this tree. It is solid in front of her, and there's no reason to fear that it will suddenly stop being a tree.

But with the arrival of the slippery knowledge of doubt, she has come to know that this tree does have the potential to lose its treeness. It could be cut down by man or beaver, or felled naturally, by wind or lightning. And once it's no longer standing, there are practically infinite things it could become. The vastness of paths for this tree, a formerly upright living thing — straight to the sun, its only job to grow — means that it has every choice and also no choice at all. It could become a chair. A house. A tooth-pick. A book. A box of pencils. A fire in someone's home, anywhere in the world.

Who put this tree here? Why? Why is it even on this earth; how has it made its way here and survived long enough to get this far? What does that *mean* — does its time on earth account for something? Who does it belong to?

Silvia feels dizzy and sad and hopeless. She feels angry with her parents for telling her that a tree was just a tree, because how can she know any answers if she doesn't even know the questions?

She gets to the lake before she realises it. It's a murky brownish blue, swampy green at the edges. She crouches, touches her fingers to the earth. Wet, definitively brown.

That's that, then. It must just be the quartz.

She takes off the cross necklace she's worn since her confirmation and shoves it into her pocket.

XXXII

A sunny Sunday, a perfect day off. They're all lying on blankets on the grass in the yard. Ibrahim and Silvia make a point of not lying next to each other.

Monique sighs so loudly she sounds aggrieved. "This is so *bliss*ful." She's wearing a white lace dress with a ripped hem, and her hair is damped down to her scalp. She looks like a punk Jean Seberg.

Bare legs exposed to the sun, open palms facing the sky, everyone lies there, not saying anything, thinking their thoughts, feeling their feelings.

Silvia is thinking about what Monique said earlier about needing "the freedom to make art." She wonders if this, now, is freedom. And if so, will she — will they — have to start making art soon? Maybe everyone else is doing their thing in private, not talking about it. When Silvia is alone, though, she is either thinking, and not in any kind of "artistic" way, or sleeping.

Then the sound of someone singing comes in on the wind — the voice of a woman.

"What's that?" Monique asks, looking up from MJ's month-old copy of *L'actualité.* (She's trying to practice her French.)

The rest of them prick their ears, like animals, to the sound. At first it's just notes — so, re, re, mi, fa, so — la, ti, ti, do, re, do — then the notes string together into a song, a song none of them recognize but one that's soulful, strangely moving. They can't hear any words from where they're sitting, but the melody carries them. The sound echoes throughout the house and spills into the yard.

"Who is that?" Silvia asks.

"It must be Cynthia," Ibrahim says.

A collective pause as this registers.

Everyone looks up to try to see the source of the sound, but they can't. They never do.

XXXIII

Down the driveway from the farm is a barn on the left partly hidden by a stand of trees — the kind whose leaves flicker with silver on the undersides when the wind draws its fingers through the branches. They don't use the building for any daily tasks, it's just where Hartford and Cynthia keep the car and pickup truck, and since it's a little removed from the main circuit of greenhouse, gardens, and house, Silvia's never really explored it before. She notices it now, for the first time really, on an afternoon walk. Having finished her chores for the day, she's decided to try to find "inspiration."

She'd looked up the word in the dictionary in the downstairs library and that's actually what it said. *Inspire* means "to breathe into life," or, more literally, "to give spirit."

Then the Lord God formed the man from the dust of the ground. He breathed the breath of life into the man's nostrils, and the man became a living person. Genesis 2:7

So it's true, she thinks, and inescapable: anything she tries to write will come from Him. In writing, she is creating; in creating anything, she is giving life to it. Can waking up every morning be an act of creation? Is she anything more than a vessel either way? She feels nauseous, powerless.

Approaching the barn she sees Cynthia, arms full of fabric, walking towards her.

"Hi," Silvia says, glad to have something puncture her thought-spiral. "Do you need help with that?" She goes towards Cynthia and picks up a floppy piece of pink wool that's fallen from the bundle.

"Thank you." Cynthia smiles as Silvia places the material back on top of the bundle. "Are you busy? Would you like to come with me?" She nods towards the barn.

"Sure," Silvia says. "I'm not busy."

She follows Cynthia inside the barn. It's dark and quiet, a totally different world from the golden, buzzing afternoon outside. Shafts of dusty light slice through the air; it smells of wood shavings. It seems bigger on the inside than it looked on the outside — the truck and car have their own space, misshapen hay bales teeter in the corners, and a bunch of unused farm equipment is rusting into paralysis along the periphery.

"I'm making a bed for the cats," Cynthia says, answering Silvia's unspoken question. "The mother will be back soon."

"The mother?"

"Toby's mother. We called her Judy, though she's not really the kind of animal who responds to a name. She comes around this time every year."

"And has her babies here?"

"For the last six years, yes. The biggest litter was ten." Cynthia clears away some hay with her foot, opening up a patch of smooth dirt on the ground.

Silvia is still confused. Answering her next unspoken question, Cynthia continues: "They don't stay. They're wild. They carry on and we never see them again. Except Toby, of course. Here, take this." She hands Silvia half the bundle of fabric, which she can now see is made up of sweaters.

Squatting from the hinges of her hips, back remaining perfectly straight, Cynthia starts placing the sweaters into a pile of flat layers.

"You don't need them anymore?" Silvia examines the one she's been handed — it's cashmere the colour of cotton candy.

"They're Hilary's. She left them." Cynthia reaches up and takes the remaining sweater from Silvia, then tucks it along the edges of the flat sweaters, creating sausagelike walls. "There we go," she says, standing up to appreciate her effort. "The kittens will like that. Did you ever have cats, Silvia?" She looks Silvia in the eye.

"My mom's allergic."

"Oh, shame."

"How long do they usually stay for?"

"Hard to say. Sometimes Judy leaves before the babies are ready. Twice I had to bottle-feed them for weeks," Cynthia says, smiling at the memory.

Silvia looks at this cozy nest, hidden in the dark, safe from coyotes and bears and whatever else. She's struck by Cynthia's tenderness. The air in here is starting to feel velvety, dark and warm and the same temperature as her body. She feels so much more at ease than she did five minutes ago. Maybe, she thinks, the things we go looking for ultimately find us. She crosses her arms and looks at Cynthia, who's still looking in admiration at the cat bed she's created.

"Do you miss her?" Silvia asks, suddenly bold.

"Who, Judy?" Cynthia smiles at the joke. "Yes. This is the first year she won't be here for the kittens."

A moment passes in silence; Silvia doesn't know what to say.

"Well, that's that." Cynthia wakes up from her reverie and goes towards the golden rectangle falling on the path from the open door. "Let's keep an eye out for Judy then, yes?"

XXXIV

The fourth week passes quickly. Another seven days of straight sun. None of the guests really notice the drought — nobody ever misses rain, at least not at first — but the one thing Ibrahim notes is how difficult it becomes to distinguish days when the weather flattens them out into one hammered stretch of golden sunshine.

Ibrahim wants to ask Silvia if she'll pose for him again, but he's nervous that she'll say no, that it was just the one-time, mead-drenched thing. He's not used to this feeling of anxiousness — he's been in three relationships, each lasting less than six months, and he's always been the one with the power — and he finds it exciting.

He approaches her in the kitchen at breakfast, managing to get to her when nobody else is around. In the past week they've had very little contact, both busy and both shy.

"Sure," she says, filling a glass with raspberries. "I'd love to." She pops one into her mouth.

She comes into his room after her shower that evening, hair still wet around her face, patches of water blossoming on her clothes in the elevated places: shoulders, breasts, hips. She's wearing a green T-shirt and jean shorts.

Her face, always fresh, looks pinker, he thinks. Newer.

"Ready?" she asks.

"Yes," he says.

She unfolds the blanket, shakes it onto the floor, and takes off her clothes slowly, turned away from him. As she unpeels and settles into her spot, he lines up the colours. Peripherally he notices the way the light falls on her body, the colours of the tartan shawl she lies on — for now he has her floating in a grey void, but he might keep it this way, as tartan is just too *plaid* — the way her hair curls down her neck. The oak-leaf wings are still right, but today they should be more yellow, so he brings out the cadmium and orange and red and gold and blue and green and white, for all these colours make up yellow, and squeezes them onto his palette with the rest.

Then he looks more, until the world becomes as he wants to paint it. Silvia is there, of course, tangible and beautiful, but looking at her he is beginning to see her as flat, colour-blocked, winged — he's seeing her as his painting already.

He starts with a thin line above her head — he uses the second thinnest paintbrush he has — and his hand follows the brush. The line, a marbled autumnal rose, turns into letters halfway down the canvas, the Arabic letters *haa,* the deep one, *baa,* and *yaa* — together this spells *habibi.* Surprised, he puts his paintbrush down.

Picking up the thickest brush, he mixes red into the remaining splotch of pink, the colour of her wings. The line he follows starts with her lips and goes down the middle of her throat to her heart, knotting there before continuing to her groin, where it disappears between her cat-curled legs.

Lips, heart, sex.

"You need me to do anything?" Silvia asks after a while, shifting, rubbing the back of her neck.

"Do you need a break?" he asks, not looking at her, focused on his painting. It's coming together. He's feeling it.

"I'm fine for a bit longer," she says, "but I

211

think it's getting kind of late. I'm a little sleepy."

"What time is it?"

"Nearly eleven."

"At night?" He looks up. She's got the blanket tucked over her feet and she's no longer propped on her arms but lying flat on the floor. The sun has long since left the sky: he can see, even from the low windows, that the stars are already midnight bright. His mouth moves into a crooked smile, jaw jigsawed. "Sorry. We're done, of course. We'll finish another time."

She gets up slowly, pins and needles all the way up her legs so they don't even feel like her own, and wraps herself in the bathrobe he has left near her. She comes around to look at the painting.

"What's that?" She points to the red-pink line going through her middle.

"I don't know," he says.

"It looks like my esophagus." She tilts her face sideways to follow it between her painted legs. "I didn't realise you were an anatomical painter."

"And those wings, copied perfectly from your anatomical self." He wraps an arm around her waist, pulling her towards him.

"And that?" She points to the squiggle down the side.

"Arabic."

"Saying what?"

"It's . . ." He pauses. "It's embarrassing."

"What is it?" She slips out of his arms and faces him, eyes bright.

"I did it without thinking. The brush just went there."

She waits.

"*Habibi,* it says."

"Which means?"

"My beloved."

XXXV

Ibrahim feels that if he jumped, he would fly. The secret inside him — love, if love is a secret — grows and swells, distributes itself throughout his body like blood, all this happiness coming from his heart.

He is on his way to the pay phone to call his dad. Walking down the path, he notices that the grass on the lot is overgrown, parched to straw in places. But from the top of the driveway, on the small rounded mound, he can see the healthy parts, the long green wild stuff, moving in the wind as if by a divine hand. It ripples not all together but as though a giant is walking through, whooshing around. Or, no, it looks like a flock of birds, the way they move in a coordinated cloud across the sky, bending pale and flashing dark.

He is bringing a handful of quarters down to the pay phone because he doesn't know how much it will be, whether it's long distance, since he's still in Ontario.

It's eleven o'clock in the morning — Abouya should be up by now.

Just before he reaches the pay phone, he sees that new flowers have blossomed along the path. He recognizes the three-pointed white ones that carpet the ground — these are trilliums, the flower of Ontario. He feels proud for knowing this. There are some pretty pink ones too, which he's never seen before. They've got a sort of basin, goblet-like, and three paler petals stemming from this. The goblet is veiny, nearly see-through; looking closely, he thinks it looks a little . . . a little like sexual organs, actually. A ball sac, he'd say, if he were being impolite. Well — part scrotum, part ovaries. He picks one for Silvia, thinking she'll find it funny too.

He boxes himself into the narrow glass rectangle and feeds the phone a quarter, then dials. It asks for another two. It rings. After two rings, silence.

"Hello?" Ibrahim says.

"Hello?"

"Abouya?"

"Ibrahim?"

"Hello!"

"What are you doing, not calling us for an eternity?" Ibrahim the Elder isn't shouting; his voice is naturally loud. "God in Moses,

Allah in the highest, you know you could have been dead and *I* could have been dead and your brothers and and sis —"

"*Dad,* I'm fine, I'm alive, I'm sorry."

"Don't call me Dad!"

"Sorry, Abouya."

"You prolific son, you abandoned us!"

Ibrahim smiles into the phone. *Prolific, prodigal.* "You know where I am!" Ibrahim knows that things are fine, that he has already been forgiven, and so goes along with this role his father is playing out. "And you *told* me to come here!"

"And then you wake me up!"

"I woke you up?" His father doesn't sound very sleepy.

"You said for the spring, Ibrahim, and now it's summer. I expected you to write or call or send a phone text to your *only family,*" Ibrahim the Elder cries.

"There's no reception on the farm," he says. Then: "And it's not technically summer — solstice isn't until next week."

Silence.

"I'm sorry, Abouya, please forgive me."

"When are you coming home?"

Ibrahim twists the phone cord. He reads the instructions: *Bell. 5¢, 10¢, 25¢, $1. Do not deposit more money until operator asks for it.*

"I don't know, Abouya, things are good here. I'm working well."

He hears his father take a deep breath. "I'm happy for you."

"How are things with you, with the kids? How are Zizi and Isa —"

"Fine, everyone is fine. I am the only one who misses you."

"Good," Ibrahim says.

The men are quiet for a while but it feels nice, not uncomfortable.

"And I'm in love, Abouya."

"In love? With who?"

"With a girl here."

"In love, in love. What is her name?"

"Silvia."

"Is she Jewish?"

"What? No."

"Good."

Ibrahim doesn't bother pursuing this. Knowing his *abouya,* it will be Anglicans or Jains next week anyway.

"So what's she like?"

Ibrahim pauses, as if he hasn't thought of this before.

Then there's a triple beep on the line and the square blue text scrolls on the screen: "Please Deposit More Money To Continue This Call."

"Ibrahim? What's this girl like, what do

her parents do?"

"Dad?" *Beep.* "Abouya?"

"Yes?"

"I've run out of quarters, I have to go —"
Beep.

"Already?" He can hear sadness fill his father's voice and thinks of him lying alone in his plush four-poster bed, the curtains drawn, full cups of cold tea on all the tables.
Beep.

"I'll call you soon, I promise, send my love —"

And then one long *bee-e-e-eep.*

Ibrahim walks up the driveway, newly aware of a feeling he has, not quite of loss or longing but of missingness. It's not a missing-home, missing-a-person feeling. More like — like he missed out on something. Missed the bus, missed his chance.

His father asked what Silvia was like. He thinks about this. What is it that he likes about her? He should know this, have it on hand.

He likes how small and tight her body is, as though everything is there for a reason. The mole on her neck. The way she looks at things and then looks back at him for confirmation, for collaboration, like a child. Her hunger — how she goes after things, even simple things, like a glass of water —

but how too she is easily satisfied. The hunger is not misplaced. She never hungers for things she can't have. He loves the logic of this; he is not like this. The craving for ambiguous things obliterates him.

But she just . . . is.

He thinks of her smile, how easily it comes, how truthful it is. Uncomplicated. And when they — when he, when she — the sound she makes. It's not ecstatic; she seems very . . . of her body. But he also loves that she's unknowable, her own whole person who surprises him. There are so many things about her that he doesn't yet know, won't ever understand. In a good way.

He gets to his room, and when he sees her reading in a tidy corner of the floor, he does love her. He sees it, he feels it. In saying it to his father, he made it true. *In the beginning was the Word.*

"Hi," he says.

She looks up at him. She's got the tailless cat, Toby, curled up under her arm. The cat is asleep, but as Ibrahim approaches it stirs, stretches. Its mouth opens in a cavernous yawn and then it goes back to sleep. Silvia looks up at him, her face full of that smile. Like a cat, she is unembarrassed by pleasure.

By this time, the strange missing feeling

has left him. There is nothing to miss on the honey farm. Everything is there, everything just is.

He gives Silvia the pink flower, deflated from the journey, but doesn't mention the resemblance to genitals. The likeness has lessened anyway.

"What is this?" she asks.

"A flower. A flower I picked for you."

"It's a lady's slipper," she says, considering it, before looking up at him. "We have them in Nova Scotia too. I thought they were endangered or something."

"Endangered?" He groans, rubbing his chin and the three-day beard that's growing there. At a certain point, nature exasperates him. "It's just a *flower* — whatever, it's just one flower. I'm not going to extinguish the entire species by picking a flower for my —" He abandons that thought. "I just thought it was beautiful," he says.

"It *is* beautiful." Silvia goes out of the room and comes back with a glass of water. She puts the flower, its papery petals as crumpled as yesterday's newspaper, into the glass. "Or maybe it would be better to press it," she says, looking at her stack of still unread books. "Anyway," she adds, leaning over to him, sitting by the window on her mattress, "thank you." She kisses his eyebrows, each twice the width of one of hers. "Just don't tell Cynthia. I don't think she'd approve."

They look at each other then, unsaid sentences passing between them. That they would keep this to themselves; that Cynthia would not know. At least not for now. Neither of them is certain that she would approve of their relationship, and they're unwilling to acknowledge their transfer of power in giving her authority to approve — or not — of their private lives.

"Why not?" Ibrahim asks.

"Well, if they are endangered —"

"Fine, fine, take her side."

Silvia shakes her head but otherwise ignores him. She moves into the V his legs make and leans her back into him. These small gestures of intimacy are coming with the ease of a mother tongue.

"How's your dad?"

"He's good. He misses me." Ibrahim shakes his head. "I miss him."

Silvia strokes his knees, wrapped around her like arms of a chair.

"I told him about you."

"You did?" She smiles, and he can hear it in her voice. "What did you say?"

"That you're nice. That I like you."

"That's nice."

"The phone died pretty quickly — I didn't have enough quarters. Have you called your parents? Do you miss them?" he asks.

"My parents? No. No, no."

"Really? Well, I'm sure they miss you."

"Definitely." She props herself up off Ibrahim's legs and turns to face him. "That's not the question. They definitely miss me, or at least an idea of me. They don't want me to be here."

"Then why don't you —"

"It's complicated."

They drop it. They're still learning about what to push and what to leave.

XXXVI

Silvia's task that day is to alphabetize the library with Monique. It's good work for an idle mind, and though it takes a long time, the time goes quickly. There's no system, no categories, and the floor-to-ceiling bookshelves are filled with English and international novels, history books, biographies, classics in French and English and dictionaries between the two languages, old copies of *National Geographic,* travel guides to countries in Central and South America as well as South Korea and Slovenia, collections of letters, and how-to manuals about gardening, cars, chess, home-brewed beer, and bees.

So many of the books are so, so old. Old in both senses: some physical copies in tatters, but also some of the texts dating back hundreds of years. Did the medieval religious poet who never left the local radius of Ipswich ever think that his writing would make it to a world — the "New World" — that he didn't even know existed? Distance, time; it boggles her mind.

If she ever wrote something, how long would it last?

While Monique is busy with a stack of mystery paperbacks, humming some pop song from ten years ago, Silvia flips open a leather-bound collection of John Donne poems, fans the gold-trimmed pages, and reads from where her eye falls.

Let sea-discoverers to new worlds have
    gone,
Let maps to other, worlds on worlds have
    shown
Let us possess one world, each hath one,
    and is one.

She thinks she likes it, but she isn't sure. She's thinking of Ibrahim upstairs, working on the painting of her. *Habibi.* Beloved. Does that mean that he loves her? If he does, what does that mean? Thinking about this is like wanting more coffee when you've already had too much.

Does she have to tell her parents about him? She doesn't want to, but she doesn't want to *not.* She was always taught that omission is the same thing as a lie, and she knows that her parents would disapprove of everything about him. It's one of the reasons she can't call them: she knows what she would say, she knows how they would respond, and she knows enough to try to postpone that for as long as possible if she wants to continue to experience this foreign, terrifying, thrilling freedom.

Just as her mind is about to get lost on that train of thought, Hartford comes into the library and sees that though the girls haven't quite finished, they're not going to get any more work done at this stage. Silvia is sitting completely still, staring into space with an open book in her lap, and Monique has poured water onto her shirt and is squatting in front of the fan in the corner of the room, hopping around like a frog to follow the blade as it rotates.

"You girls can go," Hartford says. "The rest can be finished later."

"Sweet!" Monique stands up and ties the bandanna that has been sticking out of her pocket around her head like a turban. She doesn't even use a mirror and it looks good. Stylish. "Let's go," she says to Silvia giddily, transformed by this sudden liberty.

"Okay." Silvia puts down the book of poems as Monique grabs her hand and pulls her out the back door to the garden. They find MJ sitting in a deck chair facing the sun, reading.

"Hey," Silvia says to MJ.

"*Salut,*" MJ says, lowering her sunglasses. With the sun beaming right on her hair, it glows like a traffic light: *stop.*

"You have free time too?" Monique asks MJ. "Amazing. What are we gonna do?"

"Why don't we go down to the lakes?" Silvia suggests.

"What lakes?" Monique asks.

"There are a few lakes down that way." She points vaguely in their general direction.

"You've been already? When?"

"A while ago, with Ibrahim."

"Oh, with *Ibrahim,*" Monique says.

The three of them walk down, Monique and MJ following Silvia. Butterflies float above the ground. Song comes from invisible birds. On the ground, the levels of life are stacked on top of one another. From the pine needles grows a carpet of vibrant moss, and from the moss spring clumps of wide, rubbery leaves. And above all that, of course, the trees stretch high as skyscrapers. The air is still, and the heat of the sun penetrates even the shady parts of the canopy. Light fights shadow, darting along the forest floor.

The first lake is farther than Silvia remembers, and when they arrive, it's smaller too. "I think it shrank in the heat," she says.

"This drought," says MJ, shaking her head, sad but noncommittal.

"God, it's hot." Monique sticks out her tongue like a panting dog to illustrate the heat. She is taking off her short shorts, now her T-shirt. "Aren't you guys coming in?" she asks, already running. She's naked but for the scarf-turban. A splash. "Cold!" she squeals, but pleasurably. "Oh, it feels so *good.*"

Silvia looks over at MJ, who shrugs. "Sure," MJ says, and, her cargo shorts and tank top suddenly in a pile, she follows Monique into the water, wearing only her underpants.

So now Silvia has to follow the others. She takes off her clothes slowly, folds them carefully, and lays them on a rock. Should she keep her underwear on? Which will be less awkward? Whose side does she want to be on?

She slides into the water, the colour of tea, with her arms stretched out before her and bends her neck backwards to keep the water out of her face. Monique is right: it is cold, and it does feel good.

"Am I the only one skinny-dipping?" Monique sees that Silvia has kept on her underpants and bra. "Oh well, your loss," she says, and plunges under the surface. She's so skinny she hardly even has boobs; her red nipples are almost as wide as each whole breast.

The lake gets deep towards the centre. The pond-weed tentacles at the water's edge fall away; out here, Silvia's legs don't reach the bottom. She opens her eyes under the water and sunlight filters through as if through smudged glass. All the life that lives here, the life that she can't see, is silent but pressing. It doesn't feel so cold anymore. She surfaces to take a breath. "It *does* feel good."

The girls swim silently, in peace, for a few minutes.

Then something brushes up against her leg. Something small, wriggly, hard. At first she thinks it is a fish, but then the thing surfaces, moving quickly: it's moss-green with spots the same colour as the lake, its eyes above the water's surface like an alligator's. Then she feels another one touch the side of her body with the texture and pressure of a fly swatter. It's a frog. Suddenly there are dozens, all swimming towards the water's edge.

"Hey!" Silvia cries, her specific surprise at

being touched rapidly turning to general panic.

Monique is floating like a starfish on her back; MJ's swimming laps. Both stop what they're doing and face Silvia.

"Do you see that?" She points to the exodus of frogs — there are now as many as fifty, sixty little heads bobbing along on the surface. There's a series of tiny *thunks,* like the vibrations of a skin drum, as they glide.

"What?" asks MJ, scanning the water blindly.

"Ugh, what is that?" Monique is vertical; her scarf, wet, has fallen into a collar round her neck.

"Frogs," Silvia says.

The three girls swim back to the shore as quickly as they can.

Now there are hundreds, and the frogs move faster than the girls. Propelled by their webbed feet and springy legs, they move as quickly outside the water as in it. It's as though they've all instantly changed from tadpoles and they too are running for their first taste of freedom.

Their croaks alternate between a cow's moo, the chirp of a cricket's string quartet, and a teenage girl's drunken laughter. The cacophony swells; the sound is all around them.

"They're fine so long as they're not touching me," MJ says. "I hate the feeling of things touching me in the water."

"What the fuck," Monique says. "This is fucked up."

"This is nature," MJ says. "Animals do get born."

"This many, though?" Silvia asks. "All at once?"

MJ shrugs.

"And why only frogs?" Silvia asks, though nobody has the answer.

They watch the frog migration from the rocks: hundreds and hundreds more little amphibians emerge from the water and disappear into the forest. It seems as coordinated as a military invasion but for the noise.

The frogs are all the same colour — moss, mud, grass — and the same size — no bigger than a robin's egg. At one point there seems to be an infinite number of them, and the next moment there are none. The sudden return to silence is confusing.

"I hate animals. You just never know what they're thinking," Monique says. She massages her ankles, rotating them on their joints with the elasticity of a science-room skeleton.

Silvia clutches her clothes against her, not

bothering to put them on. There's something funny flipping around in her stomach. Lighter than sadness, simpler than nervousness. Unease.

The three girls walk back to the farm in silence, following the path the frogs took, each thinking about how she will tell the unlikely story of the amphibian exodus.

XXXVII

Cynthia is at the front door when the girls get back. She emerges onto the front step, holding out three clean towels. "Hartford said you girls went swimming," she says. "Wasn't it too cold?"

Silvia is first to get to her, and Cynthia wraps a towel around her shoulders like a cape. "No," Silvia says, aware that she's wearing only her damp bra and underpants as Cynthia rubs her back. "Not too cold." She's wondering how, or even whether, to mention the frogs when Cynthia moves on to Monique and wraps another towel round her.

Silvia notices the sound of bees, a low, pervasive whine stitching a web in the air.

Dryish, still in her underwear but with the towel wrapped around her chest, Silvia runs into Ibrahim in the hallway near their bedrooms.

"Hey," he says, pleased to see her. "How's it going?"

"We went swimming," she blurts.

"Cool," Ibrahim says.

"And all these frogs came out of the lake, hundreds of them."

"Really?" Ibrahim is unsure why she's uneasy. "Well, it is nearly summer, I guess," he says. "This is when they come out of hibernation, right? I think?"

"But what should we do?"

"They're not dangerous, are they?"

"They're coming through the woods — they're on their way to the house." She speaks with great urgency.

"It's fine, we'll just clear them out. I'm sure Cynthia has nets or something."

"But aren't you worried about what their coming means?"

Ibrahim pauses and tries to tune into her wavelength. "You mean, like, climate change or something?"

She shakes her head. "Never mind." She looks behind her, down the hall. "I'm not that hungry," she says, "I'm not feeling great, actually. I think I'll skip dinner and just go to bed."

"Oh." Ibrahim follows her gaze, trying to find what she's looking at. When he turns, Silvia is already walking into her room. "I hope you feel better, then," he says, finding himself staring at her shut door.

Inside her room, Silvia opens her notebook and spreads the pages flat. She wants to write about the frogs. The way their eyes appeared above the surface of the water; the way their rubbery, muscular legs felt against her skin; the way their orange eyes stared off into nothingness in the same way Toby the cat's do. Her pencil is in her hand, but nothing comes out.

She turns instead to Cynthia's book of poems. She cracks the spine and flicks through the pages, yellowed but fresh.

XXXVIII

Silvia is no longer reading but swiping her phone open, locked, open, locked. She keeps it charged — most people do — as a timepiece, as a habit. Sometimes she listens to songs she's already downloaded. Sometimes she hopes she might catch a wave of errant signal and receive all the texts and emails suspended in the ether since she arrived. Her homescreen is her favourite view of the harbour, and seeing it now, for the first time in ages, she finds she doesn't miss it. She feels blinkered to the present in a way she never truly has before.

Then there's a tap at her bedroom door.

"Hey, you awake?" It's Monique.

"Yeah. I can't sleep either."

Monique scuttles into the dark room wearing a baggy purple T-shirt that says *Make Muffins Not War.* "Ugh," she says, shuddering as she hops into Silvia's bed alongside her. "Fucking frogs."

The girls sit hunched with their knees up under the thin comforter. The sound of croaking permeates the air. It seems as though the frogs are everywhere, invisible in the tar-black night: in the ceiling light, in the window frames, in the trees. And maybe they are, Silvia thinks. Stranger things have happened.

"It's weird, isn't it?" she asks.

"Ugh, everything is weird here. Don't even get me started."

"But, like, this is different weird. Weird like the blood in the taps."

"I know, that's what I'm saying — this place is fucked up."

"Do you think it's the drought?" Silvia asks, hoping Monique thinks so.

"How should I know?"

Silvia looks at Monique, her profile glowing in the light of the stars, silver hair electrified at all ends. She feels such fondness for this girl who was a stranger only weeks ago. Monique might be crazy, but she's so profoundly herself. Silvia has never met anyone like her, and she feels as though, if it were really to come down to it, Monique would protect her from anything.

"I'm heading out tomorrow."

"Out?"

"Yeah."

"For, like, ever?"

"I can't be here anymore." Monique shakes her head. "Bad vibes."

Silvia is startled but tries to be cool. "Where are you going?"

"My last apartment was in Toronto, but I sublet it and don't get it back until the end of the summer. I don't know — I'll figure it out once I'm on the road." She is quiet for a second, and Silvia doesn't say anything either. "Don't tell anyone, though. I hate goodbyes."

"Oh," Silvia says, not hiding the disappointment in her voice. She wants to ask more, she wants to ask why, but Monique seems to fall asleep instantly, and her ragged breath weaves into the sounds in the night. Frogs, wind, leaves, breathing.

Silvia doesn't sleep for hours, Monique's body an unfamiliar shape next to her, the sound of the frogs mounting as they get nearer and nearer. She tries to repress the feeling that they're coming for her.

XXXIX

Bell. 5¢, 10¢, 25¢, $1. Do not deposit more money until operator asks for it.

Silvia is standing in front of the pay phone at the end of the road. With an automated motion, she feeds the box some coins and dials the number (the line, contrary to what Monique said, is unfortunately not dead).

"Hello?"

"Mom?"

"Silvia!"

"Hi."

"*Honey!* Honey, it's Silvia, Silvia's on the phone, pick up! Honey, I'm getting your father. Silvia, where have you been, we've been worried sick —"

"Silvia?"

"Hi, Dad."

"Silvia, where are you, we've been worried sick."

"Haven't you been getting our emails? Our letters? What's going on?"

"Emails? No, sorry, there's no Internet on the farm, but —"

"No Internet? Where is this place?"

"I haven't received any letters either . . ." Silvia trails off, wondering.

"Why haven't you *called*?"

"I'm calling now."

"We were worried sick, honey, your father was concerned that —"

"Sorry, there's no cell reception either. I'm calling from the pay phone at the end of the —"

"No reception? Silvia, have they abducted you? We called the police, but they said they couldn't do anything since you told us where you were and had chosen to go yourself, so we were just about to come out ourselves."

"Dad."

"Silvia, I'm so glad you're fine. What your father is trying to say is just that we would have *appreciated* —"

Silvia holds the phone away from her ear for the duration of two whole breath cycles. In, out. In, out. When she puts it back they're still talking over each other. She coughs. "Hello?"

"Hello! Can you hear me? Silvia? Honey, I don't think she can —"

"I can hear you, I can *hear* you, can I just

239

talk for one second? This phone is eating up all my money and I want to actually talk to you."

"Yes, please, talk to us, honey, of course, we just —"

"Okay. All right? I'm sorry for not calling. Really. But it's only been like a month, and —"

"*Seven weeks,* Silvia, honey —"

"As I said, I'm really sorry you were worried. I'm sorry I made you worry. But I haven't been abducted, and I mean, you know exactly where I am, and I'm really enjoying myself. I like it here. Things are good."

Remarkably, for a moment there is silence at the other end of the line.

"When are you coming home, Silvia?"

"I told you, Dad — I'm staying for the summer. It's better than a job here, better than camp or a coffee-shop thing anyway, I have zero expenses, I have my own time, and I —"

"Have you found a local church? Bruce hasn't heard from you either. I spoke to him just the other day, and he asked —"

"There's a church in town, I think, yes."

"Oh good, that's good, honey, isn't that good?"

"What have you been doing?"

"Are there many people there? Are they Christian?"

"Did you get the Bible I left in your bag? I want to send you —"

"Arc you writing anything?"

Her parents' questions interrupt each other, as though the answers aren't as important as the asking. She knows they love her, of course they do. But she's realising that perhaps love means something different to them than to her.

"It's beeping, the phone. I've run out of coins, so I have to —"

"Honey? I can't hear you, it's beeping."

"We're praying for you, honey, we love —"
And then over.

She walks back to the farm, feeling vaguely but distinctly sad. Sad because she knows she's letting them down. Sad thinking of the sadness they would feel in thinking their daughter won't be "saved," that she'll end up in their worst visions of hell for the choices she's making. Sad for not feeling as guilty as she should about that. Sad for being reminded of why she'd said she was coming here: because it was an "artists' colony." And sad because after seven weeks she has nothing to show for herself: no product, no art. Sad because she didn't get

241

to talk about any of the nuances, any of the *sort of*'s, any of the strangeness or specificity — in brevity, everything had to be just good, fine. Sad because parents remind us of who we once were and who they expect us to be. Sad because of the distance between that and reality. The sadness comes in waves and then leaves like the tide, so gradual you can't see how dramatically it moves.

She sees the farm up on the hill, the same way she saw it when she first arrived. It's the same building and the same vantage point, but everything's different now.

Silvia wonders why Monique left, really. If it was only because she was restless or if, like Toby the cat, Monique could perhaps see something that none of the rest of them could.

XL

There are hundreds, maybe even thousands, of frogs hopping around in the garden. They're underfoot in the kitchen, croaking in the bathroom sink. The terror they arouse is effectively eight hundred times their size.

The men are charged with their removal, both inside the house and outside it. It's strange that the frogs made it all the way up here, especially since there is no body of water within the limits of the property: ponds are where frogs live, and there is no pond here. Removal tactics include snake repellent and butterfly nets, but mainly the men just have to catch the little buggers with their hands.

Ben, Dan, JB, and Ibrahim spend a whole day running around, chasing the hop-hopping amphibians as they aimlessly try to escape whatever fate to which they're doomed.

"Do you think this is why Monique left?"

Ibrahim asks.

"What do you mean?" asks Dan. He's on his hands and knees, rummaging in the low leaves of the zucchini plants, trying to see if any frogs are hiding there.

"I don't know — all this?" Ibrahim isn't looking at Dan; none of them are looking at each other; they're all pursuing their victims. "This . . . stuff? She completely freaked out over the red water. Now frogs . . ."

"I think Monique was lonely and we were not enough," JB says.

The others are struck silent for a second.

"Whoa," Dan says, moving from all fours onto his knees and sitting back on his heels. "Deep."

"Shut up," says Ben.

"I don't know," JB says sensitively. "This life, it is not for some people."

"Do you think it's for you? For us?" Ibrahim asks. He has an irrepressible belief in other people's insight.

"I cannot say." JB shrugs. "It's fine."

Ben is holding his spritz bottle of snake repellent like it's an AK-47. "Monique was right, though. I mean, it isn't normal."

Ibrahim doesn't know what's normal and what isn't — he's not used to country life, after all — but also he's too busy to consider it. He and JB are lumbered with the ineffective butterfly nets, and the two of them pace up and down the herb patch. The sun is going down so they'll have to finish soon, whether the frogs are gone or not.

The following day they find a couple of fugitives croaking around the drainpipes, but after that there are no more.

And after all that, nobody can bear to talk about the frogs, not just because of their amphibian hop and slime but because they are forever linked with the idea of Monique leaving, and they all loved Monique in their own way.

Each mourns her loss, privately.

XLI

Like plants, hair grows faster in the summer, and everyone's is getting wild as weeds. Nobody really noticed at first. There aren't many mirrors about the place, and besides, their hair is always sweaty, or capped, or tied back, or hidden underneath a protective beekeeper's hat. In general, nobody spends very much time on personal hygiene: the men let their beards grow, the women leave their eyebrows unplucked and their legs unshaved.

Ibrahim's hair, long and soft with curls even at the beginning, can now, to Silvia's amusement, be pulled into a full topknot. Her own grown-out toadstool, on the other hand, just gets prettier as it burgeons around her face.

The Frenchies are unaffected, JB being bald and MJ with such slow-growing hair that after all this time only about half an inch of her natural brown colour appears at

246

her roots, like a trunk beneath autumn leaves.

It's the twins who make the communal haircut necessary. Their hair, birchwood blond, is growing over their ears, and as it's straight as a tree, it's sticking out over their earlobes. The effect is one of children who've been forgotten by their parents.

Silvia once mentioned that she worked at a hair salon when she was in high school. She didn't say as a hairdresser, though. She'd been the weekend receptionist and had worked her way up to shampoos. For this reason, she is given the kitchen scissors and full responsibility. The scissors have that silver/slither/scythe sound as they slice, and she snips them in the air. "Who's first?"

"Let's go to the bathroom," says MJ, inadvertently volunteering. "It'll be easier to clean up."

The bathroom is by the front door. Grimy green tiles, walls a colour some people might call *cream*, a ceramic claw-foot tub, a thermometer, and the six remaining tooth-brushes. A dead yellow jacket is stuck in the soap dish.

They collectively decide that each *client* — funny, Silvia thinks, how certain situations can change a person's title: daughter, student, tourist, resident, girlfriend, hairdresser — will sit in the bathtub, at Silvia's feet.

With MJ sitting cross-legged in the tub, Silvia tries to create an image of professionalism: she pulls the hair up and straight, as she saw it done at the salon, measuring two chunks against each other. She starts small, cutting diagonals into the bottom. Then she pulls both sides of the hair again. They are the same length. Confidence growing, she makes larger, sharper cuts. She feels competent, omnipotent. Then a little foolish: no need to get overexcited. She doesn't touch the bangs.

"Finished," she says after a few minutes longer than necessary — she'd been cutting invisible hair for a while.

MJ gets up quickly to examine her reflection in the dirty mirror above the sink. She preens herself, fluffing her hair up, making a mirror face she never makes in public: half pertness, half pout.

"It's fine," she says, surprised. "Perfect."

Truth is, it doesn't look any different.

Easing into things with her second client, Silvia starts hairdresser chat with Ben. Their questions and answers overlap; it's not like listening, it's like killing time.

The hair starts to become something other than hair, it seems. As she cuts it, trunk-straight strands of it, they fall in clumps like pick-up sticks. She sees herself as that size, the size where an inch of hair could be a foot-sized stick. She sometimes places herself in the perspective of other people, things. She doesn't really think about doing it or know exactly when she started it — it's more of a distraction, to get her out of her own head. To become a stick: to have no desires. To become a flower: to desire something new.

After a while Ben resumes the chatter. "How are things with Ibrahim?"

She blushes all the way down to her shoulders. Then she smiles. It comes unwillingly, in spite of herself. "Good."

"Yeah?"

"Yeah."

"That's good."

When she's finished, Ben looks exactly like he did when he first arrived but with a duff cowlick (he doesn't care so doesn't mention it) and a long-hair tan line, skin paler around his ears and the downy nape of his neck.

When both brothers are finished, with oppositely ruined bangs, they leave Silvia and Ibrahim to it.

"How's it going?" Ibrahim touches her shoulder.

"Good."

"What?"

"Nothing."

"What is it?" He pulls her face up so he can look at her eyes.

"It's nothing."

"You're being weird."

"I'm not." She pauses. "Am I?"

He looks at her, his eyes saying yes.

"It's just — do you think Cynthia knows? About us?"

"Does it matter?"

She accepts his kisses. "Okay, fine, sit down," she says. She climbs into the tub first. "You should take off your shirt too," she says, trying to be professional, not flirty.

"Did you make everyone do that?"

"No," she says, rinsing the kitchen scissors under the tap, "I used towels for them. But yours is longer. It would stick all over your clothes."

"Just my top, then?" he says, his head already inside his black T-shirt.

"That'll be fine for now." She's coy again.

As he sits at her feet she feels this hunger coming from within her bones. The feeling is satisfied only when he leans his naked back against her legs and she can feel his warmth.

She starts by touching his head all over,

examining this part of him which is usually so far above her. His hair is thick, and what with the curls, snippets of it will make not sticks but grapevines, maybe, or clematis. Something twisted, still living.

"Cut it all off," he says. "I'm sick of it, so hot. Make me look like a real man." He tilts his head up to look at her, his eyes sparkling.

"You sure?"

He reaches behind him and wraps his arms round her legs. Something about this position makes him look like he's a swimmer, frozen before the dive. "Positive."

"But I like it like this. And you are a real man."

"If it's terrible, it'll always grow back."

Curls fall around her bare feet. She cuts it off in clumps, carelessly at first, just to get rid of the bulk. Fistfuls of it fall around her until she's up to her ankles in hair.

She feels sad. He feels light.

"I feel like I'm Delilah," she says, "and you're Samson."

"Who?"

"You know, Samson and Delilah?"

He tips his head up to look at her. "If I did, why would I ask?"

"They're from the Bible."

"Then no, I don't know."

"He was a strong man," she says, touching the newly revealed skin behind Ibrahim's ears, "an impossibly strong man, and she cut his hair because she knew that's where his strength came from."

"That's not where *my* strength comes from."

"She betrayed him." Silvia puts the scissors down.

"I *asked* you to do it."

"I know, I know, it's just a thing I thought of."

He kisses the palm of her hand and leans his head against her knees. "Try not to worry about it," he says, sympathetic but also, she feels, somewhat uncaring.

She looks at the sink, dirty with so many people's spits of toothpaste. She looks in the mirror, crooked above the sink, and wonders whether her parents would recognize her anymore.

Afterwards they throw all the hair out the windows so the birds can make nests. But they find it later, clumped where Toby sleeps.

XLII

Delilah was a pretty girl, but she was not the first to break Samson's heart. Samson was known throughout the land for his strength, but nobody yet knew its source.

Samson is on his way to ask his first love, a Philistine from Timnah, for her hand in marriage when a lion jumps out of the bushes on the side of the dirt road. Samson grabs its front legs and simply rips the lion apart. The roaring, the ripping of fur, of bones; the sudden rush of blood.

The girl — well, her father on her behalf — says yes. Samson is overcome.

A few weeks later, on his way to the rehearsal dinner, Samson takes the same trail and finds the lion is still there, splayed in two, its carcass hollowed but filled with something.

Getting closer, he hears a sound.
Bees. Honeycomb. Honey.

The bees are buzzing, the roar almost equal to the lion's, and honey is dripping from the rotting, drying flesh. Samson scoops out a handful, comb and all, and eats the lot of it: wax, bees, blood. It tastes perfect.

Something about the experience with the lion so moves Samson that he vows never to tell anyone about it.

At the feast, though, buoyed on pride, Samson proposes a riddle:
Out of the eater, something to eat; out of the strong, something sweet.

Nobody gets it, and they start to get angry, so he tells them. He's surprised by how readily he gives in. After that, the night feels not quite right.

The next day he finds that his beloved's father has married her off to another man. There are no hows, no whys, no wherefores. His heart, suddenly cold and huge, feels like it will kill him.

It turns out that heartbreak makes Samson even stronger than anger. He burns three hundred foxes and scorches all the town's crops.

Later the Philistines propose Samson a riddle of their own:
What is sweeter than honey? What is stronger than a lion?

Tortured, he can't find the answer.
He never will.

Years later, Delilah betrayed him. But he was already only half a man.

XLIII

It's a milky-tea afternoon and Silvia is watering flowers in the garden, trying to think of cool things. As she goes down the row for the herbs, nearing the beehives, the buzz gets disproportionately loud. A cloud of bees lifts from one of the hives and a few fly towards her.

"Hey," she says reflexively. Two bees land on her outstretched hand. "What are you two doing?" Then there are two more, and two more; her arm is filling up. They feel like small beaded earrings, just as finely constructed, just as fragile. Silvia is amazed by how they come to her, but for the moment she is too curious to be afraid. The sound is all around her; she is within the sound.

What is sweeter than honey?
What is stronger than a lion?

"Come here," she says, testing, and the bees respond as one by slowly climbing up her arm, towards her bare shoulder. It's only when one flies ahead and lands on her cheek that she starts to freak out and tries to shake them off. With her empty arm she tries to brush them off without touching them, scared of being stung; her instinct takes over her rational mind and she doesn't think to move them gently away, as she had brought them to her, but instead panic-swipes the bewildered insects until they are all gone.

"Go," she whispers. "Go home."

The bees fly back towards their hive. Silvia turns to watch them and thinks she sees, in her peripheral vision, Cynthia standing on the back step, watching her. But when she looks properly, Cynthia isn't there at all. It must have been just a trick of the light.

XLIV

The trees are starting to crisp around the edges. Burnt-brown, not fire-red. This isn't from any premonition of autumn but rather from the scorching summer heat. Many of the plants in the garden are surrendering their fruits earlier than usual. Silvia wonders whether the farm is in some kind of microclimate or whether the drought is affecting the whole province. By the end of June, the fuzzy-headed clover will have finished its season. The bees will have sucked the purple straws dry. The buckwheat — flowers the colour of a baby girl's room — will be ready to harvest as well. Goldenrod has bloomed early this year too, so its peppery nectar will bleed into the rest.

"It's baking out," says Ibrahim as the group walks towards the back lot for the next harvest. "We'll all turn to banana bread."

Once they've got their suits on and Silvia

and Ibrahim are preparing the tools, Ben starts singing "Tupelo Honey" through his veil. *"You can't stop us on the road to freedom, you can't keep us 'cause our eyes can see . . ."*

His voice is nice; he doesn't sound like himself when he sings.

Silvia does the smoking while Ibrahim extracts the frames. They move in rhythm, not touching, swiftly swooping around each other. Ben stands to the side, observing. When the frames are out he'll uncap the wax cells and drain the honey, but until then he just watches everything, singing and feeling pretty productive.

Once the honey has been drained from the combs they can see that the buckwheat honey is much darker than the "flower of the honey" they first harvested, darker even than the yellow-gold they were expecting. It's the colour of molasses and smells of beer and farm. The goldenrod adds a certain bitterness.

Silvia dips a finger into the bowl as the uncapped comb drains. "Ugh," she says, her face crumpling. "It tastes of cow."

Ben, at first offended, as if the taste were a result of his draining, dips a finger in too. "That's gross, man," he says, shaking his head. "Who would actually eat that?"

Ibrahim takes some, licking his finger like a lollipop. "Different strokes."

Cynthia has said that this one is a best-seller at the farmers' market. The three of them decide this is because when things don't taste good, people think it must be better for them.

They work through the peak heat of the day, finishing off twenty hives in five hours, ten frames per hive, two hundred frames in total, nineteen huge plastic buckets of honey extracted, which Hartford will later bottle. After the two-hour mark, everyone stopped talking, focused intently on the tasks at hand. Silvia's T-shirt is soaked through with sweat, and when it reaches the point where it begins to cool her off, she marvels silently at the natural workings of the body.

When they've finished, Ibrahim and Silvia go back to his room and fall asleep among the wet canvases, like children, body-tired from the heat and the hard work.

XLV

Silvia has never thought about whether Cynthia is rich or poor. It's as if the farm is entirely outside a world where those two categories apply and is instead governed by weather, capricious as moods, and time, which also seems to operate on its own schedule here. The capital Cynthia owns is greater than money: she has land, she has life.

It's morning. The group is in the kitchen, quietly eating their breakfast before their chores for the day, when Cynthia enters and catches Silvia's eye.

"The kittens," Cynthia says to her.

"Kittens?" Ben asks, turning to the others.

Silvia stands up. Nobody else knew about the kittens — thinking about it now, she actually doesn't even remember mentioning it to Ibrahim. Cynthia looks tender with tiredness, eyes small and neck sloping forward like a tulip on its stem. It's clear she's been up all night.

"Is Toby a girl?" Dan asks, but nobody answers.

Cynthia walks out the front door. Silvia follows her, and the rest of the group follows Silvia. A low fog hangs around the grass as the dew evaporates in the hot July sun. The smell of tomato leaves as they walk down the driveway makes no sense to Silvia; it's more intense than she's ever known.

"Did you know about this?" Ibrahim catches up to Silvia.

"Cynthia told me that there would be kittens soon, yeah. I guess I forgot, though," she says.

They arrive at the barn, and Cynthia stops in the doorway. "They were born in the night. Seven of them. They're sleeping." She turns and looks into the barn. "Or some of them are. You must be quiet." She stands aside, arm stretched to hold the slatted wooden door open on its hinges, and the group slowly, tentatively, enters.

The mother cat is stretched out long, lying on her side on the bed of cashmere sweaters. Judy looks put-upon but proud; in fact, so does Cynthia. She's looking at the scene with bliss spread across her face.

"It's Toby's mother," Silvia whispers to

Ibrahim. "They call her Judy."

"Toby has a mother?" Ibrahim says instinctively.

The kittens line up along the mother's belly, a few sleeping but most scrabbling with their tiny paws and mouths to find something, they don't even know what, but instinct is pushing them towards their mother's milk. One of the babies is blindly climbing over the body of its mother, hoping for a nipple on her back.

"He's an explorer," Cynthia says.

Judy reaches back, clasps him by the neck between her jaws, and places him within range of the milk source.

The kittens sound like tiny sirens when they mewl, and their tails, narrow and nearly hairless like rats', move with the same random jiggling as their legs. Three are tabby; two are black with white patches on their feet and faces; one is calico — orange, black, and white; and one is all-over grey.

"Hey," MJ says, "there are seven kittens, and seven of us!"

"Plus 'artford is eight," JB corrects. "Where's 'artford?"

"Errands," Cynthia says, "in town."

The kittens' eyes are still sealed shut, their noses neon-pink, and they're smaller than butter sticks with legs, toes still clawless and

263

spread apart like outstretched hands, their fur damped down from the newness. They're so adorable and fragile it's like a cartoon. Ibrahim crouches down to look at them closely and thinks his heart might actually explode.

"Should we name them after ourselves?" Ben asks, looking around at the others, their reverent faces raptly looking upon the scene. "One each?"

Judy protectively stretches out a paw to herd in her litter, covering them from the looming strangers now encircling them.

"You shouldn't name them," Cynthia says, crouching down to stroke Judy's head — a sign of trust — before she gently scoops up the dark grey kitten. "They'll leave as soon as they're ready. It's best not to get attached." She holds the grey baby up to her chest so tenderly, so carefully, it's as though it will replace her heart.

Silvia watches Cynthia hold the baby cat and kiss its damp forehead and becomes aware, as if for the first time, that there is so much outside her control. That you become a hostage to fortune when your heart is outside your body.

"If they all leave," Ibrahim asks, "why did Toby stay?"

Cynthia is quiet for a moment, still absorbed by the kitten she's holding with both hands, then belatedly registers the question. "Toby was attacked by a coyote when he was just a few days old. That's why we had to chop his tail off."

Silvia is taken aback by this news; she'd presumed an entirely different narrative.

"He never wanted to leave after that," Cynthia says, gently placing the grey kitten back down at its mother's belly. Everyone is still staring at the kittens, which are taking turns falling asleep and falling on top of one another, nursing and finding their voices. "Well." Cynthia stands up, still looking at the babies. "I think the kittens need some alone time with their mother now."

They all look at each other, remembering that the day of work is still ahead of them. JB, nearest to the door, leads them back out into the world to start the day. Silvia has a feeling that they'll each carry this moment with them for a long time.

"Do you think she loves them?" Ibrahim asks Silvia as they walk back to the house.

"I don't know if it's about that," Silvia says. "I think it's about something more than love."

XLVI

It is now early July and the solstice has passed, unremarked. The drought has now persisted for five months and six days.

"We haven't had a drought like this since 1954," Hartford says at the dinner table that night. "That one had lasted seven months."

"We?" Ibrahim asks. "How old are you?"

"I mean the region," Hartford explains, impatient.

Cynthia interjects to say that there was a twelve-month drought — longer — in 1931, and another in 1952. Several shorter droughts — three months, four months — scattered in the seventies and again, more frequently, throughout the nineties.

"But we're still here, right?" Ibrahim says. "The world didn't end."

"Most droughts end by March," Cynthia continues. "March is the most reliable wet month."

"Surely we can last until March, no?" JB

says, mouth full.

"We won't be around to see what happens then," Ben says, "but yeah, I'm sure the world of Smooth Rock Falls will not end before March."

Silvia wonders where she'll be in March. The distance between now and then seems insurmountable. The future feels like one unified, unknowable thing, like Europe, though she knows it's all composed of minutes and days, like today and tomorrow.

Everyone eats their spaghetti squash in silence.

"The Cochrane Farmers' Market is next Saturday," Hartford says. "It's a nice one, very big. We'll need all your help to sell the latest honey harvest."

"Hey," Silvia says to Ibrahim, "why don't you frame some of your paintings and take them to market?" He has nearly thirty canvases now, and Silvia keeps telling him that this means something, that it all adds up.

"With the vegetables and artisanal cheeses?" Ibrahim asks, putting down his fork.

"Well, it might not be a gallery, but it's a start. People will see your work."

"I don't know. They're not done."

"Ibrahim."

"How would we even transport them?" he asks, "They're huge, and none of them are framed."

"I could help with that," JB says. "And we could bungee them to the roof of Hartford's car."

"But it would have to be sunny," Ibrahim says, hesitating. "It couldn't rain."

Eventually, somehow, he concedes.

They get to work after dinner, everyone teaming up for a common cause. The atmosphere is immediately lighter. Ibrahim dances circles around JB, who stands still as a flagpole, welding gear in hand and mask over his face.

"Je sais ce que je fais," JB says. When he's concentrating on anything else he can't concentrate on English, and now he's concentrating on welding an iron frame for one of Ibrahim's canvases. JB's beard is so long now that it inverts the proportions of his head.

"Holy," Ben says, his camera right up next to JB's iron.

"Careful," says Dan, nodding to the camera, "the sparks." Ibrahim sees them: flickers flying like miniature fireworks.

"Yeah, careful!" Ibrahim looks tortured. "The sparks! My painting!" All his muscles are stretched like elastic bands about to snap.

But Ben stays in his place, and JB explains that the sparks lose their heat quickly. *"C'est bon. T'inquiète pas."*

Silvia sees Ibrahim flapping helplessly like a bird in a cage, splays her book on the floor, and goes to him. She wraps her arms around his waist, strapping his arms to his sides — she doesn't know this is the manoeuvre to immobilize a maniac, she just does it out of instinct — and leans her head on his back, her ears at his shoulder level. "Come on, he knows what he's doing," she says, then repeats it, rubbing Ibrahim's upper arms, nuzzling into the space between his shoulder blades.

Then: "Ow! Oh, oh, ouch!" Silvia pulls her hand close as though recoiling from a flame.

"What?" Ibrahim asks, and they all look at her.

She inspects her palm, trying to find something between the lines. Then she sees a bee on the floor, nearly dead, still fritzing with a dwindling buzz. "I think I got stung."

"By a bee?" Ibrahim asks, incredulous.

"Of course by a bee," she says, nodding at the dying insect on the ground. "I didn't even notice it." Silvia juts the heel of her hand into Ibrahim's face to show him the spiky black stinger sticking out like a splinter. "Look."

"You'll be fine, babe," Ibrahim says, and though he says it lovingly, he doesn't do any more to console her, absorbed as he is in his own drama.

Nobody else is paying her any attention either.

"I'm gonna go find Cynthia," she says, irritated with him, with everyone.

Cynthia is sitting at the kitchen table with a notebook, her back to Silvia. Silvia stops for a second before announcing herself, not wanting to interrupt, but Cynthia turns before Silvia can even say anything.

"Everything all right?" Cynthia asks.

"Yeah, fine. Well . . ." Nervously, Silvia puts her hand forth and follows her palm to Cynthia. "I got stung. By a bee."

"Really?" Cynthia looks astonished. Bees sting only when the hive is in direct danger from an intruder, in order to protect their colony. Cynthia knows this; Silvia knows it too. "Does it hurt?"

"Not really." Silvia lies. "I'm not allergic or anything."

"In that case, I'll remove the stinger and then we'll get some ice on it."

270

Cynthia gets the first-aid kit from underneath the sink and extracts from the red plastic box a long needle. She uses the needle to open the skin enough to prise out the stinger. A fine sheet of white cotton smudges away the blood that blossoms at the prick. Silvia is too riveted by the procedure to feel any pain.

"Look," Cynthia says, holding up the slender specimen between her thumb and forefinger. It's as long as a fingernail clipping. "I have some cream we could put on it if you like. Homeopathic, a traditional beekeeper's trick."

"Sure."

Cynthia asks Silvia to accompany her to the honey house, and Silvia follows in her wake as if they're birds and she's riding in the vortices of Cynthia's wings. Out the front door, across the yard, down a gravel path she's never trodden on.

Looking straight ahead, Cynthia speaks in a confiding tone. "Have you any sisters, Silvia?"

She hesitates before replying no.

"Me neither. I've never had a sister," Cynthia says, as though this is a distinction from not having one currently. She swipes a bee away from her shoulder without touching it.

The women arrive at the door to the

honey house. Plain wood, a simple lock, a slot below the handle like an extra-large mail flap. Cynthia slides her hand underneath her collar, along her breast, to fish something out. The key. Without removing the thin white string, newly visible, from around her neck, she lowers down to keyhole height so as to unlock the door. At the click, she replaces the key in its place under her shirt, over her heart. "Wait here a moment, will you?" She opens the door and goes inside.

Silvia waits, feet planted in a dancer's third position on the gravel path. She doesn't feel anything resembling irritation or even curiosity; she accepts the situation as readily as she accepts the weather. She feels comfortably aware of information that she is outside of — the honey room, this conversation — but it's more like an iceberg than anything else. Though we only see the top of it, there's always the full knowledge that the greatest expanse of ice is unseen.

"Here we are." Cynthia is back already. "Sorry about that. We'd do this inside, but it's just utter chaos in there. Can't see a thing."

"It's fine." Silvia looks up to the periwinkle sky.

Cynthia has a squidge of jelly on her finger

and a small square of porous gauze draped over her wrist. "Give me your hand," she says, holding hers out.

Silvia surrenders the wounded palm and watches as Cynthia performs her nurse's work.

"There we go," Cynthia says, patting the top of Silvia's hand. She looks at the girl for a moment, then says, "I know how hard it must have been for you, Silvia, to leave your old life behind. It's the kind of thing that stays with you, isn't it? But I want you to know I think you're adjusting brilliantly. You're doing so well." She pats Silvia on the arm maternally, then she touches her heart, feeling the key there: reassurance. "Thank you, Silvia."

"Oh. Um, no problem. I mean, thank *you*."

Dismissed, Silvia goes back along the gravel path, wondering what it is exactly that she has to be grateful for.

XLVII

"Last night I dreamt I murdered everyone here. Hartford, Cynthia. You."

"God."

"I know."

"Why did you do it? In your dream."

"I don't know."

"Was it scary?"

"Yeah."

"So were you alone at the end?"

"No."

"Then you didn't kill everyone?"

"No, I did, but I had a baby. I was pregnant when I did the murders and then I had a baby right after. But then I killed us both."

XLVIII

Ibrahim is thriving on the farm. Now that he's gotten used to the seclusion, now that he's not expecting anything else, now that his time is only his. He works constantly and feels it all, everything, moving inside him, as if his blood is red paint.

He no longer misses the messy movement of the city or the detritus he used to take and make new. He's found a replacement for this in the forest. Bark, moss, mushrooms; leaves, eggshells, twigs. And unlike cardboard, there are so many different kinds of bark, so many different colours of leaf.

When he can't sleep, or if he's working through the night, he goes out to sit in the yard to take his mind off things. The stars are like nothing he's ever seen in the city. From the lawn, any time of night, he can see the smooth-speckled Milky Way clotting near the North Star. And Silvia taught him how to find Cassiopeia and the Pleiades, the seven sisters.

To really comprehend the fucked-up magic of the universe, someone once told him, you have to look up at the sky and think about the fact that you're actually looking *down*.

It's the middle of the night and he's just gotten back to his studio from one of his night walks. Working, not insomnia. He's covered in paint — even the skin underneath his clothes is blue- and yellow-freckled — and his studio is covered too: canvases are propped on all the walls, cardboard palettes lie half abandoned, paint crusted over, all of them unusable but undiscarded in the event that he runs out of any of the colours squirted on them, in which case he'll revitalize the shellacked splatter with some paint thinner and scrape it off the soggy board.

He's been up for twenty-nine hours.

He has been working constantly to finish ("finish") enough paintings to show at the market. He's been painting through the night, through the morning, had just one little power nap in the afternoon, and then started again in the evening. Even if he hadn't actually *done* much to them — he knew Silvia, for example, wouldn't notice any changes at all — he needed time to look at them, tweak them, daub on black and

276

white for hints of light and shadow, and spend time considering them as full, complete. But at this rate he'll have Yves Kleined his body before finishing any one of his paintings.

Spinning in a slow music-box circle at a fixed point in the middle of the room, Ibrahim lets his eyes fall and then stick on one of his smaller paintings, propped in the corner by the window. He stops spinning. Something is off. He stares at it, takes one step back.

Green. It needs emerald green. Where's his tube of emerald green? He marches to the other end of the room and looks behind the canvases on the wall there. How can he not have any emerald green?

Before he can rage there's a knock at the door. He doesn't answer. He takes a thin brush from behind his ear.

Another knock.

"Hello?"

It's Silvia's voice. He doesn't turn.

"Ibrahim? Please come to bed."

"I'm working."

"You've been working for two days straight."

He turns. "And I only have one more day to finish all this."

"Exactly, you have a full day. So come to

bed. Please. You need sleep." She's leaning against the doorframe, wearing only his T-shirt. "I get it, I do — but you're not helping anything by not sleeping."

"But —"

She walks into the room, avoiding the spots of wet paint on the floor. Even though he doesn't walk towards her, she hugs him, rests her head against him. "It'll be fine. I promise."

"You don't get it. It's not like — it's the first time this is going to be outside my head, in the *world,* you know?"

"I do know, I do."

"How would you know?"

Silence.

He shakes his head and shakes her off him. "Sorry, sorry, I didn't mean that." He runs his fingers through his hair and, having forgotten his body for too long, feels a loss when he finds it short. "I'm just — I guess I am tired. I'll be right there, okay?"

She nods.

He says, "Really, right there," and looks into her eyes as a promise.

She slinks back to bed. She doesn't fall asleep, though: she listens to him continue working, grunting, breathing, moving. The moon is new so the sky is dark, and the room is less visible to her than she's used to. She thinks about what Cynthia said about leaving her life behind and for the first time since arriving thinks about how she'd like to, maybe, find the local church. An anchor could be helpful.

XLIX

Market day is bright, and Ibrahim and Silvia wake up at the exact same moment with the sun waterfalling through the window.

"Sleep well?" he asks, kissing her warm shoulder.

"More weird dreams." She presses her ear into the pillow, not as quick to alertness as he. The events of her dreams have disappeared and left her with only an unsettling, transient feeling.

Ibrahim kicks off the blanket and goes, naked and unusually sprightly even for him, to flip around a canvas that had been facing the wall. "Check it out!" he says, trying to bring Silvia along with his enthusiasm.

It's the painting of her. "Is it finished?"

"Yeah, I'm really pleased with it." He looks at it. "I'll get them to add it to the stack to take to market."

She feels extremely exposed. The painting is amazing, but it's confusing. It's her, naked; it's him, honest; it's them, a blend of them, together. Silvia wraps the comforter around her like a cape and moves until her face is in the warm yellow light of the sun. "I'm glad you're happy," she says.

"Get dressed!" Ibrahim says, wandering around the room looking for his favourite shirt. "Or we'll be late!"

Breakfast is simple, serve-yourself, as everyone is getting ready to go to the market. Hartford has already left with Ibrahim's paintings, and Cynthia is preparing paperwork in the office. The silence that presses around them is easy as heat.

In the presence of others, amid the buzz of productivity, Ibrahim is suddenly much calmer. He's making jokes and chatting, but she does notice that he doesn't eat any of his cereal. As some of them finish up and start putting their dishes in the sink, Cynthia enters, hands in her pockets.

"Good morning, everyone."

"Morning," they mumble.

"Silvia," she goes over to Silvia and sits in the empty seat next to her so she doesn't have to speak so loudly. "I'm wondering if you would stay behind to help me. There's a special harvest that needs to be done today, and I'd really appreciate your help."

281

Silvia looks at Ibrahim. He stares back at her, with an "obviously not" look on his face. She wants to go with him, she wants to see the people who look at his paintings, she wants to see how much everyone loves them. But she also knows that Cynthia wouldn't ask for her help if she didn't need it.

"Can I think about it?" Silvia asks, looking at Ibrahim. "It's just that I was looking forward to, uh, to the market." To seeing a new place, to spending time with Ibrahim outside the purview of the farm, to seeing if a little bit of distance from this place will help settle her heart.

"Of course." Cynthia presses her hands to the tops of her thighs as she stands up, looks between Ibrahim and Silvia, and walks away with the slowness belonging to only the most confident people.

Ibrahim looks at Silvia and she's not sure how to read his expression. Confusion, rejection, anxiety. "This was *your* idea," he says, once Cynthia is out of earshot.

"I know," she says, and she does feel guilty for that. "But you'll be amazing whether I come or not, right? And it's probably good that I put in some time doing bonus work."

"So you're doing it?" he asks, baffled by how quickly the situation has pivoted.

Silvia shrugs. "I think I have to." She is apologetic without apologizing. Though her feelings are not uncomplicated, underneath it all is delight, as ever, at being the chosen one. She stands, pushing her chair back, and picks up her not-quite-empty cereal bowl. "I won't say good luck, so *break a leg*!" She is too shy to kiss him in public.

Never having heard this expression, Ibrahim registers nothing. Ben and Dan have to explain what it means after she leaves. Silvia finds this hopelessly adorable when he tells her later.

Silvia knocks on the door to the honey house.

"Silvia. Perfect," Cynthia holds the door open as Silvia walks in, tentatively. "Thank you for staying."

"Sure."

"No, I really appreciate it."

Silvia looks around the room. It's plain wood, like the bedrooms, and lined with shelves that are full of things: bottles, Mason jars, papers, pipettes, Tupperware boxes. Some of the vessels are full, but most are empty. There are cupboards and filing cabinets, all of which are closed. Despite the dirt floor, everything is so organized it's practically sterile. It could be a hospital hut from *M*A*S*H:* makeshift and brushed tidy. She wonders what it must have looked like before, when Cynthia wouldn't let her in.

Cynthia continues, speaking confidentially now: "I need your help with harvesting the royal jelly." She explains that this, the food that transforms any ordinary bee into a queen, "is one of the most profitable things an apiary can produce. But" — she eyes Silvia up and down — "please don't tell anyone about today. I don't want it getting to Hartford. It upsets him." She looks at Silvia meaningfully.

"Royal jelly can be sold for up to thirty-two dollars an ounce, wholesale — honey is sold for between one and three dollars an ounce, for comparison." She continues, using terms like *profit margin, bandwagon, placebo effect.* "You start by encouraging the hive to produce its own queens." She shows Silvia the special frames — longer, deeper than normal cells. "The nurse bees feed all the larvae in these cells the royal jelly, and we harvest it before the bees fully develop."

Silvia watches as Cynthia takes out some plastic tubes from a cupboard under the sink.

"Every bee in a hive gets fed some of this during its incubation. But the ones that will be queens never stop. They consume it exclusively. That's what makes them queens."

Cynthia has set up a special hive behind the garage to fill with the victim queens. "So this hive will produce exclusively royal jelly."

"But how do they make it?"

"Make what?"

"Sorry, how do the bees make the royal jelly?"

"They secrete it from their glands."

Silvia's face registers the appropriate disgust.

"Here." Cynthia brings up the frame she'd placed on the countertop to show Silvia. "To harvest it, the queen larvae must be removed before they have the chance to fully develop but after their cells have been injected with the maximum capacity of royal jelly. It's vital to find the precise moment. You use a long thin wooden spoon, like this" — she reaches for the spoon to show Silvia — "to remove the larvae, and then a syringe to suck up the jelly."

"Where do we put them?" Silvia asks.

"Put what?"

"All the baby queens."

"Oh. We won't need them beyond this stage."

Silvia shuts her eyes and takes a deep breath. She tries to imagine light engulfing her. In a past life she would have called this a prayer.

To produce a kilogram of royal jelly, two thousand queen cells must be emptied. *Sacrificed,* Silvia thinks. Cynthia will do the removal with the spoon and then hand the frame over to Silvia, armed with a syringe to mine the honeycomb.

The comb is the burnished colour of graham crackers, chanterelle mushrooms — the same colour as Ibrahim's skin. Each hexagon is perfect. It's impossible to imagine these being built by bees, impossible to understand their organic symmetry.

"I loved your book, by the way," Silvia says as Cynthia prepares the supplies.

"Did you? That's nice of you to say."

"No, really, I loved it. Did you write it here? There's something about it that feels very much . . . I don't know how to say it, but almost, well, *of* this place."

"I did write it here, yes. Thank you."

"You're the first poet I've ever met. All my parents' friends are real estate agents or dentists."

"Well," Cynthia replies, smiling, "everyone needs a home and good teeth."

Then the memory of a thought comes to

Silvia. "Who's Leila?"

Cynthia stops humming. She puts down the thin spoon and tray of honeycomb she was holding and looks at them.

"The dedication in your book — I just noticed and wond—"

"Right. My daughter. Our daughter."

"Oh." This wasn't what Silvia was expecting. "I didn't know you had a daughter."

"Hilary took her away."

"When?"

"Just a few months after Leila was born. Hilary left to be with Tom, a friend of ours. The baby's biological father, actually. We'd asked him to donate his sperm and then Hilary left me for him. Ironic, isn't it?" She smiles.

"That must have been terrible," Silvia says. "I'm so sorry. I can't even imagine."

Cynthia picks up a honeycomb and coughs to clear her throat. "It was difficult. She was quite unstable at the end. Anyway, what about you? Was it what you expected?" Cynthia licks her lips. "Here, I mean."

Suddenly Silvia has that feeling of the iceberg approaching. She tries to think about what it was that she expected and then realises that she hadn't thought that far, where practical plans intersect with prospective futures. "I guess so. I don't know what I expected. But I do like it here, so much."

"Good. And you're finding it inspiring? Are you getting lots of writing done?"

"Oh, well — no. Not really. Not at all, actually. I don't know where to start, I guess."

"Well, if you ever want to sit down and discuss your work, I'd be happy to, Silvia. I think you have a lot to say. You just need to let it out."

"Really?" Silvia puts down the honeycomb she's been idly holding.

"Of course."

It's then understood that it's time to get back to the work at hand; Cynthia puts her hands on the high countertop work station, and Silvia follows her lead.

"First I'll take these out." Cynthia deftly manoeuvres the unvarnished wooden tool and flicks the little white globules — they look like snots — off into a plastic bag hanging from the counter. Ten cells are emptied quickly. "You have the syringe?"

Silvia nods, then takes the small frame of cleaned-out comb. She sticks the pipette down to the bottom of a cell, squeezes the black rubber nipple dropper, and sucks up the mucous-coloured gunk.

"Perfect, just like that," Cynthia says. "Do

you want to try it?"

"Try what?" She thought she was doing it.

"Taste it. The jelly. Here —"

Cynthia's got her finger right in front of Silvia's face before she's made a decision. Reflexively, she opens her mouth. A hard fingertip along her arched tongue, and a sour, sickly taste of sweet creamy vinegar.

"What do you think?" Cynthia asks, grinning, as she extricates her finger.

Silvia coughs. "I . . ." She swallows. "It's weird."

"People love weird." Cynthia laughs. "So, are you planning to stay for a while?" Cynthia turns back to work on a new honeycomb. "I mean, you can. You and Ibrahim, you two can stay. You're welcome to stay here as long as you'd like."

"Oh," Silvia says, her head catching up to this. How long has Cynthia known about them?

Cynthia continues: "I know you're from out east, and if I remember correctly, Ibrahim lives with his family in Toronto. Logistically, if you want to stay here for a while, find your feet together —"

"That's very nice of you to offer," Silvia says.

"I'd enjoy having you around," Cynthia

says. "It would be nice — you know, calmer. Without all the others around all the time. And you'd be able to get more work done after the work of the harvest season is through."

"We haven't really thought about that stuff yet — I mean, we don't really have plans yet. I don't even know if he . . . but, yeah, I'll talk to him about it."

"There's no rush, Silvia. I just thought I'd plant the seed."

After this they work in silence.

An hour or so passes, and after emptying what feels like hundreds of trays of honeycomb, they're left with a mustard jar filled only a quarter of the way — about the amount of an egg yolk but paler, more viscous.

Cynthia holds it up to the light. "Perfect. That'll be enough for now."

"Okay," Silvia says, wiping her hands on her jeans though there is nothing to wipe away. It will still be several hours before the others return from the market.

The two women are not sure how to acknowledge each other and this new thing between them. Cynthia nods; Silvia looks at her feet.

Silvia is about to leave, but then, turning

on her thoughts, she says, "I was going to make some tea. Do you want some tea?"

"Tea?" Cynthia replies, baffled. "No, no."

Outside the honey house, Silvia finds a plastic grocery bag on the ground. Opening the bag, she sees the minuscule translucent bodies of queen foetuses. Gelatinous white, like aliens with their big eyes. Hundreds of them. No, thousands. She suppresses the need to retch until she gets inside the house, skips the kitchen and the tea, and heads straight to the bathroom.

L

Feeling unsettled, as though she's just seen something she shouldn't have — some elemental fibre of the universe — Silvia goes to her room, thinking she'll try to write. Ibrahim had talked about material, and he was right — there is plenty of material here, but Silvia can't make sense of it so as to create anything logical, let alone meaningful. It's all just fabric, everything flat, everything equal.

Bees. Queens. Dead babies. Their tiny see-through brains and their unformed, cold hearts.

No.

She closes her eyes. When she opens them the page is still blank. She opens up Cynthia's book and turns to the poem about Leila. "Mine." Does it feel different now, knowing the context? There is no giveaway that indicates the poem is about a baby, let alone Cynthia's baby, but as she reads it again — she reads it three times now — the sharp hurt of loss comes through.

She hears a sound coming from outside and gets up off the bed to look out the window. Hartford's car bumps over the rocky driveway, and a few seconds afterwards the shadows of bodies follow behind it.

They're back.

She hurries down the stairs, nervous; she hopes, as though the hope is her own, that Ibrahim will be happy with how the market went.

At the bottom of the stairs she finds Cynthia waiting, arms crossed. "Get some writing done?" she asks Silvia, her voice chirpy, chitchatty.

"Mmm." Silvia slips down to the ground floor as Ben and Dan burst through the door.

"We sold *all* the honey!" Ben cries, carrying the folded-up banner Hartford made that says HONEY — MIEL in delicate cursive writing.

"And Ibrahim nearly sold the portrait of Silvia for five thousand bucks to this lady in Crocs!" Dan adds.

"Sucker," Ben says loudly, making sure Ibrahim hears as he walks in, trailing the others.

"Thanks. But she didn't buy it, so I guess that makes me the sucker."

Silvia looks at him, wanting to go over, but Cynthia is in the way. She's trying to detect any indicators that will point to what mood he's in. She can't tell.

"Well, she was gonna," Ben says, feeling a little bad now. "Maybe she still will."

Then Cynthia speaks. "Would you sell the painting to me, Ibrahim?"

There's an instant, onomatopoeic hush. Everyone in the group looks at Ibrahim, who's carrying his canvases with his back-bungee system.

"Really?" Ibrahim asks, thunderstruck.

"I should buy some of your work while I can still afford it." Cynthia chuckles. "You certainly are a rising star!"

"Well, I mean, yeah, if you want to — that would be great," he stutters.

"You should be able to afford it with all the profit you've made off our slave labour," Dan says, muttering loudly enough for everyone to hear.

Cynthia only smiles magnanimously, staring at the group until they start to walk, one by one, up the stairs to their rooms. When only Silvia and Ibrahim remain, Cynthia goes over to Ibrahim.

"I'm glad you're so productive here, Ibrahim."

He nods, looking at Silvia.

"I wondered if you would both want to stay longer," Cynthia continues, "through the fall. There'd be even more time for your painting, and —"

"Wow!" Ibrahim cries, not returning Silvia's meaningful stare. "That'd be great!" Then, finally turning to Silvia, he says, "That's so generous, isn't it? I'm sure we'd love that!"

Silvia doesn't respond — she just lets herself be taken into a sideways hug and looks at Cynthia.

"Wonderful," Cynthia says. "Good night, you two." And she's gone.

LI

"I don't get why you're so upset," Ibrahim says. He and Silvia are on opposite sides of her room, trying to keep their voices down. "I mean, we're living in her house — she would have found out we were together eventually."

"Why didn't you ask me if I was okay with staying before you —"

"Are you not okay? I thought you liked it here."

"Yes I *like* it, but maybe I had other plans, other things to do in the fall! And maybe I like it for now but not forever!"

"Oh. Well, do you?" Ibrahim sits on the mattress. "Have other plans?"

"That's not the point." She looks down at him but does not join him. "Cynthia asked me if we wanted to stay when we were working this afternoon, and I said I wanted to talk to you about it. You know, because people have to *talk* about these things."

He sighs an elaborate sigh.

"Ibrahim, please. I didn't know if you wanted to stay here, with me, whether that's something that's on the table, and —"

"What? Are you saying you don't know whether I want to be with you? Have I not made that clear? I think you're the best. The fantasticest." He kisses her loudly over her ear. "Plus, we haven't committed to anything. We can always leave with the others if we want to. We can leave whenever."

"Okay, if that's what you want," she says.

"Is that what *you* want?" he asks, trying very hard to be patient.

"I don't know what I want." She finally sits down.

"How were things with Cynthia this afternoon?" He is eager to find a change of subject, unaware that this subject will only narrow his path further.

"Fine." She brushes him off. "No, not fine. It was weird. We had to kill all these baby queens to get their royal jelly. It was like we had to abort all these alien pregnancies. And she made me try the royal jelly too, and it tasted . . . like nothing I've ever tasted before."

"Oh." He doesn't know what to say. "I've heard of royal jelly. It's pretty expensive, isn't it?"

"Yeah, and I guess it's 'cause you have to murder for it." She's upset, she knows she's more upset than she should be, but she can't rein herself in.

"And did you get any writing done afterwards?" He tries another subject.

"Ibrahim, honestly, there's no need to ask me that. Ever. I did not get any writing done. I never do. That's always the answer — *no,* so there, you never need to ask it again." She stands up but doesn't go anywhere. She has nowhere to go.

"Silvia, hey, come on, what's the matter?"

"Sorry." She doesn't look at him. "I don't know what's got into me." She has that feeling in her gut that you get when you're walking down stairs and miss a step. "I just feel exhausted."

"It's okay, it's fine. Come here." He takes her in his arms and brings her down to his level. Her ears rest right between his collarbones. "I just don't want you to forget that I think you can do it. I think you can do whatever you want."

"And if I don't want to? Would that be okay too?"

It feels awkward between them, as if there's another person in the room observing them.

With her head still pressed against his

chest, her thoughts suddenly somewhere else, she empties and fills her lungs before saying, "Don't you ever feel, like, isolated here?"

"On the farm?" He pulls back to look at her.

"Yeah. Without Internet. Without phones."

"No. I know I can leave if I want."

"What do you think she wants?" She is nervous asking him this; she feels vulnerable.

"Who, Cynthia? I don't know." He shrugs; he hasn't considered this. "She's just offering, no? Who's to say she wants anything?"

"I just feel like if she's offering this, it must be because of something. Don't you think? Maybe she wants us to stay for —"

"What do you think?" He pulls back to look her in the eyes. "That she's making us stay here — for free, in her home — so we can, what, keep her company? Help her with the work? How sinister."

"I'm just trying to tell you how I *feel*, Ibrahim." Silvia feels like she's about to burst into tears. "But you don't seem to be the best at listening to that sort of thing."

"I'm just having a hard time picking your feelings apart from all the words that you're saying, honestly," he says.

"Okay, fine."

That night Ibrahim sleeps alone on a folded blanket in his studio, leaving Silvia and Toby to the double-mattressed bed in her room.

LII

Cynthia hangs the painting of Silvia in the library. About four feet by five, it fills the whole wall. Ibrahim and Silvia are present for the hanging.

"The colours — the colours are simply lovely." Cynthia looks at it from up close, pleased, then steps back to admire it from afar. She crosses her arms and tilts her head. "Are those wings?"

Though the painting is of Silvia, it's not obviously of Silvia, so it seems less strange. It's less of a portrait and more of a feeling. This is what she tells herself.

Nothing has changed between the night that Ibrahim painted it and now. It's just as raw, just as intimate. Her breasts, nipples bright pink, are right there. However, hanging it on the wall gives the painting a sense of finality — it's become more than just that moment. It's now an official "painting." Especially with the title, which Ibrahim told

Silvia only yesterday.

The Other Woman.

Is she the other woman? Or does the title refer to a different woman? He'd told her that he just made up the title on the spot; it was the first thing that came to him when the woman in Crocs asked. He said the title referred to his mother, and while Silvia didn't really understand, she knew better than to ask. He'd alluded to the fact that his mother had died, and she knew he didn't want to talk about it; that was fine. She didn't want to talk about her parents either.

Silvia's eyes meet the eyes of the painting: they are exactly the same colour and shape as her own — pond-green, oval — though the colour changes so often, she wonders how he picked which one to preserve in paint. But in the painting they take up more space in the face, and one is much larger than the other. It's not realistic, but it feels real. Silvia looks deeper, and something pulses. Vital. It feels like the painting is looking at her, seeing right through her.

She leaves the room without excusing herself, feeling newly unmasked.

LIII

July turns to August. Time is round, stretched, redolent. A camera out of focus. The pollen from all the flowers is mixed in the late summer, when the bees go everywhere and everything blooms at once.

With this dry heat, the air clinging to their skin and throats, the people on the farm feel a mixture of pity and jealousy for the bees. Jealousy because they probably don't feel thirst, pity in case they do.

When the September winds come in from the east, they bring a terrible smell with them. The smell gets inside Silvia's head, makes it feel swollen and misty. It gets inside her stomach, makes her feel nauseated. Her eyes swell and turn cloudy red as though she's allergic to something. But finally, when she's convinced that the smell will slice her brain in two, she has to ask what it is.

"Cynthia?" Silvia approaches the curved

form of the woman, hunched over some papers on Hartford's desk.

Cynthia looks up and puts her hand to her chest — a tragic inhalation. "Oh!" she exclaims. "I'm sorry, Silvia. I didn't see you."

"Sorry, I'm sorry to bother you — it's nothing, it's just —"

"Yes?"

"Just, I was wondering, what's that smell?"

"What smell?"

"Coming from outside — it smells of sewage or something."

Cynthia stands and looks where Silvia is pointing. Something clicks.

"Oh! That. That's the canola."

"What?"

"Those yellow flowers in the field, canola. Rapeseed. For oil. It also makes delicious honey. I'm so used to the smell I don't even notice it anymore."

"Oh." Silvia looks out at the yellow fields, picture-perfect in the early autumn light. She'd seen canola fields back in Nova Scotia but had never noticed a smell. "Okay."

"Are you feeling all right?" Cynthia asks. "You look a little off-colour."

Silvia places her palms below her navel, to where her centre of gravity has shifted. "Fine." She tries to smile but feels it's a lie.

"I hope you know you can tell me anything, Silvia," Cynthia says. "If things aren't going well, or if Ibrahim, or . . ." She shrugs, trying to make light of it. "You know, I'm here."

Silvia feels dizzy as a drift of the sickening smell comes through the open window. "Right," she says. "Thanks."

When she leaves, she goes down to the fields to see for herself and finds it's true: the disgusting smell does come from those yellow flowers. The wind, when it's strong, carries the stench all the way up to the house, but close up it's absolutely intolerable. The smell of rotten milk, dead animals, and human shit.

LIV

It's a Monday. Silvia's decided to go into town. Actually the decision was made partly by her and partly by others: everyone's letters home had been sitting in their envelopes for days, and Hartford asked her to drop them off at the post office and pick up some things from the store.

Silvia's never actually left the property other than to go to the lakes. This realisation smacks her in the tight V between her eyes: Why not? She has everything she needs here, and there is always something to do, and the town is far, and . . . Being on the farm, she feels like a child: taken care of.

In her tatty Trident tote bag she's got a long letter for her parents. She hasn't called them since that first time. In a letter, she doesn't have to answer any questions. In a letter, she doesn't have to feel their sadness at her having strayed from the straight and narrow path to heaven.

It's bright, no interruption of clouds. She should have worn sunglasses.

Heat. Headache. Seasickness, but no sea.

Though there's a bus, she'd rather walk. But she finds there's no sidewalk along the whole stretch of road, only a gravel gutter that feeds to small shrubs, then descends into large, latticed evergreens. All of a sudden she has to pee. So badly. The sudden weight of it burns in her bladder. She looks around in a panic: she's far from any bathroom, but there doesn't seem to be anyone around, so she hurries into the shrubs that line the path and pulls her jeans down below her knees, carefully places her feet parallel, as if for takeoff, and squats, directing her stream into the Queen Anne's lace. The relief is ecstatic.

Silvia sees the water tower before she sees the town. It's the only man-made thing on the horizon — nearly all the houses around are bungalows with slapdash siding, built quickly as if for a passing fair. OOTH RO / ALLS. The letters wrap around the tank. The tower looks like a chess piece, a rook; it doesn't look like it can hold very much water. She wonders how much is left inside, if any, and if they (whoever *they* are) are hoarding it greedily, not sharing it with the thirsty masses.

When the town finally appears, the highway forks into Fourth, Fifth, and Sixth Streets.

WELCOME — BIENVENUE
To/À SMOOTH ROCK FALLS!

She takes Fifth. The post office is at the corner of Fifth and Hollywood Avenue. There's a small cement church, St. Gertrude's Catholic. It looks uninhabited, but she knows that it will be open: it's the church's rule that sanctuaries be accessible at all times. Right now, though, she doesn't feel like going in. There are eight squat houses placed equidistantly along the block, and at the end of Hollywood is the trailer park. There are two gas stations, one post office, and three shops: the LCBO (she imagines the liquor store must get the most business, considering); the Sears depot (but she wonders if that counts as a real store); and Blanchette Freshmart + Pharmacy, which sells groceries, tools, and prescription drugs. The only restaurant, Smoothy's, is at the entrance to the trailer park.

Ibrahim talked about the exciting feeling of possibility in the "real world" when he went to the market a few towns over, but if this is the real world, here at Hollywood and Fifth, she doesn't feel any excitement or possibility at all.

Next door to the post office is a white clapboard bungalow where a woman named Valerie has set up a beauty salon. VALERIE'S NICE BEAUTY. Funny, Silvia thinks — she's finally found it! *"Beauty lives with kindness,"* that numinous place in Shakespeare's poem! And, ironically, it lives here, in the abandoned flatlands between rocks and hard places.

"Allo!" a cheerful teenager greets her as she walks into the post office. His hair is striped from Goth to Smurf to marshmallow. It's captivating.

She pulls the letters out of her bag and puts them on the counter, thus setting off his chain of small, industrious tasks: he weighs each letter, taps on his computer, fixes things in drawers. This, mailing letters, is the kind of basic chore that she's been doing her whole life, but today she finds it confusing and pointless.

He files all the papers and then smiles. "Thank you, *merci*!"

Silvia doesn't know which language to reply in, so she frowns. "I'm also wondering, do you have any mail here for me? My name is Silvia, I'm staying on the Honey

Farm, my parents . . ."

"With Cynthia? Ah, yes. Family name?" he asks.

"Richardson."

"A moment." He disappears behind a shelf, then returns promptly with a stack of envelopes. "*Voilà!* Lots of mail!"

A stone in her belly. There are at least twenty letters. She takes them and stuffs them into her tote bag, where she plans to let them fester, and thanks the teenager with the tricolour hair as she leaves this hot cramped space for the hot open space outdoors.

Outside, the queasy, stomach-twisting feeling is starting to spread, like dandelion seeds in the wind, through her whole body. The sun is so bright it contrasts everything into light and dark. She feels lightheaded. Blanchette Freshmart + Pharmacy is at the corner; she goes in to get something to drink.

"Lemonade, please," she says, leaving a loonie on the counter. A dour-looking woman, probably around fifty, takes the coin slowly and throws it, clanging, into the old-fashioned metal cash register.

Before drinking the lemonade, Silvia brings the bottle to her forehead and holds it there. The cold shocks her body; she feels it shiver down her back, making an eel of her spine.

"Are you working up on the honey farm?" the woman asks. "For Cynthia?"

"Yeah." Silvia opens the bottle and drinks most of it in one go.

The woman gives a laugh that means the opposite of what a laugh usually means; Silvia senses she doesn't think anything is funny at all. "I saw an ad in the Barrie paper when I was visiting my aunt."

Silvia nods, not interested, and starts making tracks. "Well, thanks."

"Did you know Hilary?"

"No, I just arrived."

"You could be her sister. Or even her daughter."

"Hilary?"

"You look just like her."

"So I've been told," Silvia says. The clenching in her stomach is coming back. She grips it, trying to be subtle, and bends over, but nothing stops the pain.

The woman puts her thumb into her mouth and bites her nail. "You okay?"

"Fine, thanks."

"Getting nauseous on the regular?"

"Just sometimes lately. I think it's the season." Silvia gestures with the hand not gripping her stomach, pointing vaguely to the outdoors as though to suggest responsibility lies outside her. "Allergies or something."

"Are your breasts tender?"

"Excuse me?"

The woman ducks down, gets something from a shelf behind her, then slides the flat cardboard package she retrieved across the countertop. It says *Clear Blue* and is wrapped with both blue and pink stripes. It's a pregnancy test.

"What? Oh no, I don't —"

"You may as well check," the woman says. "Better safe than sorry."

Silvia takes the test without even thinking she needs to pay for it, and the lady doesn't stop her. She walks out of the store wondering which of the two outcomes is the safe one and whether it's a little too late for that.

Outside, the heat of the sun is poisonous. Silvia feels stricken with sunstroke, heat exhaustion, dehydration. As if she's out of her element. She thinks about the word *element*. Elementary, basic. Fundamental, essential. Component, community. If a fish isn't in its element, it dies. She thinks of that joke, or maybe it's an allegory, where two fish are swimming downstream and one says to the other, "Hey, how's the water?"

and the other one's like, "What the hell is water?"

There's a gas station on the corner and she walks briskly through the aisles of jerky and chips to the wheelchair-accessible, single-stall bathroom. She rips open the packaging, doesn't read the instructions, and assembles the device with a canny intuition, wondering whether all girls just magically know how to do this.

She pees on the tricky stick and then waits for her entire life to pass before her eyes until the results come up.

Two thin blue lines.

The reality of this thunderbolts her; she feels it in her whole body to be true. She accepts it instantly. She vomits into the toilet, buries the stick under heaps of toilet paper in the garbage bin, and walks blindly to the bus stop.

They'd been using condoms, and she'd thought they'd been careful, but well, perhaps, thinking about it now . . . maybe they hadn't been as careful as they could have been. She knows she shouldn't have let this happen, but she also doesn't feel regret. It's as though some primal survival instinct has kicked in and she's not able to see beyond the next step. All she can think of is getting back to the farm. Whatever's after that will come on its own.

As she sits there in the direct sun, her head feels like it'll either explode or float away. She feels like she'll vomit again, so she directs all her energy towards quelling the seas inside her. She bows her head until it's between her knees.

LV

The bus drops Silvia at the end of the dusty road to the farm. Walking up the path she can see that all the lights are on, every window yellow-gold against the dusking September sky. Even from outside she can tell something is off.

She walks in the front door, which is unlocked and swinging open. Footsteps, banging. MJ and Dan run down the stairs holding tangled bundles of sheets; Ben follows them with the linen curtains from the bedrooms. JB throws some forgotten pillowslips down the staircase and they fall like daisy petals.

He loves me, he loves me not.

Nobody notices her arrival.

"Hello?" she says. Someone says hi back, but she can't see who, as they're all rushing around; nobody stops, nobody greets her. "Where's Ibrahim?"

"Dunno," Ben says, appearing from the

kitchen carrying an empty plastic laundry basket.

"Haven't seen him in a while," says Dan, plopping a bundle of sheets into the basket.

MJ dumps her sheets on top of Dan's, then goes back upstairs for more.

Silvia notices that all of them have unusually shiny hair: in the light it looks shellacked, with ridges of grease slicking it back to their scalps.

"What's going on?" she asks, still standing in the open door, letting the yellow light from inside fall onto the dusky grass.

"Lice," MJ says without breaking her rhythm. "First it was frogs, today it is lice. We came only for *bees*."

At first everyone assumed it was dandruff. They weren't washing their hair often, what with the water rations. Reasonable deductions, reasonable explanations. But when the itch came that made each of them feel like a mad person, such an itch that it penetrated their skulls and couldn't be satisfied with a simple scratch, they could no longer bear it in silence. The subject was raised while Silvia was in town.

"Lice?" Silvia looks from MJ to Dan. "But what's on your head?"

"Oil," says Dan. "It's supposed to kill the bloody buggers."

Silvia is standing there, itch-free, with her news swelling inside her. "When did this happen?"

"Today," MJ says. "We just found them today."

"But do you know the date when the lice arrived?" For some reason she feels sure that the lice arrived when she murdered the baby queen bees. The frogs came after she'd slept with Ibrahim, the red water immediately after she confessed, out loud for the first time, to maybe not believing in God.

"No," Dan says, "but it probably takes at least a week for hatching or whatever. Why?"

"Let me search you." MJ pulls a fine-toothed comb from her pocket and stands next to Silvia, pushing her shoulders down so as to see better.

"I haven't felt any —"

"Better safe than sorry, don't they say that?" She turns Silvia's head with her fingertips, inspecting. MJ flips over one strip of Silvia's hair, thin as a Venetian blind, and starts combing the next strip from root to tip.

Silvia, panic constricting her throat, can't bring herself to say anything.

"So how was town?" MJ asks.

"Not really a town." Her mind is elsewhere.

MJ drops the clump of hair she'd been holding and selects a fresh strip. "Looks like you're clear. Lucky. The itch is making me crazy."

"I don't have them? Why not?"

Dan calls over to her as he shuttles another load of laundry between JB and his brother: "If you want some, I'll give 'em to you."

"I'm going to bed," Silvia says. "If you see Ibrahim, can you tell him to come find me?"

"Don't you want anything?" MJ asks. "Water? Dinner?"

"I'm not hungry." She floats up the stairs to her bedroom, Toby following two steps behind.

She feels entirely, corporally different with the knowledge of what's growing within her, and the image of this is equal parts terrifying/thrilling/maddening/exhilarating/ enlivening. She lies in bed, falling in and out of dreams, trying not to think through all these feelings, trying to keep them all balanced above her, not allowing any one of them to inhabit her yet.

LVI

Ibrahim comes to her in what seems like the middle of the night. She's asleep, having yet another dream suffused with vague doom.

"Hey," he says, curling up to her from behind, pressing his knees into the backs of hers, feeling the heat of her body. He presses his cheek to her spine and his lips find unkissed parts of her. Back of the neck, triceps, between the shoulder blades.

She turns around quickly. "Hi," she says, still soft. Then, harder: "Where were you?"

"I was painting."

"I'm pregnant."

The moon is bright and its silvery light falls into the room. She can see the news travel from his forehead to his mouth, the smile freezing as the eyes melt. "Is this — are you — serious?"

Silvia nods in the dark. "I did the test in town."

"Oh my God."

"I don't know what you're thinking, but I can't kill it." She pauses, takes a deep breath down into her belly. "I don't expect anything from you. If you don't want to do this, I'll do it alone. I've decided."

"I'm not asking, I don't want you to, I mean — how do you feel?"

Silvia is quiet for a moment. "I shouldn't have let it happen."

"It's not your fault. Holy shit."

"Yeah," Silvia is still avoiding his eyes.

Ibrahim is quiet for a moment, thoughts running through his mind at the speed of light. "Well, I guess this is a sign or something."

"A sign?"

"There's no reason why we shouldn't do this."

"Really? But how would we . . . where would we . . . for work, and living, and —"

"Hey, hey, one thing at a time. I think, well, let's stay here for now. We can take our time to plan what's next, but at least here we have a home. Together. And it's free. Yeah?" There is silence. "Weirdly good timing with Cynthia's offer, right?"

Silvia says nothing.

"Silvia? What do you think?"

She falls into a hug, then pulls away to

look at him. "Why weren't we infested like the others?"

"What?"

"We didn't get the lice. I don't understand why not."

"We were lucky, I guess. Don't worry about that, it's only a good thing. Everything is good things." He kisses her forehead.

Fucking is just like it was before, each hungry for the other, trying to make their love something they can hold on to, knowing that in some sense it soon will be. A baby, an actual product of their love, is becoming alive. Ibrahim pins Silvia down and tastes every part of her, confusing calf with biceps and shoulder with knee, leaving a line of salty kisses all along her belly. Then he reaches the heart of her. At any rate, it feels like a heart. Hot as, wet as, vital and pulsing. This poor girl, he thinks: her heart inside out.

They are breathing at the same time until the moment when neither of them is breathing at all.

"I love you, you know?" he says, feeling his love for her swell inside his chest and his heartbeat in his ears.

"I love you too," she says, feeling it in her

lower belly, and she closes her eyes in a
vestigial sign of prayer.

LVII

Harvest day. A morning sharp and gold. Already the leaves are like embers in a fire, flickering softly between orange, red, and yellow. The world is ablaze. During the days the sun heats up the world like a greenhouse, but at night the cold falls hard as glass.

This is the last full day that all six of them will be together. MJ, JB, Ben, and Dan are leaving the following morning, sharing the bus to Timmins and then catching their respective trains. The brothers will go west, the Frenchies east. But for the moment things feel normal. Well, normal but accentuated. The golden sharpness of it all made somehow more acute.

Silvia and MJ are sitting off to the side, under the birches, letting the boys do all the work. They're close enough to be a part of it, though, and between the six of them there is all the warmth of a group of friends who've known each other for years but haven't seen each other in ages.

Quietly MJ asks, "How are you doing?" Her hair is even redder than the leaves, and the light from behind makes it look like flames.

"I'm *fine*!" Silvia says, disproportionately exuberant. "*So* fine." Then: "Well. You know. Sad you're all leaving." She knits her fingers together.

"So you're going to stay for a little while longer? With Ibrahim?"

"Yeah. We've decided that we will stay here for a bit. It'll be nice here when everything is quiet."

"Don't your parents want you to come home?" MJ asks.

"I haven't spoken to them." Silvia shakes her head. "I can't."

A bee lands on Silvia's left thigh, and with her right hand she gestures, without touching, for it to fly off. MJ doesn't notice any of this. The small hum of the bee's wings carries with it a certain sadness that doesn't leave when it coasts back to its home.

The autumn honey draws from a wide mixture of wildflowers, all of them darker than the clover and fruit blossoms of the earlier, milkier harvest. There's still some dark, earthy buckwheat flowering, and this tints the honey amber; there's also golden-rod this time around, complicating the flavour with its particular spice; and there are grapevines nearby too, from which local farmers make a bright red wine. The bees have collected nectar from all these flowers, and the resulting flavour — blackcurrant, maple sugar, peaches both plump and gauzy — would have a sommelier in tongue-map raptures.

This particular harvest normally happens in the beginning of October, but this year's heat and drought mean the honey is ready earlier than usual. Silvia has long stopped questioning the ways in which time and nature here follow different rules from the ones she used to know. Despite the desiccation, they find that the harvest yields nearly twice Cynthia and Hartford's expectations. The hives are full, sticky, flowing.

Ben and Dan raise a comb high, each grasping one side of the frame, and hold it up to the sun. It's kaleidoscopic, mathematical perfection. Golden honey trickles from the cells before the men have even unsealed the caps. A couple of bees hover around the honeycomb, still possessively, lazily, clinging to their wealth.

Ibrahim and JB uncap the cells and Ben and Dan drain the honey. They fill 174 jars.

It's the colour of healthy urine, just as it should be.

Everyone has done their best to keep the flowers healthy and the bees provided for, and this time their best was enough.

The success is duly celebrated over dinner. Hartford has made roast goose, its legs tied up in string, its skin, with its plucked pores, crispy and golden with honey.

"I killed it myself," Cynthia says. "Every year Hartford says he'll do it, and every year I have to do it for him. You have to wring their necks, and he just can't bear to do it." She smiles at him.

Hartford, blushing, carves the bird tenderly, each pink slice falling light as a sheet of paper.

Cynthia serves them, adding mounds of buttery potatoes, sprinkling them with chopped chives from the garden. There is Niagara wine too, and mead and wheat beer brewed locally.

"A toast," she says, holding up a glass of red. "To all of you, to thank you for your help this season. We couldn't have done it without you." She pushes her glass forward into the air; everyone cheers without clinking.

Hartford clears his throat; it sounds like a horse braying. "I second that." He swallows.

"Thank you, all of you."

"Cheers to Hartford," Ben interrupts. "To the goose!"

Glasses up again; laughter on the air.

Cynthia nods at Hartford, then goes on. "We hope you all got what you wanted and wish you luck in your future endeavours, right, Hartford?"

"Right. That's it, yes."

"So this is farewell, but not to . . . all of you. Hartford and I are . . . delighted that Silvia and Ibrahim" — her speech is full of pauses, but she doesn't seem out of breath — "will be staying on for a little while. And we hope that the rest of you might . . . come back and visit sometimes."

It's hard to say exactly how, but something about Cynthia is different. She seems happier, pink-cheeked. Girlish. Eager.

Everyone toasts, clinking properly, looking each other in the eyes.

The evening passes, full of laughter and idle chatter. The food is delicious and copious; there's much too much for them to handle, though they all go back for seconds and thirds.

Ben and Dan tell stories of epic injuries, canyoning in Central America and caving in Hungary. They laughingly explain that they don't have that twin connection of empathetic pain. "Thank God," says Dan, "else we'd feel it all twice." MJ and JB talk about the nightmarish client commissions they've had, vowing — "Again, we are always making this promise" — only to work on their own terms, ever.

Throughout the meal Silvia is quiet, observing. She has her bell jar back on, Ibrahim notes. She takes a glass of wine so as not to be conspicuous, but she doesn't drink it.

"Would you like some milk, Silvia?" Cynthia asks. "Hartford, get her some milk."

When the glass of milk appears, Silvia thanks him, nodding, looking at Cynthia as if to ask why she is doing this. She doesn't drink the milk — the idea of another animal's milk repulses her right now.

The candles on the table shrink from fingerlength to thumb stumps. The pale yellow beeswax pools on the uncovered tables.

Everyone talks about the past months, remembering only the best moments, swapping stories that have become either fables or inside jokes. There is no mention of goodbyes or the future, but everyone knows, for the most part, that they will never see each other again.

As the evening closes with the velvety depth of focus that alcohol and closeness bring, Silvia feels she's on the outside, looking in with a clarity unusual to her. Despite her sober lucidity, though, the pattern of it all escapes her still. The lines blur.

Next there will be more solitude, this much she knows. She understands and fears the power that can come from that. There will be too a parallel of freedom and intimacy, but she does not yet appreciate this balance, and so she cannot fear it.

■ ■ ■ ■

PART II

■ ■ ■ ■

God heard their groaning.

— EXODUS 2:24

I

Silvia stands in the back doorway, looking out at the lot. Toppling boxes of hives, the shaggy vegetable garden, spindly birch trees turning every shade of flame. She takes a deep breath of the autumn air. Crisp and peppery, fulvous and sweet, she feels it crackle down to the bottom of her lungs. Fall has always been her favourite season. In the fall, time is transitioning to silent hibernation instead of the mad rush of life that comes in springtime. There is a relief as the world starts to settle in on its heels.

The sky is cloudless, but a few airplanes have made tracks. The sun is warm on her bare arms, but the heat is laced with something hostile: the beginnings of what she can already tell will be a bitter winter. A wind whips up, setting all the leaves and flowers dancing. Silvia exhales, feeling as if the gust comes from her own lungs.

Though there has still been no rain, Cynthia has impressed upon them how proud she is of how they've been handling things. The well is essentially empty — the stone test is now up to six and a half alligators — but they've made it work with bottled water, recycled water, grey water, any water but normal water. They would have collected rainwater had there been any rain; there are buckets at the ready under the eaves.

She slips on a pair of Cynthia's Birkenstocks and walks into the vegetable patch. Rutabagas, parsnips, onions, potatoes. Carrots, cauliflowers, Brussels sprouts. There's a hardiness to the autumn vegetables that she respects. The leaves of the zucchini and tomatoes have furled inwards, the first stage of their annual death.

Ibrahim is upstairs working on a new series inspired by their baby. This time, instead of Moroccan religious symbolism, the images he's implanted in the work are dream-catchers, full moons, and weaving strands of DNA. He was inspired when he learned that the farm was so close to the Abitibi Indian Reserve, and though he's never actually gone out to visit it, every day he thinks about making the trip. Silvia features in many of them too: the profile of her face filled in with strings, like veins or textiles — she's not exactly sure, and she doesn't like to look too closely.

As she walks deeper into the garden she sees several bees fumbling about a hive, their movement so quick and aimless they seem to just float there. They come to her, and when she parts her hands — like Moses, she thinks — they leave. The effect is getting stronger. When they're gone, she's left with a longing, a craving she can't specify.

Before the first frost, Cynthia and Hartford will wrap the hives with fibreglass and tarpaper with a final twine binding. Cynthia explained that they'll cut a small entrance through all these layers so the bees can go in and out — worker bees leave the hive daily to get rid of personal and collective discharge; they are the cleanest of creatures. But every winter a few bees will embark on a suicide mission. There is no preventing this. It's programmed in their genetic code, and one cannot mourn their loss.

Once wrapped up, the colony of bees will slumber all winter long. Bees don't hibernate, though — they huddle. Placing the queen in the centre, the others cluster to keep her warm. They shiver — so human — to increase temperature through friction. The workers and drones move around the cluster, from the inside to the outside, so no bee gets too cold in the outer layers.

Silvia wonders what will happen for her this winter. Can the huddling bees be an allegory for her situation? If so, is she the queen, or is the baby the queen? If it's a boy, as Ibrahim wants, can it still be considered a queen, for the sake of this analogy at least?

It doesn't matter. Nothing matters.

She tries to dislodge the thought from her mind, but it clings. She's given up so much of the big stuff, she finds it's sometimes harder to let go of the smaller things. There's so much more emptiness now that whatever comes is more reluctant to leave.

It's been months since she's spoken to her parents. She's been sending them regular, generic letters to keep them from hounding her, but she knows that will keep them away for only so long. She still hasn't been able to face opening their letters. She has no idea what they'll do when they find out. Not true: she has many ideas, but can't bear to entertain them. Her imagination ignites too quickly.

Within days the temperature drops an octave. The sun seems to have been turned off, and the world closes in on itself. The sudden shift in temperature — from oven-hot to a cold so strong they can feel it in

338

their nostrils — will be temporary, Cynthia and Hartford say.

"It always happens like this in late September, doesn't it, Hartford?"

But the heat does not return.

In no time at all, rime beards the grass and remaining flowers every morning. The sun burns it away in the day, but it beats back every night.

The thing about change is that it can sometimes blind you to the things that stay the same. Focused on their baby-to-be and on the cold, like a vise round their heads, and on the loss of their friends, their allies, Silvia and Ibrahim don't see, don't think to look at, the constants in their lives. Cynthia. Hartford. The farm itself. And how those constants may or may not have changed amid the rest of it.

This will creep up on them, like footsteps with no source.

They have yet to share their news.

II

There is little work to do on the farm other than maintain survival. The bees don't need them until spring, and so Silvia and Ibrahim have more time to themselves. To each other.

Silvia's stomach is still flat; the baby is just a little apple seed.

Ibrahim thinks about this little seed — his, theirs — all the time.

It's night and the sky is black. The kind of black you can't get in cities. The kind of black so dense it would look exaggerated if he were to paint it.

Ibrahim prefers to paint without any artificial lighting, so he flicks a match and cups the flame to some white emergency candles. He's siphoned a stash of candles from the cupboard by the front door, where Cynthia and Hartford keep flashlights, wool blankets, nails, and rubber sealant, and lights them one by one, gradually lighting enough for either an attic shrine or a raging fire.

One candle and he can see her, smoke-lit on the tartan. The second cuts shadows in her cheekbones and arches her eyebrows — look, she's a painting already. Three and the light pools in her navel, in the dip above her upper lip.

He lights all seventeen of them, until the room is liquid gold.

Then he pulls a fresh piece of paper onto his easel and tapes it in place. "You okay?" he asks.

"Yes," she says. She closes her eyes.

Ibrahim holds the piece of charcoal between his right thumb and index finger and keeps an HB pencil between his teeth, sideways, as if it were a rose and he a tango dancer. He uses this nib for fine details, and he prefers these erasers for their fineness too. He pulls the charcoal through the air, looking simultaneously at the page and his subject, following the line of Silvia's profile. Her small nose, her big mouth, her hard chin. Already preparing for nursing, her nipples are growing long like the eraser on his pencil. (He can't focus on the detail of them for several reasons, but mostly because the charcoal draws too wide a line and not because of the impossible distraction of them, those perfect pink nipples.) Her pronged hipbones, her belly button like a drain, all the flesh elegantly, casually, sloping towards it.

"I can't do this," he says suddenly, putting everything down.

"What?" she says, her voice sleepy.

"You have *life* inside you."

"So what?"

"So *what*? What do you mean, so what?"

"Why does that mean you can't draw me?"

"Because . . . because you're this whole new mystery with a tiny human growing in your belly, and I don't know what that means! I have to understand something, or feel like it's *possible* to understand it, if I'm going to paint it."

She turns onto her side, towards him.

"I've been thinking about something," he continues. "I think Cynthia needs to know about the baby. I mean, she is going to know eventually. And she'll probably be helpful, can help us plan for . . . I don't know, I just want to make sure everything will be —"

"Ow, fuck." It's rare that Silvia curses, and she sounds ashamed but purposeful.

Ibrahim looks up. "What?"

"This *fucking* candle." She squeezes the top of her right index finger until it swells with blood, then she pops the tip in her mouth.

"What — what happened?" He goes over to her; the wool blanket scratches his knees.

"Beeuuund," she slurs, her tongue compressed beneath her finger.

"Show me," he says, holding out both his hands.

She plucks her burned finger from her puckered lips and places it, already a little pruney from the hot dampness of her mouth, into his cupped palm.

"How did that happen?"

"I just — I just reached for it. I didn't mean to touch it — I thought it was going to fall." Her face is like a freshly painted doll's and her voice is mournful.

"It'll be okay," he says. He puts her finger in his mouth.

They stay like that for a while, him sucking her finger, her naked and sullen and cross-legged.

"Do you want me to read to you?" he says, returning her finger with a kiss on its tip.

"I'm not an invalid, Ibrahim." She wraps herself in the tartan.

Another candle goes out for no reason. From seventeen to fifteen, but still it's bright.

"Do you ever think about the others?" he

343

asks, zipping up his hoodie. "I sometimes wonder what they're doing, what their normal lives look like."

"No," she says. She misses them but doesn't think of them.

"What's the matter?"

"Nothing." Everything.

"Do you want to go for a walk?" he asks, though he doesn't want to go for a walk.

"No," she says. Then: "Why are we staying?"

"Silvia. Come on."

"Why are we even here? How did this happen?"

"Do you want me to answer that?"

"That's why I asked it."

"Well . . . why not?"

"That's not an answer."

"Why do we do anything? Why did we come? Why do we go places? Why do we fall in love? But we've got something here. Maybe that's all it is — that we're used to it or something — I don't know, but I like it. I'm working well, I'm with you, I love you, and life here is *free,* Silvia, you can't underestimate that. We don't pay any bills. They buy our food, we don't have any responsibilities —"

"But we do have responsibilities, don't you see? To stay, that's our responsibility.

They don't want us to leave."

"Come here." He scoops her up and takes her, so tiny, to cradle her in his lap, and weaves her long hair through his fingers. He strokes her forehead unconsciously, as though she is a child and he is a father already.

Her tears make a wet patch on the thigh of his corduroys. Her whole body shudders, obeying its own rhythm.

"Hey." He tilts her face up towards his own. "Look at me, come back to me." He's staring at her intensely, trying to see through the veil that's formed over her irises and find her again. He kisses her ear, salty, and then her cheek, shiny wet.

"Sorry," she says, her voice a wave crashing onto the sand. "I'm sorry."

Her body is pliable and it bends as he stands, holding her the way a husband carries his wife over the threshold, and takes her to the bed. "Sorry for what? Sorry for nothing! Everything's fine!"

Her body is soft; she seems not just to welcome him but to need him to fill her up.

She tilts her head to the side and feels her tears slide down her cheek. The drawing Ibrahim was working on is propped against the wall, abandoned at the point of the burn but finished enough to be recognizable. She recognizes her shoulders; he caught the circular slope of them. She would never have thought about parts of her body like her forearms, but there they are, and in seeing them she realises that she does know them after all.

She closes her eyes when he enters her. Hard in soft.

She feels skin and sweat and fear and guilt and the throbbing pain in her fingertip. Will this affect the baby? Does that matter? The tears are running down her neck and puddling in the cavity between her collarbones.

She opens her eyes and meets her drawn self, unfinished and larger than life. She's been split in two.

III

Hartford has made porridge for breakfast. The oats are overcooked and blurry, no longer the shape of oats. "Morning," he says cheerfully as Ibrahim and Silvia walk into the kitchen. "Coffee?"

"Please," they say at once. The whites of their eyes are pink and the skin around them puffy; they hardly slept.

There are dates, almonds, and raisins on the table. Milk and honey to add to the porridge. The garden has yielded almost all it will this year; the season for fresh fruit is over. Bananas and oranges — the imported, thick-skinned fruits — are all that's left.

"Sleep well?" Cynthia asks.

"Fine," Ibrahim says quickly, trying to cover any doubt.

"What happened?" Cynthia asks, noticing the white pad of dead flesh on Silvia's right forefinger.

"A candle," says Silvia.

"Oh no. Does it hurt?"

"A little, yeah." She is using only her left hand to hold her mug, her spoon, her glass of orange juice. Everything takes longer.

"Wait a second." Cynthia puts down her coffee and goes to the cupboard. She takes a pot of creamed honey, a roll of 3M medical tape, and some paper towel. "Give me your finger." She holds out her hand expectantly. "Honey is good for burns."

Silvia hands over her wounded finger and Cynthia presses the blistered pouch lightly, examining the severity of the burn with the tender precision of a mother. "Not as bad as it could be." She opens the jar and takes a glob of the sponge-coloured honey on her finger, then smears it onto Silvia's.

"Feel good?" she asks.

"Yeah, actually."

"Good. Honey is cooling. And antiseptic."

"Honey cures everything," Ibrahim says, his half-laugh stilted, awkward.

When Cynthia has finished, she wraps a rectangle of paper towel around the burn and seals the whole thing off with tape.

"That'll do you," she says with finality.

"Thanks." Silvia stares at her mummified finger as though it doesn't belong to her.

They all eat quietly except for Ibrahim, whose life is always out loud. He's even able to chew oats at a volume; his sips and swallows are equally amplified. Silvia feels like the opposite of him in every possible way.

"Looks like a nice day today," Hartford says, gazing through the screen of the back door. It keeps swinging open and banging shut with the small breathing of the wind. "Any plans?"

Ibrahim and Silvia look at each other. Ibrahim wipes away his milk moustache with the heel of his palm. "We're having a baby," he says, then rushes on. "Well, Silvia's having the baby, but yeah, we are going to, together, be — yeah. A baby."

Silvia's expression peels open. Her eyes are still shrunken from the night of crying. She stares at him, begging the question: *Why didn't you wait for me?*

Hartford lets his mouth hang open as this sinks in. "Congrats!" He swallows, then looks at Cynthia.

Everyone looks at Cynthia.

Her face has all the nuanced drama of a sunset. "What wonderful news!" she cries. "That *is* wonderful news." She looks at Silvia's belly and pauses in thought for a moment. She softens her voice, and as Hartford shakes Ibrahim's hand, she asks Silvia, "How are you feeling?"

"Oh, fine. I'm good."

"Is this what you want?"

Silvia nods. "Yes." She looks at Ibrahim, who looks back at her. "It's what we want."

"Good." Cynthia says. "So where will you have it?"

"We haven't really discussed that yet," Ibrahim responds for them.

"Well, you should stay here, of course," Cynthia says. She reaches out to grip Silvia's unbandaged hand and clasps it tightly, encouragingly. "My offer is still on the table. Of course. The air is good here," she says. "Fresh. You *must* stay — the calm will be good for the baby. For your pregnancy. We have everything you need here. There's a midwife in town and a doctor just outside Smooth Rock. If there's any emergency there's a big hospital in Timmins, but that surely won't be necessary."

"Oh," is all Silvia can say.

"Where else would you go?" Cynthia asks, probably meaning only to be polite. Silvia thinks she looks like . . . like a young girl. Expectant, hopeful.

"You'll save money staying here too," Cynthia continues after a moment. "No rent, of course. And I could even hire you two to help Hartford and me with some work. We can get the Internet, start selling online — we've been planning that for a while, and you two would be so good at that, young technophiles . . ." Her eyes start to bulge with excitement.

As Cynthia continues, Silvia thinks in the back of her mind that it's a little odd that Cynthia seems to have this all planned out.

Then Silvia remembers something she learned in a high school drama class, about how all characters are motivated by either love or power. When the students were preparing for their roles, they would have to decide which one motivated their character and explain why. It was subjective, of course, and a certain amount of crossover was expected, but to simplify and strengthen, and possibly even subvert, the students had to argue — and then exaggerate — just one.

Juliet: power.

Evita: love.

Joan of Arc: love.

Delilah: power.

Silvia wonders which one she's driven by, and which drives Cynthia.

IV

Silvia and Ibrahim go down to the pay phone to call their parents. It was his idea — he can't wait to tell his father — but she didn't disagree. She recognized it was necessary, though she didn't tell him just how much she dreaded delivering this news.

Silvia goes first, and while she stands inside the phone booth, Ibrahim watches her from outside. He looks through the glass to try to assess her face for reactions. She holds the receiver to her ear, listens more than talks, and after around two minutes she hangs up.

"What did they say?" he asks, antsy, when she comes out.

"Nothing much."

"Really? It looked like it got kind of . . . intense?"

Silvia shrugs. "I have a headache. Do you mind if I head back?"

"Oh." He thought she'd want to wait for

him, as he'd wanted to wait for her. "Sure," he says, and kisses her cheek. "Get some rest."

Ibrahim cannot understand how Silvia's parents could be so removed. From the little he knows of them, or maybe just from his impression of religious parents in general, he'd have thought they'd be opinionated, at the very least.

For his part, his father is angry not to be more involved. "You should come home," he says. "You should have the baby in the city. You should introduce me to your wife."

"She's not my wife, Abouya."

"Where are you, anyway? You're in the middle of nowhere! It's not natural! So much isolation. What will the baby think?"

Despite these protestations, Ibrahim the Younger can hear the joy in Ibrahim the Elder's voice. The Abdullah line will continue! From Ibrahim's infancy, this has been his father's ultimate wish.

"I have to tell you," his father says, and when his voice becomes magnified and echoey, Ibrahim can tell that he is cupping the phone in case any of his other children are listening at his door (which of course they never would), "I'm glad for this news, to be quite honest, because I don't know where else a progeny would come from. I think your brothers might be homosexuals, Ibrahim. And your sister is such a *feminist.*"

"Dad."

"Hey!"

"Sorry, I mean Abouya."

"So yes, I am glad *you* are here to continue the family tree. *Inshallah,* he will be a healthy boy."

"Silvia wants a girl."

"The Abdullahs have boys. Tell her. Did you tell her that?"

"I did." Ibrahim looks through the glass wall of the phone booth, instinctively wanting to see Silvia, having forgotten that she's not there.

"Siiiiiiiillllllllllviiiiaaaaaaa." Ibrahim the Elder stretches the name slowly. "Not Jewish, you said?"

"No."

"Muslim?"

"Da— Abouya. Silvia? A Muslim Silvia?"

"Well, you never —"

"No."

"So Christian?"

"Does it matter?"

"She's Christian?"

"Her parents are." Ibrahim the Younger sighs. "She's figuring it out."

"Figuring it out? Well, what is she in the meantime?"

"I don't know — nothing. What are people who are nothing?"

"They are nothing."

The line is silent.

Then Ibrahim the Elder forfeits. "What does she look like? Silvia."

"Oh she's beautiful, Abouya." Ibrahim smiles, seeing Silvia in his mind. "Light brown hair — you can tell she was blond when she was little. It used to be short but it's grown out now, curls a little round her shoulders. Good bones in her face. Pale eyes that always change colour."

"You must be careful of that, Ibrahim. Changelings. Can be bad news."

"A little nose, a good chin. She's so small all over, but she's really strong, actually. Light-footed, like a dancer."

"She's got the recessive genes, then. Fair, small. Good. The boy will be dark and strong like you."

"And she's smart, and curious, and open-minded. She loves things, she isn't critical, but she's thoughtful, you know? Reminds me a little bit of Ma sometimes in that way, actually."

There is silence on the line. Ibrahim knows this particular silence.

Abouya finally sighs. "Is she an *artist*?"

"No. I mean, well, yes. She's a writer."

"Novels?"

"No, not exactly. She reads them. She writes . . . poems."

"She's a poet? Oh, Ibrahim."

"She's not *really* a poet. Not like that."

His father's sister is a poet, and she drowns everyone else in her sorrows. Ibrahim the Elder has an understandable prejudice.

"She doesn't even really write poems, she just likes them. She hasn't written much yet."

"So she's not an artist?"

"Well . . . I guess not really. Not at the moment."

"Does she understand you, Ibrahim? You need someone who can. I was never able to." His voice fills with flamboyant sorrow.

In his mind, Ibrahim sees the memory of Silvia rather than the way she is right now. He sees her as a naked angel on his tartan rug, as a girl who asks him questions; he sees her reading to him, her mouth making the shapes of the words as if she were a small child learning to speak. He holds this memory above the current murky shape of her. She will grow back into this person, he thinks. He trusts.

V

This is how Silvia's side of the conversation went:

"Hello?"

"Mom?"

"Silvia! Oh my dear Lord, we were just talking about you! *Honey,* honey, it's Silvia —"

"Wait, Mom?"

"Pick up the phone. *Honey?*"

"Actually — *Mom,* stop — can I just talk to you for a second? I have to —"

"Hello?"

"Hi, Dad."

"Silvia! Where on earth have you *been?*"

"Did you get my letter?"

"Of course we got your letter. Silvia, what are you running away from? I don't understand. Why won't you come home?"

"I'm still here, Mom. On the honey farm. I would have told you guys if I'd left."

"This is ridiculous — what's going on?

Do we need to send someone, the police?"

"It's autumn now, you need to come home, life can't —"

"It's been almost six *months,* and —"

Silvia inhales. This kind of thing is like a Band-Aid, really: all about the ripping. "I'm pregnant."

Silence.

More silence.

"And I'm having the baby."

"You're *pregnant*? But —"

"Who's the father? I'll kill him."

"Sweetie, we're just a little . . ." She can hear tears in her mother's voice.

"What's his name?"

"Ibrahim."

"He's a *Muslim*?"

"Dad, please."

"I'll kill him. Did he do this to you? Did he —"

"*Dad.* Stop it. We're together, and we're having this baby. Together."

Her father's gruff breathing comes through the line. Silvia knows he's huffing so she'll know exactly how he feels about this: Not Good. Not Good Enough for his littlest, preciousest, onliest daughter. "We're going to come," he says. "We'll come to get you, won't we, Miriam?"

"No! No, Dad —"

"Yes, honey," her mother says, her voice wavering. "Yes, we'll come to get you and bring you home. We can find a place for you to have the baby, nobody has to know, and God forgives all those who seek repentance. We'll come get you and sort out everything."

"No!"

"You've been abducted, Silvia." Her father sounds calmer, having taken away his daughter's responsibility in the situation and thereby also removing her guilt. "You've been brainwashed there, at this honey cult — it's not your fault, you're not in your right mind. We can sort this out and everything will be fine, I promise. We'll get on a plane to Ontario tomorrow and come, we're coming right now —"

"You're not *listening* to me. Listen. Please. Mom, Dad, I am here because I want to be. Ibrahim and I love each other, and we are going to have this baby. And we're not going to give it away, we're going to keep it and raise it together. In a family. And if you don't want to be a part of that, fine, but don't tell me what to do. I'm an *adult.*" But she knows that when one has to assert the fact of one's adulthood, one hasn't quite made it to that stage.

Silvia hears her mother inhale sharply. Then she hears her mother's signature warbling sobs, soft at first but gradually growing loud as an opera solo.

"Silvia." Her father's voice sounds watery as well, but Silvia knows he won't be crying — he never cries. "You don't know what you're talk—"

"I know exactly what I'm talking about. I'm sorry I didn't turn out the way you wanted me to, but this is what I'm doing. We are going to have this baby, me and Ibrahim, and we're going to love it with everything we have. And I hope you can find it in your big Christian hearts to accept that."

Before they can say anything else she hangs up and walks out.

VI

Hartford is painting one of the closed-up spare rooms pink. The room is on the ground floor a few doors down from the library. It's the colour of carnations and ballet shoes.

The first coat of paint goes on in a wide, porous stripe; the second fills the holes. He doesn't make patterns with the roller, spelling out letters or anything of the sort. He doesn't think to. He works steadily until a whole wall is covered, then starts another. He hums pleasantly, so fully absorbed in his task that he doesn't notice Silvia in the doorway.

She stands for a while, listening to Hartford's angelic melody. She recognizes the song but doesn't know where from. The sound is pure and light; the ladder of scales turns into a descant, then words:

I see the stars, I hear the rolling thunder

Thy power throughout the universe displayed

As she listens, she notices that a patch of plaster on the wall outside this room is peeling, cracks emanating from a misshapen hole, revealing the brick beneath.

Hartford's voice builds, tremulous but powerful, and Silvia feels overwhelmingly moved. She clears her throat to announce her presence, and Hartford jumps back, spattering paint from the roller onto the floor.

"Hey." Silvia stands tentatively in the doorway. "Don't stop," she says. "You have a lovely voice."

Hartford looks as though he's been caught masturbating. He goes red, stumbles over his words, and ends up saying nothing.

"I'm sorry I surprised you," Silvia says, getting closer, looking at the pink walls.

"Innocence," Hartford says.

"Sorry, what?"

"The paint colour. That's the name. It's for the baby."

"Oh, nice." Silvia looks at the room differently now, thinking of her baby in here, and then two things hit her separately: "But why did you make it pink? We don't know it's a girl," and then: "And why is the room downstairs and on the other side of the house from ours?"

Hartford shrugs. "Cynthia," is all he says.

VII

Silvia is lying on the floor of the library, trying to calm her stomach, Toby at her side. Ibrahim is sitting in the corner of the room, flicking through a book on Basquiat. She watches him, envying his raptness, then closes her eyes. Nausea punches through her belly before and after eating. At all times, really. And this fills her with a constant, watery sadness. Every time she moves she must be careful not to spill the liquid inside her, just barely held in by her skin. She is unable to think of the child inside, the food he or she (she, Silvia still hopes) hungers for, or the bones she is growing. Silvia can think only of her nausea. Of the nausea ending. Of feeling like herself again. She hopes that being horizontal will create a more stable, shallow base for all the water inside her. That it will calm the strange tides and warping undercurrents.

Toby has started delicately licking her

fingers with his rough tongue when Cynthia appears.

"How are you feeling, Silvia?"

Silvia doesn't know how to answer. She docsn't want to undercut her response with qualifiers: "Okay but," "Fine except," "Good although." If water could instantly turn into Jell-O, that's what it would feel like. Aspic in her insides, holding together all the disparate parts. Good, is she good? Physically yes, maybe. Emotionally, no: this nausea is nearly spiritual. Instead of answering, making yet another hole in her body through which the water could come forth, she smiles with her lips closed. This seems to be sufficient.

"Are you busy?" Cynthia continues.

Ibrahim looks up from his book.

"I'm never busy," Silvia replies.

"Oh good," Cynthia says. "I haven't any plans either. I was wondering if you wanted to — might want to watch a movie with me." She holds out a box to show Silvia. Silvia moves only her eyes to find it. It's got a black-and-white cover.

"Sure," she says, still unmoving. It doesn't matter to her what the movie is, so she doesn't bother asking.

"Wonderful!"

"Now?"

"Or later, if you prefer."

"No," Silvia says, reluctantly pushing herself up onto her elbows. "Now is fine." Toby bangs his head against her body in a self-petting technique he's developed in recent weeks, nuzzling into Silvia's ribs, full of the irrational affection of animals.

"Wonderful." Cynthia helps manoeuvre Silvia into a sitting position.

Ibrahim gets up and comes over too, standing tall above her. "Can I get you anything, Silvia?"

She looks up at him, a giant. "I'm fine."

He puts his hands in his pockets and looks out the window to see Hartford struggling past with a huge load of stuff — ropes, wood, tarps. "What's Hartford doing?"

"He has to finish winterizing the hives," Cynthia says. "Make them waterproof and warm for the bees."

"Should I give him a hand?"

Cynthia brushes him off with a falsely high voice. "You're busy with your own work. Don't worry — that's what you should be focusing on."

Ibrahim starts to go towards the door. "It's fine. I'm happy to help out."

"Well, that's very generous of you," Cynthia says.

"Not at all." He feels kind of guilty but

can't explain why. "You okay, Silvia?" he asks one more time.

"Mm-hmm."

"Okay. I'll be back in a bit, then."

Silvia doesn't feel a loss when Ibrahim leaves; she's too busy working to stay as horizontal as possible as she moves herself from the floor to the corduroy couch.

And Cynthia is there, Cynthia will keep her company.

"Do you want a snack? Something to drink? Water?" Cynthia scans Silvia's body as if to locate a particular need.

"No, no water." She is already full of water and already has to pee every forty-five seconds; if she puts more water in her body it will rupture.

"May I?" Cynthia asks, her hand hovering above Silvia's stomach.

Silvia looks down at her belly. It's still fairly flat — you might think she was pudgy or maybe a little bloated — but to her it is enormous, unrecognizable. Her body is not her body. "Sure," she says, tasting vinegar at the root of her tongue. When did she stop feeling like herself? What did her *self* feel like to begin with?

Cynthia presses her hand over the thin black cotton T-shirt Silvia wears most days. Her palm cups around the subtle curve of

Silvia's body. Her hard black eyes are cutting diagonals — the sign of someone listening closely. "I feel something!" she cries. "A beat, like a heart, or a kick. Oh!" Light comes from within her dark eyes.

"Let me," and Silvia pushes Cynthia's hand away to try to feel for herself. She pats her hands all over her abdomen as if she's packing a suitcase. "I don't feel anything." She only feels jealous.

"Maybe she's stopped."

"She?"

"The baby."

"Oh." Silvia is gently, absent-mindedly, stroking Toby's soft purple-grey fur as he purrs next to her elbow.

"Are you all right? You look a bit pale," Cynthia says.

"I don't understand." Tears fill Silvia's eyes.

"It's all right." Cynthia sits next to her on the sofa. She wraps one arm around the girl and pats her knees with the other. "I'm here." Silvia looks to where Cynthia is patting and lays her head down. "Shall we watch the film?" Cynthia looks down at her.

Silvia nods.

Her hair is spread out on Cynthia's lap like a mermaid's under water. Cynthia looks at it, puts her hands out towards it. She hesitates for a moment, then picks up a lock of Silvia's hair and twists it around her fingers.

VIII

When Silvia hits the eight-week mark, Cynthia sets up an appointment with the county midwife. Just a routine checkup.

The midwife's skin is rough and red, as if it has been scoured with sandpaper. The redness spreads from the apples of her cheeks to the jowly bits under her ears. It must be some kind of condition, Silvia thinks. The woman's hair is dark, tightly curled but puffy. Like a brushed-out poodle's.

"Hello, Cynthia." The midwife greets Cynthia with a manly handshake. "Long time. You're looking well." She steps back, nodding appraisingly.

Cynthia smiles. "Meg, come in." She gestures to Silvia, who is now sitting on the sofa just through the open library door.

Meg is squat and sporty in black tearaway pants, the kind that kids wore in Silvia's grade school. She's never seen an adult wearing them. Meg takes off her shoulder bag and black windbreaker and puts both on the back of a chair. There is something efficient and loveless in her manner; she's the type of woman who wouldn't coddle a baby but would make it stop crying faster than anyone. Silvia realises that it's been weeks since she's seen a human being other than Ibrahim, Cynthia, and Hartford.

"You must be Silvia." Meg greets her with the same vigorous handshake. "All going well so far?"

Silvia nods.

"And how have you been?" Meg turns to look at Cynthia, standing with her arms crossed, overseeing.

"Me? Fine, thank you."

"You know everyone wanted to help," Meg says. "We just didn't know how. We were all so sorry to hear what happened, and with the baby —"

"I appreciate the thought," Cynthia says, cutting her off.

Meg rolls up her sleeves and pulls up a chair to sit beside Silvia's belly. "Eight weeks, eh? 'E'll be about the size of a kidney bean. Less than an inch, crown to rump."

The softness of the personal pronoun Meg uses implies genderlessness. This must be practiced, so as not to give anything away;

it's all intuition at this point anyway. Silvia feels an immense swell of nausea at the thought of a kidney bean in her womb. She feels like a stranger in her own body.

"How are you feeling?" Meg asks, scanning Silvia from head to toe.

"Now or in general?"

"Both."

"Fine." She hopes Meg can't read minds but wouldn't be surprised if she could.

"No nausea?"

"Yes."

"You do have nausea?"

"Yeah. But isn't nausea normal?"

"Almost everything is normal these days" — she raises her eyebrows — "but we want you to be comfortable." Meg takes two hard candies out of her pocket and pats them into Silvia's palm. "Ginger. It helps."

Silvia notices that Meg's not wearing any makeup. Not that Silvia has worn any in months either, but still. This is a woman on the job. Silvia puts the sweets on the floor.

"Shirt off, please," Meg says, rifling through her big black bag.

Acquiescing, Silvia pulls her T-shirt over her head.

"Bra too."

Cynthia is standing right in front of her, Meg sitting at her side. Silvia avoids the women's gaze as she removes her bra.

With Silvia naked from the waist up, Meg gives her another once-over. Navel, belly; she lingers on the breasts. She nods. Then she puts her right hand on Silvia's stomach. Above the belly button, where it bulges. Meg feels her way along the flesh and taps the back of her right hand with her left. She explains that this makes an echo she can feel through all three of their bodies — Meg, Silvia, Baby. She tilts her head to listen to, to feel, the silent reverberations from her tapping hands.

Silvia can see the crosshatched shadow of a fine moustache on Meg's upper lip. The sound her hands make is softer than a tap but less accidental than a thump: *dump, dump, dump.* Silvia makes a face.

"Hurts?" Meg asks.

"No."

Then breasts.

"Swollen?" Meg asks, squeezing them as though testing for ripeness.

"A little."

"Painful?"

"Not too bad."

"Good."

Silvia's nipples have grown longer and thicker than pencil erasers and have darkened to the colour of milky chocolate. The colour of Ibrahim's lips. Meg taps around the areola as though it were cookie dough.

"Everything okay there," she declares bluntly. She goes back to her bag and withdraws a plastic, book-shaped device, what looks like a microphone and tape deck for children.

"Oh good," Cynthia says, relieved. "Isn't that good, Silvia?"

Silvia closes her eyes.

"This is a Doppler," Meg says, "so I can hear the heartbeat."

Meg presses the round plastic next to Silvia's navel and listens for a while. "Would you like to hear the heartbeat?" she asks softly.

Silvia opens her eyes. "Me?"

A glimmer — condescension, amusement — crosses Meg's matte-brown eyes. "Yes, you."

"I'm sure she would!" Cynthia cries.

Silvia thinks about it, then nods. Meg unhooks the earpieces from her own ears and holds them up to Silvia, who looks at them, decides they look okay, then puts them in.

She hears the sudden rush of water, the sonic wallow of blood, *thump-Thump, thump-Thump,* moving at its private, rhythmic pace.

At that moment she doesn't think of the

thing inside her as a bloated bellyache or an unwanted grain that's making her ill. It's a tiny human baby. While this brings with it a sense of relief, the collision of their two heartbeats reminds her of the cacophonic skin-drum vibration of the frogs, and she realises that in a few months she will be no longer herself but a mother.

IX

"How did it go?" Ibrahim asks, his voice on edge as he puts down his paintbrush. He had been forbidden to attend the checkup, but honestly, he hadn't pushed very hard: the whole thing makes him feel a little queasy. He didn't want to tell Silvia this, though — he knows how hard it's been for her, and that he deserves no sympathy for his own nausea, vicarious or not.

"I heard the heartbeat!"

"Come here, come here." He goes to her. "Let me hear." He presses his ear to her shirt. Hearing nothing, he lifts it up.

"Do you hear it?"

"No." He sounds annoyed. He's on his knees, his ear tight to her skin.

"Oh, Ibrahim," she says, her voice floating, "it was so . . . so *good* to hear it, to know that it is *alive*. A real thing."

Ibrahim looks up at her, his face hot with love. He kisses Silvia's belly. And again.

"That one's for the little guy."

"I felt so much love for the baby then," she says. "It was such a relief."

Ibrahim stands up. To him, she still doesn't look pregnant at all. Maybe a little thicker round the waist, but that could just be normal winter padding. "I'm so, so happy," he says. "Hey, why don't we go for a walk down to the lakes?"

"Now? Won't it be cold?"

"It's not bad."

"Oh." She isn't sure how she feels about this; it doesn't seem possible, but she also doesn't know any better. "Sure."

Ibrahim cocoons Silvia in wool. He wraps scratchy scarves and his *abouya*'s sweater around her, ties a holey afghan he found in the candle cupboard round her neck, and insists that she wear three pairs of his red-striped work socks.

"Three? Ibrahim, my shoes won't fit."

"You can wear mine."

He stashes towels and a thermos of hot chocolate in a borrowed backpack, tucks his red scarf into his sweater, and flips up the visor of his Raptors cap. "My little baby's inside there!" he squeals, rubbing Silvia's belly. He's just finished a new painting, so he's feeling particularly buoyant.

"Hey," she says, "my baby too." Silvia

hasn't finished anything of anything at all, and the sinking feeling inside her has become so habitual she can almost forget about it.

"Let's go, baby," he says, taking her hand.

Though summer is long gone, it's warm for mid-October. By now, Hartford tells them, there's often a foot of snow shielding the world, but the permanent layer of snow and ice they've been anticipating has not yet arrived. The drought continues. Anticipation magnifies everything.

Leaves crumple into mulch on the ground. Abandoned nests rest in the crooks of bare branches; knots in trunks are stashed with acorns to tide the squirrels through what is sure to be a long winter. More than this seasonal shift, though, there is a whole new climate in the forest: moss wraps the stones in green fur, and beards of lichen cling to broken bark. The air has the clarity of an ice cube.

"Careful," Ibrahim says, putting out his arm like a mother would at a car's sudden stop.

"What?"

"I just don't want you falling. The ground's all uneven."

And for a bit they walk in silence, Ibrahim

378

two steps ahead.

"It's so good to get out of the house," Silvia says, sighing a little. "I love forests in the winter."

"Why?"

"Isn't it amazing how they look dead but they're actually alive?" Her cheeks, pinked, lift to the sky, to the tops of the trees.

The lakes are patent-leather black, darker than in summertime. No ice has formed round the rim of the first lake, and the edge seems to have stayed in the same place: the drought has not affected the size of the Black Falls Lakes. (Their true name was revealed by Hartford a couple weeks ago. Not revealed, Ibrahim reasons — it was never hidden. But he still thinks of them as Big and Little Cynthia.)

Silvia remembers Monique, the frogs. Now all the animals are hiding from the winter they'd known was coming — which they'd been preparing for — since the last one ended. The frogs, any of the survivors, will have buried themselves in the mud and be sleeping at the bottom of the lake.

She walks to the water's edge. Her body feels unbearably heavy. Her legs, her groin, her belly, her breasts, her arms, her eyelids;

her tongue is like an anvil behind her leaden lips.

Ibrahim is watching her. She can feel him watching her.

"What are you thinking about?" he asks.

"Nothing," she answers, looking up at the sky. "Just that . . . well, I think there's something about Hilary and Cynthia and their baby, but I don't know. Meg said something about how she was sorry about what happened, but it was hard to follow what she was talking about. I didn't understand."

"Huh." Ibrahim is quiet but she can tell he's alert. "I'm sure she was just trying to be polite. I'm sure it's nothing, but either way, it must be hard for Cynthia to talk about. Hilary took the baby away, right? That would be hard, for sure."

"Yeah, but it didn't seem like that was it. I don't know."

They wordlessly agree to simply stop talking about it, perhaps knowing that they can't — or don't want to — know the answers.

"I'm cold," Silvia says, feeling it suddenly all through her bones.

"Really?"

"Ibrahim, I'm freezing."

"Okay, sure, of course. Let's go back and

get you warmed up."

He wraps his arm around her shoulders and they make their way back to the farm-house.

X

Though winter came on slowly, it has now hit full on. There's that expression about being cold to the bone, but this presupposes that the cold stops there. This far north, it goes straight through — bones, marrow, everything. Moisture in the air turns into snow crystals, even though there's still no precipitation; the wind picks up the fine frozen powder; it sparkles in the light.

Ibrahim was meant to help Hartford that morning, but he woke up late to chalky sunlight filtering pale through the window and Silvia's light snoring. As he starts out of bed, she shuffles under the covers.

"Good morning," he says, oddly cheerful.

"Not good yet," she grumbles. "What are you doing?"

"Late for Hartford." His head pops out of his brown scratchy-wool sweater.

"Oh." Another day stretches empty ahead of her.

"What's the matter?" Ibrahim asks.

"Nothing," she says, shaking her head, "I'm just still half asleep." She had a dream, she's remembering now, in which she was a child playing in her backyard, the sound of the ocean turning into the sound of the bees. She was only a child, so she obviously wasn't pregnant — none of this new world existed. In the dream she'd had the freedom of a child and her body was her own. Nostalgia isn't enough to cover the feeling she has now, upon waking, upon pulling her foot firmly out of the dream-ether; neither is regret. It's a feeling that has become dulled by fact, the emotion of it all chewed out. She blinks.

He kisses her on the forehead in a way she finds patronizing. "See you later!"

She slumps back onto the bed and tries to escape the remnants of the night and her dream, of which she can remember only the feeling, and the darkness that's swarming.

Hartford and Ibrahim are in the toolshed, the only place on the farm that has an unadulterated warmth, as it's where the heater is located. Outside, a thin layer of frost covers everything, but inside they work without coats, only one layer of socks and sweaters. They've used a handsaw to remove a piece of drywall, exposing a swarm of bees within the walls.

"Come on, you guys." Hartford speaks pleadingly, cajolingly. He's wearing thick canvas gloves, and his hands move across the bees without touching them. They do not move in response.

"Holy shit." Ibrahim is just seeing the mass of insects from which the vacuum-loud buzzing is coming. He's also wearing gloves, but stands back.

"There we go." Hartford's voice is straining slightly; the bees still do not move. He grunts. "Cynthia is so much better at this — I don't know why she asked me to do it."

"Do they do this often? The bees?"

"Once in a while. If the old queen leaves before the new queen has taken her place, then she takes the colony with her."

"Why?"

"That's just the way it is. Power, trust, I don't know."

"What if the new queen was already there but the bees just liked the old one better?"

"Never happens."

"Never? Really? How do you know?"

"Science." Hartford stands back, puts his hands on his hips. "Here, you give it a try."

"Me? What am I supposed to do?"

"Just pick them up. With your hands. Try to get as many as you can and put them in that bucket there."

"What will we do with them once they're in the bucket?"

"Take them back to the hive."

"Why can't we just let them stay here?"

"Ibrahim." Hartford crosses his arms and looks down at Ibrahim, crouching over the bucket. "Not only would it ruin the whole structure of the building, but bees are valuable, and they belong to us, and so we need them to work for us."

"Right." Ibrahim squints a little. "Okay."

The funny thing about Hartford's face, Ibrahim realises as he stares at him from this vantage point, is that his eyes start farther than halfway down his head. He can see now, with sharp clarity, how the bare expanse of Neanderthal-boned forehead stretches an extra inch or so down Hartford's head, thereby squeezing his eyes, nose, and mouth — the only valuable parts of a face, really — into a space too small to seem at all right. He wonders if Hartford knows.

Slowly, by persuasion, the men are able to place the bees in the bucket. But it is by magic that the bees stay in the bucket, or at least that's how it seems to Ibrahim.

As the men work, they talk. It's always easier to talk about serious things if your given task prevents you from looking the other person in the eye. Driving, walking, working. Given this distance, Ibrahim feels he can ask anything he wants. "How did you hear about it here?"

"Cynthia put out a call for a private singing instructor."

"Oh yeah? When was that?"

"Twelve years ago." Hartford speaks very matter-of-factly as he scoops bees from the wall and smoothes them down into the bucket.

"So when did the singing stop?"

"Excuse me?"

"Like, did you and Cynthia ever have a —"

For the first time Hartford stops what he's doing. He looks at Ibrahim, his face red with heat, his eyes dark. He shakes his head. "Ibrahim. No. It's never been about that."

"Okay, okay, I'm sorry." He wants to ask, of course, what it *was* about, but doesn't.

Silence for a moment. Neither of them gets back to work.

"Hey." Ibrahim points to the ground next to Hartford. "Can you pass me the water bottle?" He glugs back half its contents, then changes the subject. "What about your family?"

"Died. That's why I wanted to come here."

"Hey, man." Ibrahim backs up in that deferential way men do when avoiding a fight with a drunken stranger on the street. "I'm sorry." His voice drops. "My ma too. Cancer, nine years ago now. It's the worst, the absolute worst."

It's true, it is the worst: a layer of sadness is the underpainting of his life and work, and while things might be bright and beautiful on the surface, they're anchored in this grief, which sometimes lends itself to mild paralysis. It's why he has to keep moving.

Hartford looks around, then flicks one last bee into the bucket. "We're done here. Thank you."

"Oh." Ibrahim stands up, taken aback. "Sure." He takes off his gloves.

He catches his reflection in the window-pane before leaving, but it takes a minute before he recognizes himself. His beard has grown lumberjack-long, and his face, thinner than ever before, is floating hollowly over the barren landscape. He blinks, imagining himself as a painting, then walks out.

XI

Having spent the entire morning and afternoon in bed, looking at the ceiling, Silvia decides to go outside on a little walk, maybe stroll the perimeter of the forest or at least go through the gardens, but when she's just through the front door, she runs into Ibrahim on the lawn.

There's the sound of bleating, almost like a moan, and then a loud crack. Then again: bleating, crack.

"Did you hear that?" she asks.

"No, I just got —" And then he hears what she's talking about.

"What is that?" Silvia asks Ibrahim. She's confused, doesn't believe what she hears. She's trying not to let the terror translate to her voice.

A new sound: a slow whine turns into a grunting shriek, the panting sounds of terror, then the crack, louder now as they move closer to the noises.

Ibrahim senses Silvia's distress, and as the two of them turn the corner of the big stone house and near the honey hut, they come across a pile of sheep, four or five of them, their legs tied, their fleece bloody and dark against the hardened grey frost. She can feel warmth coming off their bodies; they must be freshly dead. Who would kill the sheep? She puts her hands on her knees and bends down, about to retch.

"Come on, honey, let's get you inside." Ibrahim tries to guide her away, but then they see it.

Blood, fleece, corduroy.

Scrambling legs and an open mouth.

The sharp flash of a silver knife.

It's a sheep — bleating, bleeding, suspended by its back legs from a tree branch. Cynthia is standing behind it, gently touching its thick body, twitching. Then she slits its throat, and blood spills into a tin bowl on the ground.

"What —" Silvia tries to speak but can't.

Cynthia notices them. The knife is still in her hand.

"It's okay," Ibrahim whispers, putting his arm around Silvia, trying to steer her away, but her body is fixed.

Cynthia walks over to them, around the pile of sheep. "I'm sorry you had to see this," she says.

Silvia shakes her head.

"It's the kindest thing to do," Cynthia continues as Silvia buries her head in Ibrahim's flannel jacket. "Hartford doesn't like it either, but they're sick. It needs to be done."

The last thing Silvia sees is the blood matting in the sheep's wool coat, and the last thing she feels is her own blood suddenly cold in her veins. She closes her eyes, seeing the pieces fit together, and then darkness.

XII

My father woke me early. I could see him, his body a shadow, standing in the doorway to the room I used to share with my brother. My father did not come into the room. "We are going to Mount Moriah," he said. His voice sounded different.

This is the mountain where we make sacrifices. I knew this. It takes three days to get to the mountain. Donkeys are required. I have been there before.

I was still in bed. I was still sleepy. "Father, what will we sacrifice?"

"A lamb, Isaac."

My father is a good man. He loaded the donkey before the sun rose. Wood for the altar, bread, water. He brought two servants.

We journeyed for three days and two

nights. My father let me sleep on the back of the donkey, where it was warm and soft. He and the servants slept on the ground. On the fourth morning we arrived at the base of the mountain.

My father said to his servants, "Stay here with the donkey while the boy and I go over there. We will worship and then we will come back to you."

My father asked me to carry the wood. I ran up the mountain. I was not tired.

The sun had not yet risen. The sky and the earth were the same colour: the colour of wine, and of new leaves. I saw a bird fall and swoop. It looked just like the fall and swoop of the scythe as it slices through wheat. I could not tell what bird it was.

"Father, where is the lamb we will sacrifice?"

"Have faith, Isaac."

I fell back to keep time with my father. The logs were starting to feel heavy on my back. Something was starting to feel heavy inside me too.

"Father, what are we doing?"

"I said have faith."

When we reached the top of the mountain, there was still no lamb. My father asked me to put the logs onto the flat stone where the slaughters are performed. I obeyed. The heavy thing in my belly got heavier. Then my father built the altar. I knew then that I could not leave.

"Father," I said, "why are you doing this?"
"It is God's wish, my son."

He took a rope from his satchel and took me by the wrists. I did not struggle. If this was what my father wanted, what God wanted —

My father put his big hand over my small face. He is an old man but he is a strong man. I did not close my eyes. Beyond his palm I could see the flash of a blade as it caught the light. The sun must be rising.

My father told me that we must fear God. But he also told me that we must love God.
I do not know how to do both at once.

XIII

Silvia wakes up disoriented and deeply troubled, her world blurred. The moon is in the middle of the window, casting silver blocks of light into the room. It feels as though light and shadow are one, even now, even in wakefulness. She blinks. She doesn't remember coming to bed; she doesn't remember having fallen asleep.

Bad dream. Someone died, or nearly. Was it her? And who was the person doing the killing? It was like her mother, but it wasn't her mother.

Ibrahim sleeps deeply, unmoved. She doesn't want to wake up, but she needs to leave the bed because the dream still inhabits it.

A knife. A betrayal.

She wants something to drink.

Her head still caught between two places, she is unaware of the walk between her room and the kitchen, unaware of whether she flicked on the light there or it was already on, but a voice startles her.

"Can't sleep?"

Silvia sees Cynthia sitting at the table, an open notebook in front of her.

"I was having trouble too. But early mornings are a lovely time to write, I find. Peaceful. May as well take advantage."

Silvia nods and looks away, not wanting to see Cynthia: something about her teeth, about her eyes, troubles her. She opens the fridge to see if there's juice, but when she turns, there is a glass already out — she doesn't remember putting it there — and it's filled with milk. She wants to say something but finds her voice isn't quite working yet — it's the middle of the night; it's the bad dream, moments of it flashing back to her; it's the surprise of not being alone.

She's trying to remember more about what happened in the nightmare, trying to figure out why she feels so troubled. She had a feeling of being hunted, but who was the hunter?

"It's okay, Silvia," Cynthia says as she stands up, moving in slow motion. "It was just a bad dream." She takes Silvia in her arms and holds her tightly as Silvia starts to cry.

"The sheep had to be killed. It wasn't a

choice. They had a fungus," Cynthia says. "A fungal plague in their lungs. We had to kill them, or else it would spread to the bees. To the baby, even."

"A plague?" Silvia repeats.

"Yes, you know, an illness."

"I know what it means."

A plague. There is a plague on the honey farm, and it arrived with her.

XIV

Back in her room, still holding the glass of milk, Silvia knows she has to leave, but she also knows that they will find her, that they will try to bring her back. And that would only make it worse. How could she explain this to anyone? Should she call her parents? Would they be able to help her? Ibrahim is sleeping soundly and she knows she should wake him; she knows he'll want to come with her, but she also knows that if she wants to protect him, she must go alone. The punishment is only for her; it is she who is bringing the plague.

She puts a sweater over her pyjamas and goes back down the stairs, avoiding the kitchen, and slips out the always-unlocked front door.

A few steps into the dark garden and she looks back at the house, unlit, asleep.

She runs.

Air catches and swells her lungs. Looking

behind her, she tries to scan the forest to find the source of the sound, snapping twigs, fast breath. She can't see anything. Then the sound gets bigger, monumental — it's coming from above. It's thunder, breaking through the vaulted ceiling of the sky. It's dark, but she can tell the dawn is coming. Through the canopy of winter-bare trees, the February sky is the ethereal grey of premorning, prelife, like a lamp behind a movie screen.

Trees flash by, and when she turns her head it seems as if the trees themselves are moving. She goes faster, until her breath runs out, until she gets a cramp. The baby — she doesn't want to upset the baby, even though she's certain that the baby is the source of the pain. But what can she do? What *should* she do?

She grabs a tree round its trunk. Tears are streaming down her face, but she's not crying, she's sure she's not actually crying, it must just be the wind, the cold, but then her chest starts to heave with choking sobs. She looks up, trying to see the top of the tree, but it's too tall. It must be hundreds and hundreds of years old. She knows she should feel comforted looking at this tree — if it has survived the world around it, maybe she can too — but there is no comfort there. It doesn't even have a name.

She folds to her knees, unable to do anything but surrender. "Forgive me," she says, tears on her tongue, "please forgive me."

If only this would stop. She will do anything to make this stop. All she wants is nothingness.

Then the sky opens. She feels it first on her skin — it's freezing, and falling so hard it feels almost painful, sharp. Within seconds her clothes are soaked through. The earth, having crusted over to protect itself, doesn't absorb the water readily, like someone who doesn't quite have the confidence to be vulnerable.

Then there is a voice. She opens her eyes, scrambles around. She's never had a reply before.

The voice is louder. "Silvia?" Ibrahim appears, running. "Silvia, what the hell are you doing?"

Equal parts fear and relief. She shakes her head, can hardly breathe.

"You're gonna get sick. Come on." He comes next to her and grips her shoulders, hugging her, pulling her, trying to get her to move.

"I'm sorry," she says, weeping into the ground, not moving towards him.

"Get up, come here."

"Please forgive me," she says.

"For what?" He looks distraught but not angry, for which she is grateful. "What are you doing?"

"I didn't want to leave without you," she says between sobs.

"Of course not — we don't have to leave, you don't have to go anywhere," he says, rubbing her back. "Come back, we need to get you inside, it's freezing. You'll catch a cold and the baby will get sick."

Silvia does not want to be moved, at least not in the direction that Ibrahim is pulling her.

"Silvia, come on — what's going on?"

"I have to leave. I'm sorry. I can't go back there."

"What are you talking about?" Ibrahim is desperate. "Silvia, I love you." His voice sounds different, less strong than usual. "But I don't understand what's happening. Please come back with me. Please let me take care of you."

By now all of heaven is black with cloud. The trees shake with the sudden rush of animals taking shelter in the branches, and there follows a great deluge. Not just rain but a waterfall of freezing water, turning the ground to a skating rink as soon as it touches earth.

As though her bones have dissolved with her resolve, Silvia lets herself be carried by Ibrahim back in the direction from which she came, her face wet with tears and rain, her clothes soaked.

Three heartbeats turn towards the farm.

The freezing rain is falling solidly, but Silvia can't go quickly and Ibrahim, supporting her weight, can go only so fast himself. This rain is new and endless. She can hardly see, her tunnel vision focusing on a fearful abstraction rather than the reality of the muddy ground before her.

As they approach the house, her breathing constricts. "Ibrahim," she says hoarsely, "Ibrahim, I can't."

"It's okay," he says. "I've got you."

The walk back seems to have taken only a few minutes, though she thought she'd been running for hours. They arrive dripping wet at the house under a shiny grey sky to find Cynthia and Hartford waiting for them by the front door, dry under the metal porch awning.

"Silvia." Cynthia is standing in the doorframe, holding the door open for them. "Are you all right? What's going on?"

Neither Ibrahim nor Silvia says anything.

Ibrahim, shaking his head, is struggling to get Silvia over the threshold and into the warmth.

"Come in, get inside." Cynthia stands aside, and Hartford is waiting in the kitchen with hot-water bottles and woollen blankets.

Silvia is guided to the table. She lets herself be covered in two blankets, one on her lap and one over her shoulders; she lets Hartford place a hot-water bottle on her lap; she stares at the mug of boiling water he's placed in front of her on a bee-shaped coaster.

"Silvia." Cynthia comes to stand behind her and places her hands on Silvia's shoulders. She fingers Silvia's wet hair and reaches behind her for a tea towel to rub away the damp. "Silvia — what happened?"

Silvia looks at Ibrahim, standing opposite, staring at her with his big brown eyes stretched to the outer limits of their sockets. She looks at Hartford, sitting at the head of the table, sipping from his own mug of hot water. She feels Cynthia's presence behind her, warm and unknowable — she is invisible, but when Silvia leans her head back, it rests just above Cynthia's belly button. "I'm sorry," she says.

"There's no need to be sorry, honey." Cynthia comes around and sits next to Silvia. She touches the girl's cold cheek. "Tell us how we can help you."

"I can't — I can't tell you." Her face is still wet from both tears and rain.

"Silvia," Cynthia says, "you know you can tell us anything."

Silvia is shaking her head as though a tick has landed in her ear. She sees it all in her head, but she doesn't know how to get it out without sounding insane.

"Silvia, please," Ibrahim says, draping his arm over her small shoulders.

"I had to leave." Silvia's voice is barely above a whisper. "I had to leave to protect you."

"From what? What are you talking about?" Ibrahim comes even closer but can't get near enough. It upsets him to be so in the dark; he wants Silvia's light back.

Silvia takes a deep breath. She looks at her hands and speaks with reluctance and speed. "This maybe will . . . I know it might sound . . . but I know, I know that God has been sending signs from the beginning, but it's only just become obvious." Her breathing is shallow. "Or maybe I was just trying to ignore it at first, I don't know, but you have to tr—"

"What?" Ibrahim looks as though he's been smacked. "*What* signs? There are no *signs.* Silvia, it's in your head —"

"Shh." Cynthia steps in, quietly brushing Ibrahim aside. "Hold on." She takes Silvia's hands in her own. "They're freezing," she says. "You must be exhausted." She rubs Silvia's hands, warming them up between her own. "Can you tell me what signs you mean, Silvia?"

Silvia nods obediently.

"First there was the red water, and then the frogs came, which is why Monique left, and the lice too, even though I didn't get them, and then the sheep got a plague, you told me that yourself . . ." She trails off and closes her eyes. She's dizzy; she's still finding it difficult to bring air into her lungs.

"So what?" Ibrahim can't keep the exasperation out of his concern. "It's a *farm,* Silvia."

"God sent plagues to punish the Egyptians," Silvia says, breathless, "because they didn't follow the true faith. Now God is punishing me for following my pleasure instead of His path."

"Silvia." Ibrahim comes and sits next to her, trying to be calm, though she can see his hands are shaking. "You have to stop this. No one's punishing anyone."

Cynthia raises her hand to Ibrahim to quiet him. "It's possible you're reading too much into this, Silvia. That you're seeing signs where really it's just nature. Have you thought about that?"

The rain is getting louder, hammering on the tiled roof and the tin eaves, pelting the hard earth.

Cynthia continues: "You come from a very different place, I know that, and we are all so proud of the progress you've made." She squeezes Silvia's hands for emphasis. "You said you felt free here, didn't you?" She pauses, looking into Silvia's eyes. "Maybe you need to learn to trust us. Trust that feeling."

Cynthia's eyes belie something elliptical; Silvia can't determine what her eyes are saying that's different from what her words are saying. Whether it's concern or something more. Her heart is beating too fast for her to breathe properly, that's what it is; it's so vast and swollen that it's blocking her lungs from filling with air. She puts her forehead to the smooth wood of the tabletop and opens her mouth, gasping.

Once she has.

Once she has calmed.

Once she has calmed down she can breathe normally again, with the inhale equal to the exhale, her lungs operating without her talking them through each motion.

Once she has calmed down, Cynthia takes her to bed.

XV

Cynthia helps Silvia out of her wet clothes as though she were a child. Silvia doesn't feel like her body is her own, so she is not embarrassed. She is the host of another life, not an independent self. Cynthia helps her sit back against the pillows, pale against the grubby cotton.

"That better?" Cynthia asks.

Silvia nods. "I'm sorry."

Cynthia shushes her. "It's okay, honey."

"I do trust you. It's just —" She stops for a moment to catch her breath. "I have no idea what I'm doing."

"You've gone through such big changes. It's normal to be scared, even a bit unstable. I understand."

That word, "unstable." She remembers Cynthia used that word about someone else. Or was it about her? Silvia looks at the ceiling, thinking about how it looks like every other ceiling she's ever seen.

"But I'd like to help you, if you'll let me."

Silvia looks at Cynthia, sensing urgency in her voice.

"Stay here after the baby's born. Ibrahim will be able to focus on his work, I'll look after the baby, and you'll be able to rest. I know this is hard for you, and you don't need to do it alone."

Silvia's brain is fizzing like a shaken-up soda. She can't speak.

"Does that sound like a good idea?" Cynthia asks gently.

Silvia looks into Cynthia's eyes, which she notices no longer seem like ice but like fire.

"The baby needs stability, Silvia. And I don't think you can give her that right now, do you?"

Silvia recognizes herself in the accusation and feels suddenly teenaged, chastened. "I, uh, I need to discuss it with Ibrahim —"

"I can talk to him." Cynthia strokes Silvia's hair gently.

Silvia nods. "It does seem like a good idea, for the moment at least."

"Good." Cynthia smiles, revealing her teeth. "You get some rest."

Ibrahim is fretting in the kitchen, treading a path between the table and the countertop. When Cynthia enters he stops walking and words pour out of his mouth as though he's turned on a tap. "I don't get what's going on with her, I don't know how to make it better — you know I've been trying, and I do love her, I love her so much, I just can't understand —"

"She'll be okay," Cynthia says, touching his arm.

"Are you sure?"

Cynthia nods sagely. "But you should leave her to rest for a few days."

Ibrahim is taken aback. "Really? You think she wants to be alone?"

"Don't you see, Ibrahim? You're part of the sin she thinks she's committing. It's best if you give her some space — her state of mind is clearly delicate."

"But —"

"Oh, I was wondering," Cynthia interrupts, "would you paint my portrait? That should help keep you occupied for the next little while. Same rate as the last one, of course."

"Uh . . ." He has never done a commission so isn't sure what it would be like. He deliberates, but can't exactly find the space to say no at the moment. And the money will definitely be helpful when they leave. "Sure, I guess."

"Brilliant. Can you start tomorrow? Bet-

ter to get it done before the baby is born."
She walks out before he can say anything in
response.

XVI

He wishes he could talk to his father, but the fact that it's the middle of the night in the last freezing gasp of winter, which makes this a logistical impossibility, fills his chest like lead. Ibrahim is alone right now — he feels more alone than ever too — sitting on the toilet in the downstairs bathroom at 3 a.m. His previous schedule has been creeping in, and there doesn't seem to be a reason to try to sync back up to a daytime rhythm. Silvia sleeps most of the day anyway. Out the window he can see moonlight falling on the grass, beveling the blades as the ice once did. It's late March, that in-between season where the damp darkness of winter is at its dullest, and yet hope is starting to grow.

Abouya, he says to the father who is always in his head. *Will it always be like this?*

Don't be so melodramatic, Ibrahim, his head-father says. *The future unfolds as the*

411

present, forever and ever.

What if the baby dies, like Mama died?

She will die, Abouya responds with a sigh. *Everything dies.* Ibrahim can see his father's sorrowful, pragmatic, heart-full face crumpling, mouth open as he considers his words. *And we have to learn to love the world anyway. Lucky for you if you die first.*

Ibrahim closes his eyes. He can feel his *abouya*'s duvet cover around him like a cape; he can see the glass teacups his mother bought from the souk refracting the weak light of the dark bedroom. *Will I make a good father? What will my son call me? Will he call me Abouya? Dad? And what if it's a girl? Will I be able to paint still? Where will we live? What will we do about money? Will Silvia want the baby baptised? Will I be able to teach him about my world too? Will he want to learn?*

His thoughts have run away from him now, and his imaginary father has stopped responding; Ibrahim can't come up with all the answers himself anymore. He just has to give it up to the unknowable inevitability of the future.

Somehow he got back to bed. Somehow he fell asleep. Morning comes, as morning always does. He puts on his shirt, and when

412

he tumbles out of bed, leaving Silvia sleeping soundly, he finds Cynthia sitting in his studio. She's wearing a black button-down shirt, sort of silky in the way it reflects the light, and black cotton trousers.

"Morning," Ibrahim says. He wasn't expecting her to be there yet. He wanted to have a cup of coffee and settle into the atmosphere first, but there's no time for that now. He shakes his head, trying to make himself more alert, and walks to his box of paints by the window.

"Good morning." Cynthia's voice sounds bright. "I brought you coffee." She points to a steaming cup on the floor. "Is here all right?" she asks, adjusting herself on the chair by the window. Though the light is pale and veiled through the thin, unending layer of clouds, the room shines with a light that seems to come not from a specific source but from within. He hopes he can capture it in paint.

"Wait a second." He's in the middle of squirting paints onto a small bit of plywood he's selected for his palette. Feeling what he's drawn to. Red and black and white, silver and gold. A little bit of yellow. You always need yellow, yellow's in everything. To get the light right he'll have to mix in a lot of white; maybe he'll try painting a translucent layer over the top of it all. His excitement is waking him up.

"Yeah," he says finally, scanning his palette and then looking up to see where she was referring to. "There's good."

Cynthia adjusts herself on the edge of the seat; she doesn't look very relaxed.

Ibrahim takes the coffee, then looks closely at her. A painter, to paint, must see things with loving eyes, so he has to adjust his perspective slightly, open himself up to love, whereas previously there has just been respect, distance, perhaps even confusion. He looks harder, trying to see through her opacity and understand whatever is within this woman, whatever it is that she keeps around her heart. As he looks, something about her softens: she looks slightly less uncomfortable than she did just moments ago.

She's sitting with her right foot crossed over her left and her arms crossed over her legs. She looks like a princess in a wedding portrait. Girlish and nervous, betrothed and dutiful. In this light she looks alarmingly young. He wouldn't call her beautiful — that's not the right word. *Handsome.* That's more like it. Cynthia's a very handsome woman. He looks at her now as he's never looked at her before. She carries herself with a dignity he thinks might have come from having lost it once. His confusion softens to sympathy.

He starts with her face. It's wider at the temples and tapers to a point at the chin. The nose is broad; he describes it using three wavy lines. His brushstrokes are bold.

Her eyes he does colourless — they are so black they hardly have any colour anyway — but he doesn't feel any colour coming from her, none at all. Except —

Yes.

He dips his brush in red and daubs a crimson dot on her forehead, like a bindi, but not.

Straight lines for her body — small; texture provides shape — and another red daub above her sternum. He steps back, closing one eye and placing his hand in front of Cynthia and then in front of the painting, evaluating size and perspective. He nods.

"I'm honoured to have a portrait done by you, Ibrahim." Cynthia sits a little higher in the chair. "You really are a true artist."

He hums, noncommittal.

She continues: "Is Silvia doing okay?"

"Yeah, I think so. She's sleeping, at least." He pauses. "I'm trying to give her some space, as you said."

"Good," Cynthia says. "That's very good."

"Can't talk," Ibrahim says. "Doing your face."

She's not used to being silenced.

His brush goes for the gold and mixes in some black. He finds himself painting wings, like Silvia's but smaller, more insect-like. A grubby gold.

When he's stopped painting for a while, Cynthia uncrosses her feet and twists in her seat.

Ibrahim doesn't move. He stands completely still, staring at the canvas.

Cynthia coughs, crossing her feet in the other direction.

"Are you done?" she asks finally. It's been nearly an hour of sitting in silence.

He's utterly absorbed in the painting, its textures and colours and feelings — the life he's given it. It worked; it's working. "For today," he says.

"That's all?"

"I'll work on the rest of it while you're not here. I need some time without the presence of the model."

When she's gone, he continues to stare at the painting. He's captured something of her on his canvas, definitely. Not a strict likeness, but an *attitude.* He's got her movement — formal and balletic — and a certain feeling that comes off her. It's hard to describe the feeling. There's that quote he often thinks of — though he can't remember who said it — about how portraiture is always a study of the artist rather than the subject, and while he doesn't agree, he does think it true that it's all a question of perspective.

The painting is tense and mysterious, but its energy is self-contained. It's complete. Her black body, hardly even a body while the same time nothing *but* a body, on a grey-white background. Her wings, so subtle you wouldn't ever call them that. It's funny, he thinks; he wonders why both Cynthia and Silvia had wings when he painted them. Cynthia's eyes — two black dots — are the same size as the brushstroke, as the red dot on her head. All three have the same weight and create a perfect constellation, an equilateral triangle that anchors the painting right in the middle. He tilts his head.

Nice. He likes it best when things like this happen unplanned. Lightness gasps in his chest, clear and shocking as if a light bulb had popped.

XVII

Rain is pummeling the dried-up land, beating a rhythm into every day. Silvia hasn't been outside since it started. Since she left the last time. Every day means the same thing to her, rain or no rain. During the drought everything was one thing, and now it is all another thing, but maybe those things are actually the same thing in that neither affects her at all.

She's gotten better at being comfortable in nothingness. She used to be propelled by hunger, a fast-moving fluidity that made adapting to change easy, and an appetite for the future that allowed her to put out of her mind any complications of the past. She was never a nostalgic person, but she wasn't exactly goal-oriented either. She also didn't "live for the moment" in a learned, New Age way. So which domain did she occupy? She thinks that it must have been a future-present sort of space, the place just in front of her nose where the carrot usually dangles from its stick — future as five-minutes-from-now.

But now she dwells in oblivion. In the space between her ears, behind her eyes; in the unimaginable, unlit vortex of her own brain.

She's standing in the hallway outside her room, looking out the window from which she, months ago, saved the bee. The view is the same but different. Same hills, same trees, but now everything looks dead. Brown grass, no leaves. She can feel her heart beating and looks down, her chest thin as the skin of a drum, as her black T-shirt lifts and sinks with the rhythm. If her heart stopped beating, would she see it? How much time would elapse between her being aware of its ending and the moment of her death? Is the heart more like a motor or more like a seed? She stops looking at her shirt and looks outside again, through the wall of water warping the landscape behind it. It's March — is it March? She thinks so — and she knows that life is lying latent in this land, buds dormant in the branches and roots and seeds lying in wait under the surface of the earth, but for now it's all invisible. It's hard to keep what's out of sight still in one's mind. This is where her faith used to come in.

She remembers her realisation about the tree. A tree used to be a tree, but then suddenly a tree could be anything. But now, this minute, the trees she sees are all just nothing. Dormant, invisible, irrelevant. Their treeness doesn't matter; it doesn't change anything.

She looks down to make sure her heart is still beating, her shirt is still moving. It is; they both are.

She can hear Ibrahim working in the bedroom that has become his studio. She steps towards his door, four paces down the hall, and looks inside.

"Hey." He turns around when he sees her shadow cast across his canvas.

"You're still working?"

"Yeah, it's the one of Cynthia. Want to come see?" He steps aside; she can tell he's eager to see her. She hasn't seen him, properly seen him, in a few days. She doesn't know why, really, though she assumes he's been busy with this portrait. She doesn't know what to say to him.

She stays leaning against the doorframe. The canvas he's working on is the same size as the first portrait he did of her, but this one gives a different impression — it *feels* bigger. It's darker and brighter at the same time, more abstract but also providing a more specific feeling of the subject. Maybe that's just because she can recognize Cynthia better than she can recognize herself.

"It looks good," Silvia says.

"What're you up to?" He comes nearer, a fistful of paintbrushes in his right hand.

"Nothing."

"You doing okay?" He takes her hand in his.

"Yeah."

"Do you need anything? Want to stay and keep me company?" He knows Cynthia told him to give Silvia some space right now, and he's trying, but he wants to make sure she knows that he's there for her if she wants him.

"No, I'm tired. I think I'll just go to bed." She wishes he would come with her, but she can't bring herself to ask. She feels she has no right to anything.

"Oh." He lets go of her hand and pushes his hair behind his ears. "Well, sleep well, then."

She goes into her room, their room, and lies on the bed, on top of the blanket. The rain is even louder here than in the corridor, something to do with the lack of insulation where the roof slopes; it's so loud it almost drowns out her thoughts. Her eyes are open, but she's looking at nothing, at the space in front of her nose, remembering the time when her mother let her stay home from school even when she wasn't particularly sick. It was early spring, probably around March too, and Silvia was in grade three. The day was this same deep dark grey and Silvia had woken to the sound of rain, falling just as hard as it is now. Little Silvia lay in bed feeling not quite right and realised after a few minutes of lying there that the feeling was sadness. She wasn't used to it. It felt slippery, as though it could uproot her. For a few seconds the feeling would go away but then it would come crashing back, this time stronger, just like the waves by their cottage in LaHave, down the South Shore. But even then Silvia knew that sadness wasn't grounds enough to miss school, and she also knew that it was something she would never be able to explain properly to her mom. Maybe to anyone.

When it was nearly time to catch the school bus, Silvia called her mom up to her room and, from her turtled position under the blankets, told her in a rushing voice that she'd hardly slept, that her head hurt, that she felt like she was going to throw up.

Her mom looked at her deeply for a long

moment. Silvia was sure she could see right through the weak excuses, but she just said, "Okay." She let Silvia watch Disney movies on repeat all day and made her plain toast and chicken soup. It made Silvia feel better, but more importantly, it didn't make her feel worse.

During the end of *Beauty and the Beast,* her mother came and sat on the sofa with a blue plastic bucket she normally used for hand-washing her pantyhose. "How are you feeling, honey?" she asked.

"Okay," little Silvia said, pulling away reluctantly as the candelabra transforms into a man. "Better."

"I brought this in case you need to throw up," her mom said, patting Silvia on the back.

Silvia looked at her and then at the bucket and was aware of the sensation of being rubbed between her shoulder blades, being cared for so tenderly. She took the bucket into her lap, and as her mom's hands continued to pat a soft rhythm through her pyjama top, Silvia, who had been feeling perfectly fine physically up to this point, vomited neatly into the blue bucket.

"There's a good girl," her mother said, and took the bucket away.

Silvia fell asleep before the end of the

movie, knowing very well how it would end. And by the next day the feeling had passed.

XVIII

The rain stops after seven days and then the skies are a perfect blue, as though nothing had ever troubled them. Tentatively, Silvia goes out to the garden, where repercussive rain filters through the branches, making cymbals of the leaves, and the earth soaks up water like someone thirsty for love.

The earth heals itself as the body does, and both refuse to give up their secrets.

XIX

After what felt like an infinite, impossible winter, spring manages to find its way through, and with all the usual proclamations of light and leaf, too: flowers are pulsing within their buds, tight like fists; bees are buzzing again, searching for life outside their tarpapered hives. The fuzz of new bloom is like champagne froth in the trees. Everything is just on the edge of bursting.

First spring morning: a tentative sun, warm on her eyelids. Silvia is in bed, head where her feet normally are so as to be closer to the window, open for the first time since the cold snap in September. A warm, gentle wind brings in the smell of everything, waxy and new. Fresh shoots through dark soil are growing so quickly she feels she can hear them: a subtle buzz. There is an ease to warmth that she had forgotten. Part of the struggle of living has gone.

"Silvia?" There's a tap on her door, and

Cynthia opens it expectantly. "Are you sleeping?"

"No." She props herself up on her elbows.

"Wonderful! I wondered if you wanted to come for a walk."

"Oh." Silvia looks at her feet, as if to see whether they're up to the task of leaving the bed — something they haven't done much for a few days. "Okay, sure."

"Wonderful."

Cynthia carefully guides Silvia down the steps, through the kitchen, and out the back door to the garden. Silvia's belly is enormous; she has to go slowly. She wonders where Ibrahim is, knowing that wherever he is, he's probably great. Better than great — perfect. She shouldn't begrudge him this. She tries to bend her envy into hope.

Outside, the sky too is perfect, the sun is perfect, the vegetable patch is perfect in its own prelife way. There is no breeze; the leaves are unruffled. Everything is perfect, and outside her. Silvia almost feels like she's looking at a painting in a museum — she can't be a part of its perfection. Even Ibrahim, perfect in his own way, is removed from her.

She puts her face to the sun, feeling its heat with surprise, and revels in the guilty pleasure of accepting, without acknowledging, the miracle of spring.

As the women walk towards the back of the lot, Cynthia still supporting Silvia's unbalanced weight, the number of bees quickly multiplies. Silvia can feel them coming before she sees them. Two, then thirty; then, the next minute, there are hundreds. They're walking towards a moving Milky Way of honeybees, each one bumbling, darting, as if the women don't even exist.

"Don't worry," Cynthia says, "they won't come near." She waves her arm and the bees part to let the women pass.

"I know. They do that for me too." Silvia stretches out an arm and a straight line of bees comes towards her. "It feels funny," she says.

"Funny how?"

"Not the feeling of them on my skin, but when they come. I don't know how to describe it. Like how I can feel it beforehand."

Cynthia nods. She watches Silvia's face as the bees land on her arm and march slowly towards her elbow. Cynthia looks as though she has an unscratchable itch.

"Is it like this for everyone?" Silvia asks, curious.

"Not at all. It takes a particular kind of person."

Without thinking on it further, Silvia moves the line of bees down from her elbow and into her palm, along her middle finger, and back into the air. A smile crosses her lips unconsciously as she feels them depart, as though there's still a string inside her that connects her nerves to theirs.

"You did that very well," said Cynthia. "Your confidence is growing."

Silvia looks at Cynthia and smiles, proud.

XX

The next morning Silvia wakes up nauseous and goes immediately to the bathroom, where she spends the rest of the day lying, clothed, in the empty tub. These days her body seems to be responding to its own tidal patterns; one moment the water is down, and she's happily walking in the shallows, but the next it's so high she can hardly keep her head above the surface. She doesn't know what she wants. Even if she did know, she wouldn't have a choice, a chance to change any of this. She watches a light flicker on the wall and tries to find where the reflection is coming from. The light is the slippery, luminous thing that bounces off water or metal, but she can't see any of either.

"Hey." Ibrahim comes in, knocking after the fact. "The painting of Cynthia is finished and hung. Want to come see?"

"Oh." She opens her eyes, not realising

until that moment that they'd been closed. "Sure."

Silvia's skin is no longer dewy, as Ibrahim once thought. It's dulled, gone ruddy in a rundown, adult way. Thin frown lines are starting to make their mark on her forehead, tracing all her worries. And from the face down, her body has dramatically changed too — and not just her belly. Her ankles have disappeared into the straight stretch of calf; her thighs are thicker, heavier; her breasts look like they're about to burst, her nipples are dark and long, thick as a pinkie finger; and her hair, which used to be so soft and downy, has gone dark and wiry. He still loves her, of course, but he does hope her body will return to the way it once was.

He comes over to help her out of the tub. "You good there?"

She nods, squinting a little with the pressure of being vertical.

He guides her slowly into the library, where Silvia steps back with a start when she sees the portrait of Cynthia. It looks so similar to her own, but at the same time completely different. There's something about it that follows her.

"How many paintings have you made since we've been here?" she asks. "Forty, fifty?"

"I don't know — about that I guess. There are a few that aren't quite finished, though . . ."

She wonders if he feels worried, if he ever has doubts — if not about God, then about life, about his art, about this baby, about her. He must. But she doesn't know how to ask about this. She's not even sure she wants to know. She's learning — or trying to learn — the value of unknowability, which is different from having faith.

"Forty paintings," she says quietly. "And I've done nothing."

"That's not true, Silvia — you've done so much." He rubs her belly.

She lifts his hand off her. "Incubating another life doesn't count. Different sort of product." She goes to look at the painting up close, seeing the life within the paint. It's mostly black and white but somehow feels full of colour. It doesn't look very much like Cynthia, but she can tell, she can feel, that it is Cynthia. "It's beautiful, Ibrahim, really. You're so talented. I'm so happy for you." Pride and jealousy aren't mutually exclusive.

"Thanks," Ibrahim said. "I'm just glad Cynthia likes it."

As though her name has summoned her, Cynthia walks into the library with the kind of confidence that can only come from ownership and goes straight to Silvia. "How are you, sweetheart?"

"Fine."

Cynthia places her palm on Silvia's watermelon belly. "Is she kicking?"

"Not now."

Cynthia moves her hand over the expanse of Silvia's stomach like a diviner, or a cartographer. With intention. She goes slowly, her palm flat but her fingertips lifting. Silvia wonders what she's looking for.

"This is going to be so wonderful." Cynthia sighs, looking into an abstract middle distance between her painted eyes.

XXI

Ibrahim is sitting on the back step outside the kitchen, looking out over the backyard. It's the beginning of May, nearly a year to the day since everyone arrived, and he's noticing the thin clouds that have formed a low-hanging ceiling over the world. The bright grey quality of light has a dizzying effect; he feels nauseous, but that might just be in sympathy with Silvia, whose morning sickness has never gone away.

Cynthia invited him to come investigate the hives for the first time that morning, opening them up after they'd been sealed all winter. Less than half the bees died this year, so on paper they did better than last, but last season she'd bought twice as many hives, she explained, so there had actually been a greater quantity of death. She'll have to hope to catch more swarms this spring, but you can't trap queens, "of course, since bees only swarm when queenless — a queen must be either bred or bought," she tells Ibrahim.

He hears Hartford walk in through the front door, back from doing the weekly shopping in Smooth Rock.

"Cynthia?" Hartford calls.

Ibrahim hears her footsteps. He then realises that they don't see him, though he isn't trying to hide. Still, he doesn't make his presence known. He feels like a little kid hiding from his parents.

"You got the folic acid?" she asks. "And the lavender oil?"

"Yeah," he says, "and I saw Meg in town. She said she could come by any time this week just to check everything's going okay."

"Right, thank you."

"She said to just give her a call."

"Yes, thank you, Hartford."

Ibrahim can hear Cynthia walk across the kitchen, creak open a cupboard, plunk a glass on the counter, open the fridge, and — this part is conjecture, but his mental image is clear from memory — pour milk into the glass.

"I'll take care of it." The fridge shuts.

Then a ruffling of newspaper.

"There's going to be a total solar eclipse tomorrow," says Hartford. "First time in nearly seventy years. The weather conditions are going to be perfect, apparently."

Silence. Footsteps. A chair pulled out from the table; someone taking a seat.

"Are you going to be all right, Cynthia?"

Quietly: "What are you talking about?"

"When she leaves. When Silvia leaves, with the baby. After Hilary, I just . . ." He trails off.

"Oh, didn't I tell you? She's decided to stay."

XXII

Silvia wakes to the smell of burning. She sits up, her movements awkward, and looks out the window. It's dark. She thought it was morning, she has slept forever, but the sun isn't there to light the world. It's not cloudy; it's as though the sky is on a dimmer switch that's been turned down. The air is misty, silver.

Nobody's around. Not Ibrahim, not Cynthia, who sometimes is there when she wakes to give her tea and toast with honey. Silvia pulls herself out of bed, toppling a little bit before she finds her balance, and pulls Ibrahim's dad's sweater over her grubby white pyjamas.

She tries to tune in to the sounds of the house as she walks down the stairs. She knows them all so well she can usually tell just from listening where everyone is and what they are doing, but now it's all a hushed blur. When she gets to the kitchen

437

it's dark there too. She goes to flick on the light switch, but by the time she gets to it she sees Hartford through the window, in the backyard, facing away from her.

"Hartford!" she calls out. He doesn't turn; he must not have heard her. He's stoking a large bonfire with wood from old hives. The thin frames still retain their shape for the moment, but the licking flames will soon overtake and consume them.

"Ibrahim?" she calls towards the library, thinking he might be in there, touching up the paintings of her and Cynthia. But there are no lights on in there, and there is no response either.

"Cynthia?" A heavy silence. "Hello?"

She goes towards the back door and looks outside. The sky turns from a matte grey to a deep, uniform slate — it's not as black as night, but it's nothing at all like day. Looking up, she sees a hole in the sky where the sun would normally be — like a hole punched clear through canvas, a wholly black centre with white light radiating from behind it.

"Hartford?" she cries loudly, and he turns.

"Silvia," he says, taking a step towards her. "What are you doing up?"

"Isn't it morning?"

"Yes," he says matter-of-factly.

The fire's neon-orange heart is the only source of light in the world, and it draws her like a moth. She shakes her head and steps, barefoot, onto the damp grass, the dew not having had any help in disappearing.

Hartford throws another stack of broken honeycomb frames onto the fire, and the hiss and sizzle of combustion shocks her back a step, and then it settles down. When she's nearly by his side he looks at her gently. "You should go back to bed," he says, sounding like her father.

Suddenly the birds, which she hadn't even realised had been singing, fall silent. Silvia pauses, feeling cold; the temperature has dropped. "Where is everybody?" she whispers, afraid of speaking any louder in this newly silent world. "Where's the sun?"

Hartford prods the fire, which is rising to the sky, higher and higher, even as the wood collapses in on itself. The first law of thermodynamics: energy can be converted from one form to another but cannot be created or destroyed. Wood becomes fire becomes stars.

She looks up and sees a disk moving across the hole punch through the sky, letting a little bit more light in from behind. She stares for a moment and then looks away, the light burning her eyes. "What's happening?" she asks Hartford, but he just shrugs.

She looks back to the house and Cynthia is there, wearing a baggy sweater; her hair, for the first time, is not perfectly brushed but kinked, as if from sleep. She's holding a glass of milk as a sort of offering. "Come."

"Where were you? Where's Ibrahim?"

"Let's get you back to bed, Silvia. You must be tired."

"What are you talking about? I just woke up. It's day, isn't it?"

Cynthia walks to where Silvia is rooted on the wet grass and puts her arm around Silvia's shoulders, giving her the glass of milk. "Just calm down, darling. Everything is fine — there's nothing you need to do."

Silvia doesn't want to drink the milk, but she picks up the glass and gulps it as if under a spell.

Cynthia watches. "There's a good girl."

"This is insane." Silvia is laughing as if something has switched inside her. Fear becomes bewilderment becomes complete absurdity and back again. "I just saw — the sun, it isn't —"

"I need you to calm down. It's bad for the baby for you to get so agitated."

"But you can see it too? It's not just me,

I'm not — ?" Silvia collapses into Cynthia's arms, her legs giving way. Nothing hurts, it's not that — she feels nothing at all. Her insides have been replaced with gauze.

"Silvia." Ibrahim is there in the doorway and rushes to her. "What's going on?" he asks Cynthia.

"Where were you?" Silvia asks him. "Do you see this too?" She points with her head to the sky, lightening back to a silvery grey but still not the colour of day.

"Of course I see it; it's normal."

"Normal?" Silvia's voice becomes dog-whistle high. "You're telling me that it's *normal* to have night in the day?" and when she says this out loud, it's as if a piece falls into place. Her body turns from gauze to ice.

"Help me, Ibrahim," Cynthia says. "I've lost control of her."

"This is the next plague," Silvia says, hardly even audible. "That's what's happening. It's the second to last one."

"I thought you'd gotten over this, Silvia." Following Cynthia's gestured instructions, he takes Silvia's other arm and helps to lift her up and walk her back to the house.

Silvia starts crying.

"Come on, honey," Ibrahim says, softening but still condescending. "We'll get you back to bed and you'll feel better." He looks at Cynthia and gets them to stop in the middle of the wet lawn, under the dark daylight. He takes Silvia's hand in his. "I'm here with you," he says. "We're right here, and everything's fine." He uncurls her tightly clutched fist, wanting to hold her hand, but in her palm he finds the small silver cross, stuck with sweat to her skin.

XXIII

Against a tar-black backdrop Silvia sees a close-up of Cynthia's face, magnified and unreadable. Her lips are hanging slightly open, and Silvia looks closely, sensing that something is not quite right: Cynthia's large teeth, perfect white squares, are covered in something red. A bright, living red, as if she has been chewing fresh flesh. The lips stretch into a dripping smile, then everything recedes into the blackness, and she's gone.

Out of the darkness now comes a spinning vortex of bees, shining and moving to form a perfect helix. A voice resounds, deep and all-encompassing like a universal loudspeaker: *"I will strike Pharaoh and the land of Egypt with one more blow. After that, Pharaoh will let you leave this country. In fact, he will be so eager to get rid of you that he will force you all to leave."*

Silvia is not pregnant and so moves differently, light again, free in her body. She feels like a child. She's in the yard, by the vegetable patch; now she's by the hives, floating among, then above them. She looks up at the tornado of bees and tries to move away, but they keep moving towards her. She's unable to control them, but this doesn't scare her. She feels at peace, she feels outside herself.

The voice speaks again, this time louder. *"For I will pass through the land this night, and smite all the firstborn children."*

Cynthia's face appears again, superimposed over the whole world. She seems kindly, still shining, and Silvia tries to say something, to ask why her mouth was full of blood — she trusts that there must have been some misunderstanding from before, but then Cynthia smiles again, revealing not just blood on her teeth but the half-formed wings of baby queen bees, stuck like pineapple fibres between her teeth.

Silvia recoils in disgust, but not horror: there must be a logical explanation, for Cynthia is nothing if not logical. Taking two steps back, she's about to ask Cynthia what's going on when she notices for the first time that she is cradling something in her arms. Perhaps she was holding it all along.

XXIV

Silvia wakes up to see Ibrahim smiling down at her. The day is bright. For a moment she can't tell where she is. She doesn't remember arriving in bed, doesn't remember falling asleep. Then she remembers her dream. She's left with less of a memory and more of a feeling. Should she tell Ibrahim about it? Could she convince him that they must leave to protect themselves from the final plague? Would it be worse not to be believed or to be proved right?

Before she can say anything, Ibrahim proffers a steaming cup.

"Tea?" He is smiling benevolently.

Silvia sits up and takes the cup.

"You okay?" he asks.

She sips, swallows. "Bad dream."

"Well, the solar eclipse passed a few hours ago, see? Look." He gestures to the sky-blue sky. "Everything's back to normal."

Silvia stares at him. "Solar eclipse? I . . . I

didn't know."

"Hartford didn't tell you? I just assumed, when you found him —"

"Ibrahim." She stops him, shaking her head, needing to speak for herself. "I'm sorry . . . for everything" — she's waking up now; the dream is disappearing and it's all coming back — "but I have to tell you something. The final plague, after the darkness —" He's about to interrupt. "No, no, please let me finish," she goes on. "I know you don't believe me, but after the darkness is the death of the firstborn," she explains, rushing on though he's trying to interrupt again. "And even if it's not true, please, what's the harm in just being cautious? Right? I really, really think we need to leave the farm."

He's confused, because she's sounding so much more logical than she ever has before, even though her logic is utterly unreasoned. He tries to hold his love for her in his head, paint it over this current reality. He tries to empathize with her circumstances, remember where she comes from, what she must be going through, but it's hard to create narrative with no context.

"Listen," she continues, "whatever you think, I know something's not right, and I would just rather have the baby in a hospital, to be safe." She's trying so hard to sound reasonable and takes a deep breath, willing her heart rate to slow down. "Something about Cynthia is making me nervous."

"Hey." He wraps his arm around her. "Honey, it's okay, calm down." He rocks her back and forth. Her needs and concerns are so pressing that they dissolve his own. This is how the world balances itself. He turns her face to his and kisses her with such tenderness, such a profound acceptance, that she can feel a seam unstitch in her heart. "Everything's fine. Cynthia's fine, the baby's fine, and besides, I'm here. I'll take care of you no matter what."

"It's not about you, Ibrahim — *please* listen to me. I —" She looks down; she feels liquid. "Oh my God!"

"What?" Ibrahim looks down too and sees the patch of water spreading out from beneath her. "Oh! It broke!"

"What broke?" Silvia, shrieking, is not just confused but terrified.

"Your water." He pads his hands around the damp sheets. He looks at Silvia, his eyes brilliant, his smile maniacal. "Baby! You're having the baby!" Ibrahim, face on, grips Silvia's biceps and tries to transmit his joy.

Silvia shakes him off. There's no time. She won't be able to leave. The reality of this falls over her, top to bottom.

"What's the matter?" He sees that her expression has changed, as quickly as the weather.

"Get Meg."

"Does it hurt?"

"Not yet." Scream-gasp. "Yes."

"The contractions have started already?" Ibrahim asks.

"I guess so."

"Isn't that a little early?"

Silvia has no idea what he's been reading up on but wants trusted authority regardless. *"Call Meg."*

"Where is she?"

"Ibrahim."

"What should I say?"

"I don't fucking care what you fucking say" — another scream-gasp — "I'm having a fucking *baby. Now.* I want Meg. Here. Right. Now." He still doesn't move. "Go!" she shrieks.

"Right, right, sorry, sorry." He scrambles up, fusses about with the sheets, leaps into the jeans he was wearing yesterday and pulls on the same T-shirt (inside out), runs out the door, runs back to kiss Silvia, (*"Ibrahim!"*), then breaks into a run down the stairs and into the kitchen. He treads water, looking around, panic growing. Then he sees Hartford coming from his office, holding a crate of honey: a salvation. "Hartford!" Hartford looks up. "Where's Cynthia?"

"I haven't seen her yet. Probably in her room."

"Silvia's having the baby. I need to call Meg!"

"I'm afraid I don't have her —"

"Oh God, never mind. I need to get Cynthia!"

Hartford continues to stare blankly, the pieces not seeming to come together for him.

"Silvia is having the baby."

"Oh, yes, of course. Well, go knock on her door."

While Hartford points to the ceiling, to all the black holes in the universe, Ibrahim thinks of how nothing Hartford could do would ever be a surprise to anyone.

Ibrahim's on his way up the other staircase, which he's barely used, at the front of the house, overlooking the driveway and sort-of courtyard. The stairs creak as he takes them two at a time. He would be rushing, running, shouting if he weren't so worried — his worry about disturbing Cynthia is currently, disloyally, supreme to his worry about Silvia's labour.

Then there is a figure at the top of the

wooden staircase; he can feel its shadow cast over him. He looks up: Cynthia.

"Ibrahim?"

"Silvia's having the baby — sorry, you have to call Meg, you have to come." The words stumble out; he's unsure of what he's apologizing for.

"Have her contractions started?"

"Yes, I think so, and her water — there's water everywhere."

"Okay. I'll be right there."

Ibrahim waits where he is, not moving.

"You go back to her, Ibrahim. I'll get the things required."

"How long will it take for Meg to get here?"

"Don't worry, Ibrahim. Go on."

He runs back down the stairs, back across the foyer — he bumps into Hartford, who nearly drops the crate full of jars of honey — and tears across the kitchen and back up the staircase to his and Silvia's room.

Just as soon as he's crossed the threshold, Silvia screams. *"WHERE IS SHE?"*

"Cynthia?"

"No, *Meg.* I told you —"

"She's coming, she's coming." He runs to her side. "What can I do? What do you want me to do? Do you want to, like, squeeze my hand or something?"

"No, no, no, *no* —"

"What's the matter?"

"What's the *matter*? Ibrahim, I'm having a *baby.*"

"But everything is going to be fine! People have babies all the time."

She just stares at him. Even her eyeballs hurt.

At that moment Cynthia arrives.

"Where's Meg?" Ibrahim asks.

Cynthia doesn't reply. She marches up to the mattress, takes one look at Silvia, squirming, and quickly assesses that the labour is too far along: there is no time to set up the birthing pool. The baby is coming so quickly, much more quickly than any of them imagined. She unfolds the flannel sheets (at the ready next to the mattress) and lays out the sponge pad underneath Silvia's legs, nudging the edge as far beneath her hips as she can manage without physically moving the girl, then props the clarysage massage oil and dried lavender stalks on the stack of books that serves as a night table.

"Silvia, can you take your pyjama bottoms off by yourself, or do you need my help?"

Silvia shakes her head, sweat pearling above her eyebrows.

Cynthia nods, then crouches as she gently

451

pulls the pyjamas down from Silvia's hips and along the length of her unshaven legs.

Ibrahim winces, and pulls Cynthia aside. "What are you — I mean, what's going on? Isn't Meg coming?"

"I've got this taken care of, Ibrahim."

"What do you mean? What are you — what if something goes wrong?" he whispers, not wanting Silvia to hear.

"She's too far along — I need to do this now. Nothing will go wrong." Cynthia snaps latex-free gloves over her hands. "You'll wait outside."

"What?"

"Outside, please. We can't have men in the birthing room."

"The birthing room? Cynthia, that's insane. This is *my* baby!"

"Not Silvia's baby, then?" Cynthia gives him a look. "I really don't think you've been much help to Silvia these last few weeks, Ibrahim. And now, since you don't seem to be able to provide a calming influence, you need to step outside. Silvia needs me. You're wasting everyone's time." She pivots to go back to Silvia. "Close the door on your way out."

Ibrahim stalks the upstairs corridor as if he's hunting for prey, and for every sound he hears through the doorway, his imagination fills in all the blanks. A shuffle could mean Silvia moving down the bed, getting up, running away; the sound of rapping glass could mean her knocking on the window, trying to break through; the groans could be the normal pains of childbirth or they could be something entirely different, something he can't imagine. He has no reference point at all.

Then, a song he recognizes. What is it? It's that song, the main one from . . . *The Nutcracker.* Tchaikovsky, that's it. It tinkles along, floating above the human sounds inside the room. He hears someone humming. Probably Cynthia. He doubts Silvia will be humming right now.

Hartford appears at the end of the hallway, and the way the light falls, only his head and shoulders are visible. He looks at Ibrahim. "How's it going?" he asks.

"How'm I supposed to know?"

"Why don't you come wait downstairs?" he says kindly, and when Ibrahim doesn't move, Hartford guides him down the stairs to the kitchen, knowing that a little space will be better for everyone.

"There we go," Hartford says. "Tea?"

Ibrahim shakes his head.

"Toast?"

Ibrahim is now pacing between the window and the table instead of between his studio and the bedroom, and he's still shaking his head.

"Right. I'll get the whisky," Hartford says, and pours two glasses.

Time passes; the song loops; Ibrahim downs his whisky and listens to the shouts and grunts and muffled words coming from upstairs; then, worse, silence. Everything inside him is poised to go towards the room — he's on his toes, he's leaning forward, his hands are clenched so tightly he's forgotten about them — like a wave as it crashes in the middle of the sea, smashing forever towards land. Should he pray? He's not sure he remembers how to pray, or really even to whom. To his higher power, to his family, to the God of All Things?

Please let everything be all right.

Then one huge, majestic scream, doubled. The scream turns to a hiccupping burble.

Life.

XXV

Black. Black and red, the pain its own palpitation. Then — a white, lightning-searing flash. Life. She is a cog in the system of creation and has fulfilled her duty, has churned forth a new seed. She is a mother machine.

When the pain has abated, absence. Her breath is a black abyss. When the life that was inside her is gone, there is no more. She's been emptied.

When the baby is gone from her womb and is replaced with a hole, the rest of the world returns to her through this opening. First: the wood-beamed white ceiling, the feeling of fabric around her ankles. Second: an unrecognizable scream. The fear evoked by this scream instantly transfers to Silvia, who screams in response.

"Shh, there, there."

Third: Cynthia's face, dark, close, deeply lined. Seeing this face brings a different kind of distress, and Silvia's insides turn cold. She closes her eyes and sees the teeth, bees' wings like floss between them.

Part of Silvia's very being is now outside herself — she feels this physically. She opens her mouth, but no words come out. The words have left her along with her child. She tries to lift her head so as to see more than what's in front of her nose, but her neck no longer seems able to support her skull.

"There, now," Cynthia says, her hands on Silvia's shoulders. "You just stay still, rest." Silvia stares up, helpless, unable to stop what is happening. "It's all over."

"Please," Silvia utters before her voice runs out again.

"Hello, baby," Cynthia says, and Silvia hears the smile in her voice. The feeling of this smile gives her a pain nearly as intense as the one she just pushed through, but this time the pain is in her heart. The pain *is* her heart.

"Let's go and get you cleaned up," Cynthia says.

The baby is no longer screaming but gurgling, as if bubbles are catching in its throat. Silvia can do nothing but lie there as Cynthia leaves the room, holding the child — *her* child, Silvia's child, Silvia's heart.

As soon as she's alone, not by choice but almost as if in a primal form of defense, Silvia falls asleep.

XXVI

Ibrahim is literally on the edge of his seat in the kitchen, and when Cynthia walks in, he jumps up. "How is she? How's she doing?"

"It's a girl," Cynthia says, smiling, holding out the baby to show him.

A *girl.* It's a girl! He dances forward to see: a perfect baby girl. Ibrahim has always wanted a girl. He *loves* girls. And this one's *his.* "Oh, she's perfect," he says, and she is. With her soft tufts of golden hair and her little pink feet, each one of her tiny toes smaller than one of Ibrahim's Chiclet teeth. With her rubbery, paper-thin fingernails, her legs like croissants, all pleated with buttery chubbiness. With her little ears like pressed clay — a fingerprint here, there, and with her hands opening and closing like tiny anemones, hungry for something, reaching for it. "Can I?" he asks as he takes the baby — carefully, so carefully — from Cynthia, and he feels love surge like an electric current, practically short-circuiting his heart. He loves this little human; he has been put here on this earth just to love her.

"How's Silvia?" he asks, remembering himself. "Is she doing okay?"

"Not too well, actually." Cynthia's tone is controlled, opaque.

"What? Really?" Ibrahim lowers his little girl, still holding her tight.

"You have to support her head," Cynthia says, adjusting his elbow. "There."

Ibrahim looks down at the face of this child, whose head he doesn't know how to hold correctly, whose mind he will never be able to read. He feels her heart beat through her body, through his body. "What happened? Is it serious? Should we take her to the hospital?"

"Silvia? Oh, no, I think she just needs some rest."

"Has she seen the baby? Should I go up to her?"

"Of course she's seen the baby." Cynthia half laughs. "She gave birth to her, didn't she?" They look at each other for a moment. "Silvia's sleeping, and given her circumstances, I think she needs the rest." Cynthia looks at him meaningfully.

He nods. The word "circumstances" lends a solemnity he cannot argue with. He looks

459

down at his baby. His *baby.* His little girl. Her mouth has been drawn with a pencil, tiny puckering lines and a wavering, grumpy top lip. The sun's framed in the window behind her head, haloing her golden tufts; the sunlight through her earlobes glows them red. He is filled up.

His love of Silvia has become embodied in this beautiful little baby that they created together. He loves Silvia, he loves the baby, and he loves the world for having made life this way.

He holds his baby up to the sky, then quickly brings her back to his chest, suddenly afraid of how far away from him she is, afraid that he won't be able to protect her if she's way out there.

XXVII

When Silvia wakes her breasts are aching,
swollen as footballs. She has no idea what
she looks like; she hasn't seen a mirror in
forever. And since she's a mother, maybe
she's completely changed. Aged. Grown up.
She can hear birds screeching outside; their
cries sound like a baby's. Maybe it's her
baby crying. Then she hears the sound of
an unfamiliar car. At least she thinks it's the
sound of a car — she hasn't heard one in a
while. She wants to see whose it is — there
are so rarely visitors here — but she can't
get up, or turn around. Fear, laced through
with a fine, small hope, that it might be her
parents. In a way, it would be a relief if they
came. The perfect excuse. All she wants is
to leave as soon as possible; she knows her
parents would want this too.

She gives up, tries to empty her mind of
thoughts and fears and hopes. Her stomach
is slightly deflated, like raw dough. There is

461

nothing inside her anymore. So much nothing. Believing in nothing, she decides, is completely different from not believing in anything. It would be so much easier if she could believe in nothing.

XXVIII

The house feels, for the first time in a long time, perfectly calm. It's late afternoon and all the windows are open, "so the house can breathe," as Cynthia said. The baby is now nearly twenty-four hours old. Ibrahim thinks that his whole sense of time will now be permanently shifted, measured only by the lifespan of his child. Hours, weeks, and years will be counted according to how long she's lived rather than anything else.

Silvia is sleeping, Cynthia is trying to put the baby down, and Ibrahim and Hartford are sitting at the dining room table finding excuses not to talk so that they can focus on their thoughts. Hartford alternates between polishing the silverware and balancing the chequebook; Ibrahim repeatedly reads, and then recoils from, the baby book Silvia tried to get through; he's still blissed out on love and doesn't want to disrupt it with this harsh, gloopy reality. Then there's a knock at the front door.

"Who is that?" Ibrahim asks.

"I don't know," Hartford says.

"You should get it — you live here."

"Right." Hartford stands up, but when he's halfway to the door he looks back at Ibrahim, remembering that he lives there too.

Hartford pulls open the heavy door smoothly but slowly, ready for anything.

"No reception up here?" Meg is standing on the front step, holding her phone up at shoulder height as if trying to capture signals that might be floating beyond her waist.

"Hello, Meg."

"Hartford, how are you," she says, walking into the kitchen, not wanting a response. She puts her black bag on the chair next to Ibrahim and smoothes down her hair, puffier than usual in this fresh spring heat. "Ibrahim, how's Silvia?" The real question. "I thought I'd pop in to see how things were going" — she waves her useless cell phone — "since you're otherwise unreachable."

Ibrahim feels a great sense of relief. "Silvia's sleeping," he says quickly. "She had the baby."

Meg pauses for a moment, her right eye twitching slightly. "Then why didn't you —"

"The baby came yesterday — her water broke, I asked Cynthia to call you, but she said — I can't remember what she said, actually. But it was all happening so fast and we didn't know what was going on and I had to wait down here, and now they're both sleeping. It's a girl." He wants Meg to have all the information; he senses that she'll be able to see answers he can't.

"Right." Meg is gripping the back of the chair with both hands. "Where are they?"

"Silvia's in her room, and the baby is . . ." Ibrahim pauses, looks at Hartford, and whispers as though he's offstage and missed his cue, "Where's the baby?"

"Cynthia's putting her to sleep in the nursery."

"The nursery?" Meg says. "But — okay, never mind. Baby first." Meg picks up her bag again.

"Cynthia," Meg says, striding into the pink nursery, making a beeline for the baby. "How is she?" She goes to the butter-yellow crib and looks in. Her manner, though always efficient, is rather more brusque than usual.

"Meg! We tried to call you," Cynthia says. "She's just gone to sleep," she adds protectively.

465

Hartford and Ibrahim are standing at the door, watching.

"You did?" Meg reaches down to pick up the baby even though she can tell Cynthia doesn't want her to. "There you are," she says as she scoops the baby into the crook of her right arm. "From the pay phone way down at the end of the road? You're still using that, right? Well, it must have not gone through."

Cynthia, silenced, watches Meg with a mournful expression that looks almost like longing as the midwife rocks the child back and forth, gently bringing her to a state of wakefulness, with no tears.

"Six pounds, seven or eight ounces," Meg concludes.

"What's that?" Ibrahim asks.

"The baby's weight."

"How do you know?"

"I've been doing this for more than half my life, young man," Meg says, jokingly scolding. "What's her name?"

"She doesn't have a name yet."

"Bad luck not to name a baby," she says, suddenly serious. She goes to her black bag and retrieves a cloth tape measure that unspools as she pulls. Wrapping it like a ribbon around the infant's head, Meg announces, "Thirteen inches."

"Silvia had a . . . a sort of attack," Cynthia says, finding her voice again.

"Not an *attack*," Ibrahim corrects, trying to smooth this over for himself as much as for Silvia. "She just got anxious."

Meg looks between them and waits for a further explanation.

"In any case," Cynthia continues impatiently, "it must have triggered an early labour, and it all got a bit chaotic in the moment. She's still very . . . fragile."

Meg adjusts the baby in her arms. "You came early, didn't you? The early bird catches the worm, you know." Meg doesn't do baby talk: she speaks to the child as though she might reply. She sticks her finger into the baby's mouth and feels around for a moment, wiggling her index along the palate. "All good there. Sucking reflex working well." Meg looks up. "Fragile how?"

"Mentally unstable," Cynthia states frankly.

Ibrahim, hurt by her impermeable candour, says, "She's just found the whole thing kind of hard. She used to be really religious, and there've been some strange —"

"Where is she, then?" Meg's patience has met its limit.

"Resting," Cynthia says.

"In her room?"

Cynthia nods.

"And this is the nursery?" Meg looks at the bassinet, the pink walls.

"Hartford painted it," Cynthia replies.

"Why is it on the opposite side of the house and downstairs?"

There's a pause for a moment. Cynthia and Hartford attempt to speak at once, offering rational reasons for the room's location, but Meg interrupts. "I'm going to go check on Silvia." She sees that Cynthia is about to say something, so continues: "It doesn't matter if she's resting. I need to check some things, and it will only take a few minutes."

Meg taps the baby on her nose, then folds her arms over her body and gently places her back in the crib. "Sleep for you," she says. All the while, the baby hasn't made a peep. "We'll be back to look at latching soon."

Hartford and Ibrahim leave the nursery first.

"After you," Cynthia says.

"No, you first." Meg gestures for Cynthia to walk ahead, but when she's in the doorway, Meg reaches out to touch her arm.

Looking at Meg, Cynthia's face is backlit by the sun, setting on the other side of the house, its copper rays stretching in from the garden-facing windows. Her dark, cropped hair is given a halo effect, and her right cheek is radiating while her left, the side facing Meg, seems to have been made invisible, an all-absorbing black shadow. Meg blinks, but the strange effect remains — it makes Cynthia look as though she has two faces, neatly divided by the central prow of her nose.

"Is everything all right, Cynthia?"

"Of course," she answers, her tone rising. "Everything is fine."

"I know this must be hard for you, not knowing where Leila is."

"Not at all," Cynthia says. "This is . . . this isn't like that," she adds, stumbling over on the hinge syllable, "is."

"I'll go up to Silvia, then," Meg says. "Ibrahim will take me, and you and Hartford can stay with the baby."

XXIX

The bees are getting restless. Over in the hives in the back lot, they scramble on top of one another in blind, hungry desperation. They are agitated; they have lost their queen, and the new one has yet to be appointed.

The beardy fuzz of fur on their faces; the hazy mirror effect of their vibrating wings; the buzz like the morning call of a muezzin; the complicated moving machinery of individuals working as one, thousands of six-leg sets tiptoeing at once towards a single desire, a common goal. It's a muddle of bees, a blizzard of bees. They dazzle, whiz; they drizzle out through the entrance to the hive and fly up, one after another, as if they're connected by invisible strings, until they form a cloud: cocoa-bean brown, pixellated grey. The horizon is dark.

This is passion, this is devotion, this is

death. Nothing at all like love.
   The suck, the cringe, the eerie drone.

XXX

Silvia opens her eyes and watches as a cloud passes across her vision. As soon as it sweeps out of her sightline another gelatinous cell floats across the world, casting shadows on her bare white walls, flattening her depth perception. She tries to hold on to them, identify their shapes before they disappear — a misguided clairvoyant searching for truths in tea leaves. She's had floaters since she was a child, but they seem newly portentous now.

She closes her eyes. The shapes disappear. She hears the low, distant sound of a machine starting up, and this fills her with dull, familiar panic.

Her room surges with a vivid gold light, so she knows it must be around sunset. The room fills with the sun's goodbye every evening; it's something she's come to love about it here. It must be dinnertime, she thinks, but she's not hungry for dinner, can't even remember the last time she ate something that could be called dinner.

There are footsteps on the stairs, approaching. Two sets, four feet. She remembers the car. She had forgotten to wonder who was here and now they're *here,* actually coming to her room. She tries to listen for the sound of a baby, her baby, but hears nothing. The usual panic turns into a swell of fresh terror. Where has Cynthia taken her child? She doesn't even know what her baby looks like. Then she realises, with a sudden sinking feeling, that she doesn't even know whether it's a boy or a girl.

There's a knock at the door but it's already opening before she's replied and Meg is there, followed immediately by Ibrahim. Seeing Meg, Silvia realises that she doesn't know how many days it's been since she had the baby. Has it been a week? Could it have been that long? When her water burst all she wanted was this woman, the solidity of her certainty, but now Silvia is resigned, at twenty-three, to her whole life having already passed her and to having no more personal wants at all.

"How are you doing, dear?" Meg walks to Silvia, who is lying straight as a mummy on the double mattress, and puts her bag on top of the sheet.

"Where is it?"

"Where's what?"

"My baby."

Ibrahim comes to her side and takes her hand, so small inside his. "Cynthia's looking after her — she's doing fine. Meg's here to check on you."

Silvia looks up at Ibrahim, so far above her. He looks so different from this angle that she hardly even recognizes him. The more we've seen people, she's come to realise, the less we're able to see them as a whole. "A girl?" She feels flooded.

"Didn't Cynthia tell you?" Ibrahim shrugs away the moment of confusion. "Yes, it's a girl." A smile comes to his face when he thinks of his girl, *their* girl. "And she's perfect."

Tears fill up to the rim of her eyelids. A girl. Silvia looks from Ibrahim to Meg and blinks, tenderness quickly turning to agitation. "And she's with Cynthia?" Then: "Why are you checking on me? Why not the baby?"

"The baby's doing just fine, love — Ibrahim's right, she's perfect. But birth isn't always easy on the mother, you know. We're just going to give you a look-over, make sure everything's all right with you." Meg doesn't have any tools, no stethoscope or speculum, so Silvia wonders what she plans on looking over, and how.

"I'm so proud of you." Ibrahim strokes Silvia's hand, then places it back on the bed beside her mummified body. "You're doing so well."

Silvia looks genuinely perplexed. "What do you mean? Why?" She props herself up on her elbows, head approaching the sloping ceiling.

"Lie back, Silvia." Meg eases her back down to a horizontal position. "Breast milk is coming, I see. How does that feel?"

Silvia just stares at Meg, eyes wide and hollow.

"It can be a strange feeling, I know." Meg starts gently tapping Silvia's stomach, working her way up to the breasts. "We'll work on breast feeding soon, but in the meantime Cynthia's got the bottles of formula going just fine."

"Can you please get Cynthia to bring me my baby?"

"Let's focus on you for a moment," Meg says.

"But I haven't even seen her yet. I'm the *mother*."

"Do you know what you're going to call her?" Meg asks, changing the subject and sitting down on the mattress by Silvia's hips.

"Oh." Silvia thinks. "I haven't met her yet.

And we haven't really talked about it." She looks at Ibrahim, hoping he'll give her an answer, some kind of a clue, but he just smiles weakly.

"So how are you feeling, Silvia?" Silvia can see how Meg's face changes, straightens yet tilts to assume her role.

Silvia looks inside herself, trying to see if she can identify a feeling in there. "I don't know." She tries to find the most benign of the multitude of feelings that present themselves. "Tired, I guess."

"Tired is normal — isn't it normal?" Ibrahim says to Meg.

Meg nods, dismissing him. "Are you in any pain?" she asks Silvia.

"Yeah."

"Where?"

"I don't know, lots of places. Here." Silvia points to her heart. "And here." She points to her belly. "It hurts there, more than it did before. You know that thing when your leg is amputated and it still hurts?"

"You just had a baby, darling." Meg's face folds. "Some level of discomfort is normal."

Silvia hears the sound of the machine again; it's getting louder, nearer. In an instant she knows what it is. "Do you hear that?"

Ibrahim and Meg share another glance.

476

"Hear what?" Ibrahim asks.

"It's the bees."

"The bees?"

"They're getting ready to swarm." Silvia didn't know that this is what was happening until she found herself saying it, but hearing it, she knows it to be true. Bees swarm in mourning, and in hope.

XXXI

"What do you mean? Where are they going?" Ibrahim asks, genuinely concerned.

"Here." This too is a truth discovered only when speaking it. "The bees are coming here."

"But . . . why?" Ibrahim's instinct is to believe her, not just because he loves her but because she is acting differently than during her attacks, he realises: mainly, she is not afraid.

"They need a new queen."

And now there are three of us, she thinks. This is when the fear comes.

Meg nods to Ibrahim. "Right, dear," she says. "You get some rest."

The two start to walk for the door.

"No, please," Silvia says, "don't leave."

"I'll be back soon, Silvia," Ibrahim says, and even though he's smiling, he sounds profoundly sad. "I'll see if I can bring the baby."

Meg and Ibrahim look at Silvia and smile, mollifying and veneered, and then Meg opens the door for Ibrahim. When she thinks they're out of Silvia's earshot, she says, "Bring her a cup of warm milk with a little honey."

Ibrahim and Meg walk down the stairs in silence and find that Cynthia is no longer in the nursery but is sitting at the kitchen table, holding the baby, who is calmly sleeping in her arms. The sun has set and the dusk creeps in from outside, but only the hanging lamp above the table is on.

"Well?" Cynthia says, staying seated so as not to disrupt the baby but clearly wanting to stand, to get involved. "How did she seem?"

"A bit fragile, definitely," Meg admits.

Cynthia's expression discloses a certain satisfaction, which she is quick to erase before asking Ibrahim, with more concern in her tone, "And what did you think?"

"Yeah." Ibrahim nods. He feels torn between telling Cynthia the truth and defending Silvia; at this stage, he doesn't know which is best. "She said she was tired, but that must be normal."

"Normal?" Cynthia's face is angled towards the baby and so her eyes, looking up at him, are deeply hooded.

Ibrahim opens his mouth, then shuts it again.

"Physically," Meg says, moving the conversation along, "she seems fine." She pauses, and a *but* is implied. "I'm sure she'll be better after a good sleep and a few days' rest."

"Thank you, Meg," Ibrahim says. "Thanks so much for coming by." He's leaning towards her but his body is slumped, as though standing on his own two feet is too overwhelming at the moment.

"Yes, I'm very glad I did," Meg says, looking Cynthia right in her black eyes. "Especially since it doesn't seem possible to reach me by phone."

Cynthia looks down at the baby, whose lips are curling into an unconscious smile; she can't help but smile in turn.

"Goodbye, Meg," Cynthia says, looking up in a state of detached bliss.

Looking at Ibrahim now, Meg says in a normal voice, "You know where to find me if you need anything, right?"

Ibrahim holds her stare for a second before nodding, understanding, and then Meg takes her leave.

"Hello, baby, baby," Cynthia coos. "You haven't thought of a name, then?" she asks Ibrahim. "I have a few ideas if you need any help."

"Uh, that's okay. I'm sure Silvia and I will come up with something. You know, once she sees the baby."

Ibrahim looks around at the room, the shadows from the edges encroaching as night falls harder. "Do you want me to turn on the lights?" He goes to switch them on. "It's so dark, but it's only, what, eight o'clock?"

He goes around flicking all the switches as if the light will cast away all the darkness that troubles his world.

Cynthia continues as though he hasn't spoken. "Postpartum depression is quite common, especially for younger mothers, and with everything Silvia's been going through . . ."

"Post what?"

"It means loss," she lies. "Latin."

"Oh."

"Silvia's experienced such a huge amount of loss all at once. A lot of mothers feel this after the birth, when it all becomes real in a different way, but Silvia's loss is, of course, compounded."

"Right." Though the word "loss" hurts him, making him feel guilty and that he is not enough, in a way this new term, "postpartum," gives him reassurance. Naming the problem puts it into a box. It means other people have been this way too. "Does the birth have anything to do with the bees swarming?" he asks. "Or . . ." He trails off when he sees Cynthia's reaction.

"The bees aren't swarming. Why would they be swarming?"

"It's just that, well, Silvia said she thought . . ."

"What did Silvia say?"

"I don't know." He tries to backtrack, but he doesn't know where he took the wrong turn. "Just that she thought the bees were coming here."

"Why did she say that?"

"I don't know why she said it." He pauses, thinking. "Actually, she said she heard something, I didn't hear it, though. And that the bees had lost their queen."

Cynthia is silent for a moment, pricking her ears to see if she can identify a sound, and then the baby starts to cry, a gut-wrenching wail. It contains the pain of the whole world.

"Silvia needs help, Ibrahim." Cynthia speaks through the screams, and though the strength of the child's wail far surpasses the volume of Cynthia's calm tone, the sounds are on two different wavelengths and so Ibrahim can hear both separately. "She's unstable. It's not safe for the baby."

"If we just give it time, though, like Meg said . . ." His whole body moves towards the baby, wanting to take her for himself and hoping that his paternal connection will stop the child from shrieking, but he doesn't reach for her, as Cynthia is holding her tightly.

Cynthia starts swinging from the legs up, twisting forcefully to rock the child from side to side. Not losing her rhythm, she continues: "Maybe in time she will be better, but right now she's not capable."

"But —"

"Think of your baby, Ibrahim."

He is always thinking of his baby, he's thought of her every moment since she entered the world a day ago, and he knows already that he always will, in every hour that lies ahead. No longer able to bear the distance, he reaches out to touch the head of his screaming child, wishing with his whole being that he had the power to make her stop, but the cries continue. "What exactly are you saying?" he asks.

"I'm saying that Silvia needs to be somewhere where she can be provided with the help she needs."

"What do you mean — like, to go back home?"

"I mean a hospital or something."

He puts his head in his hands, shaking. Words have become so weighted. First *loss,* now *hospital.* He feels the heaviness in his forehead and at the back of his neck.

"Don't you agree?" Cynthia's voice is oppressively rational; it doesn't make sense to him that she is so impervious to emotion in this moment.

"I don't know. This is all just happening . . . I think Silvia needs to see the baby before we make any decisions. I want to take her up." He tries to impart the same strength into his own voice, and though he nearly manages, it wavers at the end.

Cynthia sighs. "Fine." She slows her rocking and touches the baby's peachy cheek; as if by magic, the screaming softens to a garbled cry and then down to a mumbling babble. "But I'll take the baby up, all right? I think that would be better. We don't know how she'll respond to you, after last time."

Ibrahim has no idea what Cynthia is referring to — he can think only of how Silvia responded to Cynthia just the other day, when her water broke — but he's too tired to argue.

"Fine," he says, sinking down onto the chair he found Cynthia in, feeling that though he's taken one step forward, he's ended up two steps back. "I'll be right here."

XXXII

Now that all the beehives are empty, the insides are a creamy colour: sunshine on fields of hay, or real vanilla ice cream. Outside, the bees have all gathered like a nimbus cloud, belly full of rain and ready to spill over.

From bed, with her eyes closed, Silvia watches them suspended and feels at one with everything. The strings that connect the bees also connect her — not just to them but to the trees, the sky, the water, the earth. She lifts the backs of her hands, as if the strings connect to the veins beneath her knuckles, and the cloud of bees moves.

Out of the dark, Cynthia returns: first her face, as before — it looks different, paler, younger — and then the rest of her body. Silvia notices that the clump of rags is still in her arms, but the baby has stopped crying now. Thank God, Silvia thinks; the love she felt from before mounts as the revulsion ebbs.

It's pestilence, Silvia.

It's a farm, Silvia.

Have you been praying, Silvia?

Different voices. All the same voice. Distorted and monotonous.

"Is it yours?" Silvia asks.

A smile, and then Cynthia, in slow motion, shifts the baby to her right arm and with her left retrieves a narrow, long blade from behind her.

"You must fear the Lord," Cynthia says, singsongy and incongruously girlish, "and you must also love the Lord." She lifts the blade high.

"Wait, no —" Silvia puts out her hand to try to stop what she knows by now, in this instant, is inevitable.

XXXIII

"Ibrahim, are you awake?"

Ibrahim sits up, startled. He hadn't realised he'd dozed off, head on the soapy wood of the kitchen table. "Hello? I'm awake — what's going on?" It's completely dark all around him, and then Hartford steps into the light.

"I just wanted to say . . ." He takes a second to choose his words correctly. "I think you should be . . . careful."

"Careful? What do you mean, careful?"

"Just, she's affected by — she isn't entirely stable. You should know."

A pause. "What are you saying?"

"Cynthia doesn't always say what she means. It's not bad, necessarily, but she doesn't always know."

"Know what?"

"What's best, I suppose. Before, with Hilary . . . it was hard."

Ibrahim waits for a moment as this sinks

in and then sets off all the consequences in his mind. "I'm going to go check on Silvia." He gets up and goes, quickly, then turns around to look at Hartford, his disproportional face, his sloping shoulders, his disappearing hair, knowing that in telling Ibrahim this, Hartford has risked compromising his loyalties. "Thank you." And then he hears his name being called.

XXXIV

There's a knocking at the door, and Silvia realises that this is the sound that woke her. The door opens, and when it's ajar she hears another knuckle tap. Already her thoughts are starting to be reprogrammed and her list of half-second instincts upon waking are now *Where is my baby, where is Ibrahim, where am I?*

"Silvia? Are you awake?" It's Cynthia's voice, strong but unformed somehow; it reminds her of wet cement and brings Silvia back into a half-remembered state of panic, but she can't place why. Maybe the voice sounds like her mother's? She can't remember what her mother sounds like; this is the only voice she knows.

Then Cynthia is there, holding the baby, a soft bundle of fabric. "Were you sleeping? I didn't mean to wake you, I just wanted to introduce you to your little girl." As she walks into the room she turns on the overhead light, and everything Silvia had been seeing in this instant looks completely different.

Girl sticks in Silvia's head as an anomaly, as if she's never heard the word before, as if she's never known its meaning. Rhymes with *curl, pearl, whirl, unfurl.* Her girl. *Her* girl. A girl is a female child, a person's daughter; hers.

And then her dream is back — she is awake in the dream and inhabits the blackness of it, sees the silver flash of light. The sound of bees like a growl, like an ache, like a hunger; it's inside her ears and lungs and heart and brain, she is the sound and the sound is everywhere. She hears nothing but the bees, and they are coming; though it's too dark to see, she can hear them like a storm on the horizon.

Silvia has yet to see her baby — how many days old now? — and she so badly wants to get up out of bed and see it — *her* — but suddenly fears what she might see. What will she look like? What if the baby doesn't look like her? What if she looks like Ibrahim, or like Cynthia instead? Cynthia's baby. Cynthia has taken the baby that she was responsible for making in the first place.

Silvia blinks. The blink lasts forever.

Eyes open, she sees Cynthia: a disembodied head, face pale, hands concealed. She doesn't know what's hiding in them. Her heart slips into her hollow belly while something else in turn fills her up: new purpose, sudden certainty. With an abrupt force, Silvia pulls herself out of bed for the first time.

"Careful," Cynthia says. "What are you doing? Silvia? Are you all right?" Cynthia's voice floats above the sound of the bees. She goes towards the girl, who is holding the window frame as she finds her feet like a newborn deer.

Silvia's face is pointing in a different direction from her eyes; she can't seem to get them synchronized, as she's trying to look in two directions at once — towards the floor, which has become as volatile as a squalling sea, and towards Cynthia and the baby. What's her name? Does the baby have a name yet? She should name her now. She needs to give the baby a name in case something happens. It's worse to leave a baby unnamed than unbaptized. She'll call her . . . the first name that comes into her head is *Cynthia,* which makes her feel as if she's going to be sick. No — she'll call her . . . what should she call her, what are people called, what was Ibrahim's mother called? She has no idea, doesn't think she's ever known but can't believe she doesn't know, she should ask him, maybe they could name the baby after his mom, maybe he'd like that, it might be nice, but then what if names contain the seeds of our futures and since his mother died, the baby will also die? She doesn't want the baby ever to die.

"Give her to me," Silvia says, standing, stumbling, pitching towards Cynthia.

"Silvia, be careful." Cynthia leans back, avoiding the outstretched arm that flails her way. "What are you doing?"

"I want my baby," Silvia says slowly, articulating each syllable carefully so as to be heard above the rising roar of the coming swarm.

"That's why I'm here, my darling, to show her to you." Cynthia speaks to Silvia as though she's speaking to a crazy person. Silvia knows this, which only makes it worse.

The surface of the world disappears, and for a moment she can see what's beneath it all. The whites of her eyes float as her eyelids flutter.

They're here now, the bees, they're at her bedroom window. Silvia can see their bodies beating against the glass like June bugs in the summer. She looks again at Cynthia's hands and sees for the first time that there's something clenched within the palms.

Something sharp and silver that catches the moonlight.

"Silvia, what the . . . Calm down, please, *stop it.*" Cynthia's voice is rising as Silvia lunges again, this time towards the child, trying to tear Cynthia's arms apart. Cynthia nearly loses her balance and drops the baby, and the bedroom key that had been in her hand clatters to the ground. Silvia had been locked in.

The door to her room is now open, and Silvia looks out to the window in the corridor, the window where she tried to save the bee; this glass too is black with bees, all trying to break though.

"They're here," she says quietly to herself, her eyes glazing over.

"Who's here?" Cynthia spins around to see what Silvia is talking about, but there is nothing.

Silvia had thought the apocalypse would be a religious thing, but at this moment God is nowhere. "I won't let you do this to her," she says, rage distorting her vocal cords; she speaks like another person. She can see so clearly what she needs to do, but she cannot coordinate her body and mind to make it happen.

Then — it must be because of the bees — the baby starts to cry, a piercing shriek so sharp it could tear a hole through the stratosphere. Silvia's chest becomes wet, she doesn't know whether from tears or milk, and all she wants is to stop the baby crying. She reaches out for her child, but then something happens and she's on the floor.

"Ibrahim!" Cynthia calls out. *Ibrahim!*

Did she fall? She doesn't think she fell. She doesn't feel hurt, but she can't get up. Was she pushed? Did Cynthia push her? Or did she faint?

The baby's screams are getting louder but still do not surpass the sound of the bees.

"You did this on purpose," Silvia says weakly, her body limp and shaking like a fish freshly tossed out of the water. "This is what you wanted all along."

Footsteps. Ibrahim appears. Silvia sees his expression of fear and concern, and then her eyes close and the world becomes sound alone. She trusts that now he is there, he will be able to do the right thing; perhaps it's this relief that allows her to surrender. Her heartbeat is loud in her ears and then it fades out, the *whump* and *whoosh* replaced by the steady, monotonous buzzing of bees.

XXXV

When Ibrahim gets to the top of the stairs, the image frozen before him at the end of the corridor looks like a Renaissance Biblical painting, something he'd love to mimic, a classical composition of Virgin, child, and Mary Magdalene, but as movement catches up with his vision the scene quickly coalesces into reality. Cynthia is clutching his baby girl, who is screaming like it's the end of the world, and Silvia is slumped lifelessly against the wall, her back to the bedroom, facing the dark window in the hallway. Cynthia turns to face him, dazed and grateful. It must have been she who called his name — funny, he's able to think even in the moment: he'd been certain it was Silvia's voice.

He runs towards them, towards the light.

"What's going on?" he asks, breathless, looking between Cynthia, whose face is puckered with concern; his baby, red-faced and wailing; and Silvia, who seems to be part of a different world. Nothing makes sense; it doesn't add up to anything.

He squats to meet Silvia at eye level. "Silvia, what's happening?" He goes to her first — she is his woman, his love; he trusts her despite everything; without his even really registering the process, she has become his whole world. The baby, after all, came from her.

She doesn't answer. He looks over his shoulder at Cynthia, who is looking down at him. "She has totally lost control, Ibrahim," Cynthia says. "She tried to attack the baby."

"What?" The air comes out of his lungs like a balloon that's been deflated. "Silvia?" He takes her shoulders and shakes her, wanting her to deny this, or at least to mitigate it with an explanation, but her head, with a fresh red mark on the cheek, lolls on her rubbery neck and her eyes are unseeing, looking right through him. Their murky colour he so loved painting has morphed into a practically translucent black: a hollow well, an abyss with no bottom.

"I told you, she needs help." Cynthia speaks with resolve.

He can see now that this is true, that Cynthia is right, but *he* wants to be the one to help Silvia. He used to be able to, and he doesn't know what's happened since. He takes his hands off Silvia's shoulders and puts them on either side of her face, her soft, perfect face, slightly hollowed in the last months despite the flush of health that pregnancy had first bestowed upon her. She looks as though she's lost some essential part of herself and the rest of her can't properly operate without this missing thing. He feels his heart as though someone is squeezing it beneath his ribs, gripping it in a tight fist.

"Silvia," he says again, "what do you want?" He's desperate to bring her back, and part of him still believes that if he acts normal, she might too.

Throughout all this the baby hasn't stopped screaming, and Silvia's face and neck are getting increasingly wet, though she doesn't seem to be crying, and Cynthia is losing patience behind him, he can hear it in the way she's breathing, and he wants to tell everyone to just *take it easy* for a second and be *quiet* so he can *think*. The truth is, he can't appease everyone; he knows he'll have to pick a side, but he can't entertain, let alone predict, all the repercussive effects of whatever ultimate decision he'll be forced into making.

He's on the point of breaking when Hartford appears at the top of the stairs and walks down the dark corridor towards them. Ibrahim feels an impossibly huge sense of relief.

"Hartford!" he cries over the baby's screams.

"Hartford," Cynthia repeats, with a pleading edge to her voice.

Suddenly the baby stops crying. The world empties of sound and the air clarifies, becomes smooth and open like a sun-warmed lake. Ibrahim can now hear his own breathing, raspy as wind trapped in a sea-shell, and his heartbeat, so loud it seems to be outside himself. He looks at Silvia, his face so close to hers that he can feel her shallow breath on his neck, and then her eyes catch the motion of his and for a second they are looking at each other. Hope fills his chest, he's exhilarated but fearful, and then she speaks, but her voice is so quiet she's practically just mouthing the words, and only he can hear them. "Don't let her go," Silvia says.

"What?" His eyes widen, his voice sharp. "What did you say?" he asks, though he knows he heard her perfectly well. But who is "her"? Cynthia? The baby? Go where? These questions happen in half-seconds, and he knows he can't say anything out loud. He doesn't know whether her words were a flash of lucidity or of lunacy.

"She didn't say anything," Cynthia says, her feet planted slightly apart as she rocks gently from the knees and gazes at the silent baby, exhausted from its crying fit.

"You should take Silvia," Hartford says, pulling Ibrahim aside. "If you leave now, you'll be in Timmins by the time the hospital opens." He gives Ibrahim the car keys.

"Timmins?" Ibrahim asks, but what he means is *How am I meant to do this, what's going to happen after that, how long will it be until everything is normal?*

"They can examine her and give her medication if required," Hartford says, looking at Cynthia and the baby, "but hopefully she'll feel much better as soon as she's got some distance from all this."

Ibrahim again looks desperately at Silvia, who still is not moving. She's in a sort of trance, staring at the window. Then he looks up at Cynthia, who is staring at him.

"What will we do with the baby?" Ibrahim asks, turning back to Hartford.

"Cynthia and I will look after her until you get back."

Ibrahim swallows, thinking of Silvia's words. Did she know this was going to happen? Is this what she meant?

"The sooner you go, the sooner you'll be able to return," Hartford continues, staring unblinkingly at Cynthia.

"Are you sure?" Ibrahim looks at his baby, now cherubic in sleep. He loves this living thing that he's made; the only thing that he wants in the whole world is for her to be safe, to be allowed to thrive. Something about this — everything about this — doesn't seem right, but when you have no control, you just have to have faith.

"Okay," he says, almost deferentially. "I'll get some things packed up." He looks at his baby and feels the fist around his heart again. He has momentarily lost his words.

He bends down and picks Silvia up, slings her arms over his shoulders like a yoke, and carries her slowly downstairs, placing both feet on each step to balance as they descend.

"We're going to go," he says to her.

"Really?" she says, hope having the same out-of-body quality as delusion. "Thank you," she says, "thank you."

XXXVI

She's descending the stairs, the stairs she's gone up and down seven thousand times by now, and yet their whiteness seems newly astounding. So white it's alive. She wants to reach out and touch the plain white walls and feel the light within them, wants to transmit the light to her own body and illuminate the darkness there, but her body doesn't listen. Her arm doesn't move. A voice comes into her head: *What is sweeter than honey? What is stronger than a lion?*

They cross the foyer and enter the library, and her certainty that the baby is coming with them overrides her awareness that the baby is not there. Silvia sees the painting of Cynthia on the wall right next to her. She stiffens, holding Ibrahim back.

"What is it?" he asks, his tone different this time.

She looks at this painting, then turns to look at the wall opposite, where her own portrait hangs. The two still face one another. The oakleaf wings, the disproportionate eyes, the twisted magenta cord.

"Why did you call it that?"

"What?"

"The Other Woman."

"The painting? It was just the first thing that came to mind."

"What's her name? The baby." She feels certain that the baby has a name and she's forgotten it.

"We haven't named her yet, Silvia."

"Oh." Silvia stares at the painting. She feels as though there are answers in the paint and that she needs to find them.

"Come on," Ibrahim says, leaning forward with her.

"What if we name her after a colour? Like the pink there, the colour of the beloved? We can't call her Pink, though. What else is pink? Like . . . Magenta? Or . . . Rose?"

"Rose is nice." Rose madder is the name of the pigment he used, which he learned somewhere was a plant used to treat melancholy humours back in the seventeenth century. "Rose. I like it."

"Me too," she says, smiling through the gloom that floats and settles like dust motes in the air between them, between everything. She continues to look at her painting, on the opposite side of the room; she can feel its heartbeat.

He tries to start moving again, but without Silvia's cooperation it's impossible to get any momentum. "Listen," he says finally, "you sit here and wait for me. I'm going to go get some stuff together." He shrugs her off his shoulders and shuffles her onto the corduroy couch.

Then she's alone again. She feels the emptiness as a presence all around her, and for a moment this offers a small comfort, but then her eyes meet her painted eyes and she recognizes herself, the Silvia she was before all this happened. When she was a girl and not a mother. When she was a different sort of nothing, a nothing that had the potential to grow into something else. Now she's the nothing that comes after a loss, the kind that can never be recovered and transformed.

She starts to fall, falling further. The whole solar system is contained within the dark hollows of her skull. She closes her eyes. The buzzing of the bees has dulled since she left her room upstairs, but she knows for certain that it has not ended. Distance has not concluded anything.

The fall starts as soon as we're born, she was taught, for all humans inherit the original sin. If only Eve hadn't eaten that apple. "In sin my mother conceived me," says Psalm 51, but this never made sense to Silvia: *her* mother could never sin, it was only other people's mothers who lapsed. The apple falls far, far, far from the tree.

Rose. *Rose, my baby Rose.* Where is Rose? Where is Ibrahim?

With the palpable feeling that someone is looking at her, she turns around and finds herself facing the portrait of Cynthia. The black feeling comes back into her belly, a sudden stone.

The stubby golden wings, just like a bee's; the red dot where a third eye would go; her round, bottomless, black-hole eyes.

They're not *her* eyes, Ibrahim would say. They're his eyes: he made them. He was the bee, Cynthia the flower, and the portrait is the honey.

Who is the queen, then?

XXXVII

"Where are we going?"

Ibrahim is back with their bags. He doesn't seem to have heard her.

"Are we leaving forever?"

His head moves in an indiscernible way. Dismissive, frustrated, despondent. Relief feels like ecstasy.

XXXVIII

Ibrahim loads the few belongings he scraped together onto the back seat of Hartford's car and eases Silvia into the front. "Thanks, man," Ibrahim says to Hartford for the second time that night. Morning.

Hartford is standing off to the side of the car, rooted at the end of the gravel path, and Cynthia is on the front step of the main house, holding the sleeping baby. The way she stands and scans the scene reminds Ibrahim of a sphinx — eyes half open but all-seeing.

"Of course," Hartford says. He holds Ibrahim's gaze and then looks behind him, at Cynthia. "You go," he says to Ibrahim. "I'll keep an eye on things here."

Ibrahim checks that Silvia is okay in the car before running up to the house to give his baby one last kiss on her forehead, nose, each cheek and palm. "We'll be back soon, two days at the most."

"Have you named her yet?" Cynthia asks.

"Oh, yes." He feels protective about giving it away, as though the name is an essential part of her identity that he wants to safeguard. "Rose," he says, smiling without thinking; he loves his baby and her name so much it spills over. "Her name is Rose."

Cynthia looks down at the baby. "Hello, Rose." The name, the first time it's been spoken in her presence, seems to shimmer on her skin.

"I'll call you when we get to the hospital," Ibrahim says out of habit, forgetting, "and either way, I'll be back to get the baby in the next day or two."

"No rush, Ibrahim. You take care of Silvia. That's your priority."

"Thank you," Ibrahim says, sincere, sad.

"Not at all." Cynthia's eyes shine.

The sun crests the horizon at the end of the driveway, and Ibrahim and Cynthia and Hartford all turn to face it.

XXXIX

In the car with the door open, Silvia can hear the sound of bees louder than before, even louder than in the upstairs hallway. It's as if they're all around her: here, in the car, in her head. She can't see them yet, but she knows they're near, they're everywhere. The sun is rising directly before her, a copper penny slipping above the horizon, and the rays filter through her. A feeling of permanence, of strength outside herself. She can't wait to leave here, to go home, wherever that is — these logistics don't worry her so long as she and Ibrahim are together. A shadow passes through the light and then Ibrahim is there, at the window and then inside the car, by her side. He puts his hand on her knee.

"Ready?" He wears an expression she's never seen on him before.

"You don't have the baby?" she asks, as though he's forgotten his arm.

What makes his expression different from any other time, she realises, is that it's as if he's wearing a mask. Usually so unguarded, he now has protection: assertiveness and stillness tentatively disguising whatever truth is beneath. "No," he says, forcing himself to be calm. "Cynthia's going to look after her while we go to the hospital."

"The hospital?" is all she's able to say before her voice sinks into her spleen and her hands start to shake uncontrollably. This isn't possible — Cynthia can't have won.

"We're going to get you sorted out," Ibrahim continues. "It'll just be a few days and then we'll be back, and we'll go home. Everything's going to be fine."

"We have to bring the baby," she says, trying as hard as she can not to cry — she wants to show him how strong she is. "We have to take the baby and just leave! I thought that was . . . ? Please, we need to leave right now and never come back."

Ibrahim takes his hand off her knee and looks at his lap. The sun casts him in bronze and the buzzing is near-deafening, but she can hear him above the high whining of wings rubbing. "Silvia." He looks at her and the mask is gone; all that is there is sadness. "She said you tried to attack her. The baby, she nearly fell."

"What?" Silvia turns around and sees Cynthia standing on the front step holding the bundle of rags, and though she also faces the sun there is a shadow over her. "That's not what happened, that's not what happened at all. I was just trying to get her away from Cynthia and then I fell — she pushed me. I know what she's going to do — she wants the baby, she's going to keep her, and —" She stops herself before revealing the prophecy of her dream. She doesn't want to scare Ibrahim; she can hold on to this burden herself; she can stop it from happening.

With everything left unsaid, Ibrahim starts the car. Silvia can't peel herself away, though — she's twisted backwards to watch Cynthia and her baby, her perfect baby Rose with ears like tiny teacups, and Hartford, standing on the path. They make a strange family portrait, those three — it hurts her heart — and then Silvia looks up: a cloud of bees, the source of the sound and the shadow, large as a hurricane. Everything is suspended.

"Ibrahim," she says slowly, carefully, "stop the car. Look."

He looks in the rearview mirror, not stopping. "What?"

She watches his eyes scanning in the

reflection of the rearview mirror, not sticking on anything. "Don't you see?"

"I understand you're nervous, Silvia, but I promise, I swear on my life, that everything is going to be fine."

Silvia shakes her head, no longer trying not to cry, and lifts her arms to try to stop the bees from descending, but nothing happens. They're not connected to her anymore; there are no strings between them. They hover there, loud as an airplane before takeoff. "Forgive me," she says, not even sure if Ibrahim can hear her above the noise. "It was never about God at all, was it? God had nothing to do with it."

Silvia stares at Cynthia as the car pulls her away down the same path she came from, into the rising sun.

ACKNOWLEDGMENTS

THANK YOU to:

Laura Dawe for truth and beauty, Caroline Schuurman for every week, Nafkote Tamirat for humour disproportionate to your size, along with Amanda Dennis and Amélie Goldberg for coming to the farm, Rose Lipton for doing the voices, Katharine Campbell for doing the listening (and for the swag, and for being my dinosaur), Stephanie Feeney for Turkey and Amsterdam, Lucy André for the quince and the understanding, Kit Brown for the trade, Sarahjane Macdonald for the instinct to persevere, Darren Frey, Julia Grummitt for the airport meeting, Hanna Rasmunds and her family for keeping me in Sweden, Anders for the tractor ride, Lauren Elkin and Anne Marsella for taking me seriously, everyone at Shakespeare & Company including Colette and Aggie, Maddie Woda for wanting to read it before it existed, Krista Halverson for making me laugh during that phone call, Lendl Barcelos for the Tarot, Katie Harris for being the only one in the book club, Billimarie Lubiano Robinson, Alice Moon, Ryan Kerr for the flamingo and the duck, Michelle Engel, Sarah Boston for giving me jobs when I needed them, Susie Fournier for knowing the characters, Dave Hurlow for driving the U-Haul, Jeffrey Greene for Burgundy and believing in me always, Ben Gallagher, Andrea Gunraj, Greg Farrell for being such a cheerleader, Nina Campbell for the Grange, Monica Russell for giving me a home, Michael Follow whom I've never met and maybe never will, Gareth Sergeant for your deeply intelligent intuition, Cal Irvine, King of Cups. My family: the Matlocks, the Lyes, the Caseys, the Robinsons, the Smiths, and the Mikhails. Martha Sharpe and Maggie Gee for being writer mums, Diana Quick for being a London mum, Margaux Williamson for inviting me for dinner to talk about it, Diane Borsato for the honeycomb. Rosa Rankin-Gee, for your big heart, for going everywhere with me. My parents — my favourite parents — for always reading to me with all the voices, and for letting me go into the world.

514

To Stephanie Sinclair for your strategy, speed, and continual support; Whitney Moran, for taking the risk of the first step and working so hard to make this feel easy for me; Katie Henderson Adams, for your confidence and insight. All the rest of the Liveright team for your sharp eyes, especially Liz, Gina, and Amy. You've all helped make this book a better version of itself.

I'd also like to thank the Toronto Arts Council and the Ontario Arts Council for their support in affording me time to write.

ABOUT THE AUTHOR

Harriet Alida Lye's writing has been published by *VICE,* Hazlitt, the *Guardian,* and more. She lived in Paris for many years, was a writer-in-residence at Shakespeare & Company, and currently works at a museum in Toronto.